Pamela Jooste spent a number of years in publishing and in Public Relations with BP Southern Africa and has written radio and film scripts and award-winning short stories. She has always lived in Cape Town. *Frieda and Min* is her second novel, her first novel, the award winning *Dance with a Poor Man's Daughter*, is also published by Black Swan.

Praise for *Dance with a Poor Man's Daughter*
winner of the

COMMONWEALTH BEST FIRST BOOK AWARD
FOR THE AFRICAN REGION

SANLAM LITERARY AWARD

BOOK DATA SOUTH AFRICAN BOOKSELLERS
CHOICE AWARD

'Immensely moving and readable'
The Times

'I could hardly put this book down'
Cape Times

'Both moving and funny . . . A brave and memorable début'
Observer

'Tough, smart and vulnerable . . . emblematic of an
entire people'
Independent

'Highly readable, sensitive and intensely moving . . . A fine
achievement'
Mail and Guardian, South Africa

Also by Pamela Jooste

DANCE WITH A POOR MAN'S DAUGHTER

and published by Black Swan

FRIEDA AND MIN

Pamela Jooste

BLACK SWAN

FRIEDA AND MIN
A BLACK SWAN BOOK : 0 552 99758 7

Originally published in Great Britain by Doubleday,
a division of Transworld Publishers Ltd

PRINTING HISTORY
Doubleday edition published 1999
Black Swan edition published 1999

1 3 5 7 9 10 8 6 4 2

Set in 11/12pt Melior by Kestrel Data, Exeter, Devon.

Black Swan Books are published by Transworld Publishers Ltd,
61–63 Uxbridge Road, London W5 5SA,
a division of The Random House Group Ltd,
in Australia by Random House Australia (Pty) Ltd,
20 Alfred Street, Milsons Point, Sydney, NSW 2061, Australia,
in New Zealand by Random House New Zealand Ltd,
18 Poland Road, Glenfield, Auckland 10, New Zealand
and in South Africa by Random House (Pty) Ltd,
Endulini, 5a Jubilee Road, Parktown 2193, South Africa.

Reproduced, printed and bound in Great Britain by
Clays Ltd, St Ives plc

This book is for Davey

Acknowledgements

My thanks to Issy Levin and Rosemary Pascall-Sive-Griesel for the help and direction in regard to the Judaic references in this book.

FRIEDA AND MIN

FRIEDA

Things You Remember

1998

There are things you remember. About people. About the first time you saw them. The time when they were just the same as anyone else and you didn't know how important they were going to be to you. Because we never know at first and by the time you realize you don't want to forget anything you're already forgetting.

Take Min.

All I remember about the first time I saw her are her feet. Bare feet shoved into African sandals. The ones made out of old car tyres with thick, rubbery soles with their tyre tread still on them and any-old-how strips for straps over the top.

They're all the fashion now but they weren't then. We used to call them tyre tackies and only chars and garden boys wore them.

In those days white people never did and certainly not doctors' daughters who attended smart boarding schools like St Anne's.

I'm never going to be the stuff a *yeshiva* scholar is

made of but I go to Jewish day school to learn Hebrew and I know a few things and when I looked at Min, Solomon's Song of Songs jumped straight into my head.

'How beautiful are thy feet in sandals, O prince's daughter!'

She wasn't a prince's daughter but she might just as well have been, we were so different. Yet there she stood with thin white feet, marble goddess feet, on those black sandals we see every day and never really see at all and all I could do was stare. I couldn't take my eyes off her feet.

Those sandals are terribly hard to walk in. Once, when our maid Beauty was barefoot behind the washing line at the back of the house and her sandals were standing side by side on the back stoep I tried for myself so I know what I'm talking about.

You can cling on as hard as you like with your bare toes. It doesn't help. With a sandal like this not even left foot and right are always in agreement. One may want to go one way and one the other. It doesn't seem to worry the Africans. They wear them all the time and they seem to take them just wherever it is they want to go.

I suppose you get used to them. They keep the stones out and last for ever, which is a lot longer than people do, and rain and sun, good weather and bad, it's all the same to them.

The only thing they aren't good for is dancing. You can't dance in a one-size-fits-all tyre tackie.

At least you wouldn't think so but if an African feels happy enough it doesn't matter what he has on his feet. If the music moves him he'll dance anyway and those tyre tackies no white man can wear will stay right where they are on those black African feet and dance right along with them.

You'd think they'd fly around and away but they don't. They rise and fall and thump on the ground right in time to the music so in the end you'd think they were a part of the song and meant to be there.

So, that's what I remember about Min.

Her white goddess feet in their tyre tackies and that thing that I knew from the very first instant.

If she made up her mind and decided to dance that minute the tyre tackies would have danced too, right along with her, just because she wanted them to.

You could see it in her face even then. She was the kind of girl who only knew one way to go which, believe me, as you go along in the world you soon find out is not the easiest way to live your life.

BOOK ONE

FRIENDS

1964–1966

FRIEDA

The Summer Min Comes

1964

It's the summer Min comes when things begin happening.

All the signs are there.

Things happen that have never happened before.

I get my first date. My father gets signed up for regular work playing the saxophone Friday and Saturday nights at the Starlight Room which is in the ritzy-glitzy part of downtown Johannesburg.

And my mother says: 'Guess what? You're not going to be alone these holidays because we're having a visitor.'

'Who's the visitor?' Aunt Sadie wants to know.

Aunt Sadie is my mother's sister who lives with us. The unmarried one. The one who lives in the hope of finding a husband. The one in a hurry to be sure this happens before she loses her looks.

The visitor, my mother says, is her friend Julia's daughter, Min, and this daughter is just about the most wonderful girl in the world and the same age I am. Most of the time she's a boarder at St Anne's School. For the rest she lives in the lap of luxury on a big sugar farm in the wilds of Natal.

'All the complaints I've had from Frieda,' my mother says to Sadie, to me, to no one in particular. 'Then out of the blue Julia wants to know if we can take her daughter for the summer and I said yes we could.'

Min we don't know, but we know about Julia.

Julia once lived in Coronation Avenue, which is where we live, but she didn't stay very long because people here don't.

They grab any chance they can to move away. They'll go with practically anyone who invites them, as long as the ticket is one way only, and my mother's friend Julia is one of these leavers.

Her father was a shift boss on a mine which is what most people around here are but she landed in clover and married a doctor she met at a 'welcome home' dance for ex-servicemen at the Johannesburg City Hall.

His name was Tom. Dr Tom Campbell. What he had was a medical degree and a pilot's licence, plenty of money in the bank and a very well-to-do old-money family.

What she had was blond hair and a nice laugh which men liked and a very pretty face.

Sadie told me there wasn't exactly a shortage of men willing and anxious to show Julia a good time but when it came to slipping a ring on her finger it was a different story.

Julia likes to say that when Dr Tom asked her to marry him she didn't say yes straight away. What she says is: 'I made him sit it out for a while.'

Sadie says it's probably true but only because someone actually asking Julia to marry him came as such a shock that just for a change she didn't have one of her clever answers ready.

She couldn't believe her luck. She thought she'd go to Sandton or Illovo or one of those places and live there in the lap of luxury with her new husband. In those days when they were girls together and neighbours this is what she told my mother.

She had it all worked out. She'd have a nice duplex, brand-new with a two-car garage and a swimming pool and a full-time, sleep-in maid to bring her tea in bed in the morning.

She'd have a part-time gardener and just whenever she wanted one or two casual girls in proper black overalls with white aprons over them and caps on their heads, standing ready to serve the soup when she had people over for supper.

She was going to play tennis in the morning and bridge in the afternoon and have dinner parties three times a week and when she went out people would point her out and say she was the doctor's wife and probably his greatest asset because she was always beautifully dressed and twice a week she'd go to the hairdresser.

The whole idea suited her. It suited her very well. There are worse things to be than the wife of an up-and-coming doctor. Only it didn't work out this way because in the end Dr Tom turned out to be not that kind of doctor.

He made no bones about it. He wouldn't be caught dead in Sandton or Illovo or any other place even remotely like them. He'd been born in the wide open spaces and he couldn't wait to get back there. All through the war he'd thought about nothing else and he wasn't going to change his mind now, not for anything or anyone.

So where another man might have used some of the money piling up in the bank to buy a nice diamond ring Dr Tom took all of it plus the money he'd saved up from being a pilot and a doctor during the war and bought himself an aeroplane instead and a nice little practice in the bush with a landing strip close by.

All he wanted was to go back where he came from and work with the natives and he told Julia she could take it or leave it because there wasn't going to be any other way.

She didn't like the idea of ending up in a mud hut somewhere but doctors in love, with money in the bank, don't come knocking on doors in Coronation Avenue every day of the week so she took him.

She said you can always make a man change his mind and because she'd managed everything so well so far people who knew her thought she'd manage this as well but she didn't.

She went to the bush and got stuck there and had two children and there were as many natives as any-one could wish for but none of them had black maids' overalls with white aprons over them or caps on their head.

Every time she wrote to my mother she said how badly things had turned out and how much she hated her life. Then things changed. She had a son and he died and she took it hard and couldn't get over it and for almost a year while he was dying she lived in Durban and we heard hardly anything from her at all.

Then the letters started arriving again and Dr Tom took his plane out on a misty day and flew into a mountain and was killed and Julia was a widow.

'But not for long. Not if I know Julia,' Sadie said and she was right.

Her husband wasn't cold in the ground when we got a letter to say she was marrying again.

'No flies on Julia,' Sadie said.

'No decency either,' said my father.

That's the story of Julia and the whole idea is terrible but still when my time comes to meet her and her wonderful daughter who's coming to stay, I'm interested. Mainly because I've never met anyone with what in our family you would call 'a reputation'. Also because I've never met a girl my own age whose mother wants to dump her on strangers so she can go off and have a good time with a man.

'What am I supposed to say to a girl like this?' I want to know.

'Don't worry about that now,' my mother says. 'You'll think of something. After all, you have all summer to do it in.'

Then for a little while despite the fact that we're all ready it looks as if after all the fuss and carrying on Min won't be pitching up at all.

Everything's ready. We're all prepared, all the arrangements are made and a special borrowed bed has been put in my room. Every time I turn around I fall over this strange girl's bed that's taking up all the space in my own room and she isn't even in it yet.

Then the day comes and there's a special supper. Soup and chicken and vegetables and Sadie's pickled cucumber and honey cakes for afterwards and even a bottle of sweet wine and some glasses behind the pull-down section of the sideboard just in case Julia and her new husband care to step inside and we would like to offer them something.

'Excuse me asking, Miriam,' my father says, 'but who exactly is it we're expecting?'

He puts down his newspaper and looks at my mother in her second best *shul* dress with her hair just out of curlers and her legs shiny in Berkshire nylons.

'You know who,' she says.

'I thought perhaps I made a mistake,' my father says. 'I thought maybe it was Mrs Oppenheimer and Mrs Rockefeller who were going to drop by and you just forgot to mention it.'

My father hates show. Anyone is welcome in our home as long as they take us as they find us and this applies to Mrs Oppenheimer or Mrs Rockefeller or anyone else who happens to come across our doorstep which includes Julia who these days is Mrs Gerald Delaney.

'We better get used to this new name,' my mother says. 'We don't want to make slip-ups and cause offence. From what Julia says Mr Delaney is a very important man.'

He might be but it's Friday night and we can wait a little while but we can't wait for him for ever. Not for Julia or Mr Delaney or anyone else either no matter how important they may be. Not on a Friday night. Not on *shabbas*.

On *shabbas* when the sun sets and the time comes we sit down and my mother lights the candles and when the moment is exactly right and we're all seated and ready she raises her hands to her eyes and says the prayers.

My father fills the big silver goblet with wine. Then he gives the blessing and although we were ready for our visitor she hasn't turned up and we can't wait any longer. We must still do what we always do.

We break our *challa* with our fingers and eat it and the soup and vegetables and the chicken and what's left over goes into the fridge where it lives for another day. Then the table's cleared and we all go back to doing what we were doing before which is passing the time and hanging around waiting and then it's time for the big complaint.

'If we had a telephone she could have given us a call,' my mother says.

This is a sore point at our house. All our neighbours have telephones. Even the out-of-work builder who lives on the corner has one and although the argument that's coming is not just about the telephone, the telephone is usually where it begins. Everyone in the entire world has a telephone but we don't because we can't afford one.

There are lots of things other people have we don't have. We don't actually go without. What we do is make the best of what we have and we don't complain. We didn't land on Easy Street and except as far as a telephone is concerned no one is to blame for this. This is the one thing that sometimes gets too much for my mother and makes her look around for someone to blame. So, she blames my father. What else can she do?

In our family when this kind of talk starts it's up to Sadie or me to change the conversation. We take it in turns and I'm never quite sure whose turn it's supposed to be but Sadie always knows so it's usually Sadie who decides.

Sadie is sitting behind a hair and beauty magazine. All you see is the sweep of hair on top of her head and her pretty white hands holding the magazine up and her neatly buffed nails but I see something else too. The perfect arches that are her eyebrows raise just a little bit and I know it's my turn.

'Who needs a phone?' I say. 'Where would we phone to anyway? How would we even know where to find them?'

'Maybe there's been an accident and they're lying dead on the road somewhere,' says Sadie.

'In which case I suppose eventually we'll get a visit from the police,' says my father. 'When you don't have a telephone the police get sent over to tell you such things.'

'Thank you, Aaron,' says my mother. 'Thank you, Sadie. That's all we're short of.'

There's nothing we can do. So we sit and wait and time ticks by and we stay awake as long as we can but eventually we decide we may as well go to bed.

So, when at last the knock at our door comes we're all fast asleep. Lights have to be put on. We have to find dressing gowns and slippers and while we're doing it the knock becomes a *bang, bang, bang* as if

23

someone is impatient and we're the ones who're a nuisance.

We stumble out of our rooms. Our whole house is blazing with light except Sadie's room because if you want to keep being beautiful at least until you find the man of your dreams you need your sleep and nothing and no one should be allowed to steal it from you. Not even an atomic explosion would get Sadie out of her room once her light is turned out for the night.

My mother and I stand next to each other right in the doorway and my father fumbles with the key and then the Yale lock.

'We're coming, we're coming,' he says.

'No need to shout,' says my mother.

Her hands are over her hair to get it tidy. Then they're pulling at the cord of her dressing gown.

My father clicks on the stoep light at the switch right next to the front door and then he opens the door and there on the doorstep with the light from the stoep all around her stands my mother's friend Julia.

She looks like a film star on the centre of the stage and behind her is tall thin Minnie, the St Anne's girl no one will have for the holidays except us.

She stands in the half-dark with a suitcase in her hand and a face you can't see properly. All you see is a square white blur between curtains of hair and we haven't even said hello or how do you do yet and Mrs Delaney is talking like a river.

'You must have given up on us,' she says. 'It's all my fault. I'm terrible and I'm sorry. The road was longer than we expected. Then we stopped along the way to get something to eat and everything took much longer than we thought.'

She's talking and laughing and kissing my mother first on one cheek and then on the other.

'It's lovely to see you, Miriam,' she says. 'I love your letters. What would I have done without you over all

24

these years? All your wonderful news about old places and old days and you and your family and Aaron.'

I thought she'd forgotten my father but I was wrong. One look and you can see Mrs Delaney isn't a woman who forgets anything. She gets to things in her own time and that's the way she gets to people too.

When the kissing's over and all the explanations are given she turns to my father and holds out her hand as if she's offering him a look at a very expensive item she knows he couldn't possibly afford to buy.

How do I know? Because it's the same look shop assistants give Sadie and me when we go into Spilhaus to look at the underneath of the china plates. Which we don't do just for fun. We do it so when the time comes, which Sadie is sure it will, I'll know what a good thing looks like when I see it.

That's how Mrs Delaney looks and my father stands there in his dressing gown and slippers looking at her and she's all laughing and happy and her hair's like gold and you'd think she was going to invite him to dance.

'This is so good of you,' she says. 'I wouldn't even know where to begin to say thank you.'

Then it's my turn. 'You must be Frieda,' she says. 'Your mother and I were very good friends once upon a time. A long time ago. A long, long time ago.'

There's a gold charm bracelet on her wrist jam-packed with charms and her arm snakes out towards me and her bracelet shines and tinkles all the way.

Light suits her. It shines in her hair and smooths her face and she talks a lot and smiles all the time and every now and then she laughs. Her hair is such real gold that her bracelet and rings and chain necklace look cheap next to it and it's long and loose and ripples down to her shoulders and she doesn't look like someone who'd even know how to find Coronation Avenue never mind someone who actually used to live here.

She doesn't sound like Coronation Avenue either. She has a funny fake film-star voice. One of those voices with nothing else to do but make men happy and catch husbands and bark back at dogs and order servants around.

'Min's been longing to get here,' she says. 'She's never been to a proper big city before, you know. Can you imagine going along all this time and never once seeing any place that wasn't anything better than a jumped-up little town?'

She pulls Min into the light and gives her a little push towards us and all you can see are her white feet sitting on top of their funny native sandals and her eyelashes making half-circles on her cheeks and the words that should belong to her are coming out of her mother's mouth.

She stands in the half-light looking above our heads and her face is like stone. Looking at her it's hard to know whether she wants to be here at all, never mind if she's happy about it, and all the time her mother chatters on and she's talking enough for both of them and a few other people thrown in for good measure.

Min's tall. Her hair is heavy and straight. It hangs down on either side of her face and a thick fringe licks at her eyebrows. She has a high St Anne's way of holding her head. To me she looks exactly the way those girls are supposed to look. As if her hair is actual gold and every single one of her bones is made of ivory.

There's been such a lot of talk about her. Now at last she's here and we've all been pulled out of our beds to see her and it costs nothing to look so I look my heart out and would go right on looking if my father didn't decide it was time someone said something and that someone may just as well be him.

'We can't go on standing here for ever,' he says. 'I think it's time we went inside. I'll get the cases.'

He goes down into the street in his dressing gown.

His slippers *flop-flop* down the steps and Mr Delaney gets out of the car like lightning because at last things are moving in the way he wants.

He says a few words to my father and opens up the boot of the car and while he's doing it he has his back to us and Mrs Delaney takes a quick look over her shoulder and she starts talking all over again.

'Gerald's the best thing that ever happened to me,' she says. 'I think I must be the luckiest woman in the world.'

I look at Min and wonder what she's thinking. I know what I'm thinking which is that her mother may be the luckiest woman in the world but her late father certainly wasn't the luckiest man. Less than a year ago he was a young man and alive. Today he's dead in the ground and his wife doesn't seem to have lost too much sleep over it. She's busy flicking her hair and every second sentence is about her new husband and she's holding her hand out to show her ring.

'Lovely,' my mother says. 'Very nice.'

A ring is a ring. What else can she say? As it happens she doesn't have to say anything because my father's back with the suitcase and Mr Delaney is standing out in the road with his shiny car behind him and he's like a racehorse at the starter's gate. He can't wait to get away.

'This is goodbye then,' Julia says.

She gives a little sigh and a big smile and her eyes shine like stars. She turns to Min and holds out her arms and her hair flies and her bracelet tinkles.

'Come and give me a big kiss, darling,' she says. 'And remember all the things I've told you. I'll write often. I'll bring back piles of presents. I'll send a card every single place we go. I promise.'

'Say goodbye to your mother, Min,' my mother says but Min stands quite still. She doesn't move one inch.

'Don't be like this, darling,' her mother says. 'I have

to go. Really I do. You know I do. I hate it when you're like this.'

Down in the street Mr Delaney makes a big show of holding out his wrist and pointing at his watch. 'Hurry up, Julia,' he says.

'Have it your way,' Min's mother says. 'Have it any way that suits you but I have to go. Really, I must.'

She turns away from Min and puts her cheek against my mother's.

'I'm so grateful to you,' she says. 'And so glad you decided to take the money. It was the very least we could do. I didn't want us to argue about it and in the end we didn't so everything worked out just perfectly.'

Then she holds out her hand and my father takes it.

'Goodbye, Aaron,' she says and when she's finished all this she turns back to Min and this time her voice is small and barky and not nearly so lah-di-dah as it was when she was being nice.

'I hate you when you're like this,' she says. 'I know you do it on purpose to make me unhappy but I'm not going to let you spoil things for me. Not this time. Not any more. Not ever again.'

Then just like that with nothing else to say she turns on her heel and she's gone down the front steps and Mr Delaney's opening the car door for her and saying, 'At long last.'

'Goodbye, goodbye,' we say.

My mother waves as if she's afraid of disturbing the air too much and waking the neighbours and Min's mother stands on the pavement for a moment longer and waves back. My father doesn't wave and nor do I and Min doesn't and nor does Mr Delaney. When Min's mother gets to the bottom of the steps he puts his arm around her and bends towards her as if he's going to kiss her but he doesn't.

'You didn't say they were Jews,' he says.

He doesn't even bother to say it softly so we can't hear except even if he whispered it we'd still have

28

heard. When you're Jewish like we are and someone says it the way Mr Delaney says it they need hardly go to the trouble of opening their mouth at all. Even if they were fifty miles away we'd hear. We always do.

We stand there and we are what we are and there isn't a thing in the world we can do to change it and the Delaneys are climbing into their car and going on their way and not even bothering to look back at us.

'Take Min in the house,' my mother says. 'Show her where she can put her things.'

I know what the matter is and it isn't just the Jewish business. My mother didn't tell my father she was taking money for having Min. I don't think she told anyone. Who knows why? Certainly not my father because he's just asked her that question.

'Because if I'd asked you, you would have said no,' she says.

The front door is open and although she's talking soft for us not to hear we can still hear every word and Min is pulling her suitcase down the passage and I'm walking in front to show the way.

'She offered it,' my mother says. 'She said he had so much money he didn't know what to do with it. When I said I'd help her she said she couldn't accept any other way. I didn't ask.'

'Are these the kind of people you're willing to take money from?' my father says and my mother doesn't say anything at all. At least nothing that I hear.

It's done. It can't be undone. If you look at it from the outside it's a very small story but at our house it's just about the biggest story there is. Something special has been broken and the pieces hang ugly in the air and there's nothing to say that will put them together again.

'Come inside,' my mother says. 'All we're short of is that you should catch pneumonia.'

'In a minute,' says my father.

We're in my room and I'm helping Min lift her

29

suitcase on to the bed that will be hers. I know I'm supposed to say something but I don't know what to say. Not because of Min but because of this other thing.

My mother comes in the house but my father's still outside and I feel what he feels and it's not a nice feeling and I'm afraid he might be so upset he won't ever come back inside our house again but after a while he does come in and when he crosses the threshold he does what he always does. He puts his fingers to his lips. Then he presses them against the *mezuzah* which stands at the doorpost of our house.

He does it every time he comes into the house only this time he takes a little longer because his mind is on other things and Min is sitting on the bed with her suitcase still closed sitting next to her and her eyes are on me all the time.

I don't know how it is you begin to know things about people but I know eyes like hers that stay on you clear as glass and faithful as a mirror and always see more than they should.

MIN

Things Left Unsaid

1964

I hate Gerald Delaney. If I could, I'd kill him.

I'd pull him apart limb from limb. Then I'd fillet him and when it was done I'd put him piece by horrible piece in a big plastic bucket. Then I'd take a walk and keep on walking until I found the mangiest, hungriest township dogs I could find. I'd look for the kinds of dog Gerald would despise most and when I found them I'd put my bucket down and walk a little way away. Then I'd stand and watch them while they ate.

It's not what I call wanting very much. Not really. Just the satisfaction of knowing that such parts of Gerald Delaney that have any value at all be put to some good use.

I sit on this bed in a strange person's house and this is the only thing I can think of that makes me feel better so I let the way I hate Gerald grow as big as it likes till it fills up my mind and I needn't think of anything else.

Let some other poor creatures have their fill of Gerald.

I know I have.

'Would you like to unpack?'

Frieda is round; a round soft girl with bright brown eyes and the kind of hair that curls any way it wants. She has a nice face, a small gap between her front teeth and some freckles across the bridge of her nose.

'Would you rather leave it till morning?' she says. 'It's very late. I'll show you where the bathroom is. Then you can go and we can go to bed if you like.'

I don't want the bathroom. What I want is to be in another place and another time. I used to think if I wished it hard enough and wanted it badly enough I could make it happen. Now I know I can't.

'Do you want to go or don't you?' she says.

I don't want to go anywhere but I shake my head yes because it's the easiest way.

'I'll be quick,' I say.

'Take as long as you like,' she says. 'At this hour of the morning no one's queuing and that makes a change believe me.'

I do believe her. About the bathroom and anything else she likes to tell me. That's one thing I'm good at these days. I know who you can believe and who you can't but I don't want to talk about it. It's much easier to open my case and scratch around for my sponge bag.

'You'll get used to it here,' she says.

I will. I know I will. I've learnt that if you try hard enough you can get used to just about anything. I know she's trying to be nice to me and I wish I could say something to her. The trouble is I don't know what there is to be said.

What I'd like to say is that my mother and Gerald don't speak for me. They never have and never will. It may look like it but that's only because I'm not old enough yet to have any real say but that will change. All I have to do is wait.

I can bear anything now but only because one day things will be different. My life will be my own and when my turn comes I'll never do what Gerald did tonight. Not to anyone. Certainly not to people who have offered us nothing but kindness and the hospitality of their house.

One day I'll be able to be myself again and say and do as I please.

FRIEDA

Life Before Min

1964

I'm fourteen years old and the major worry in my life is that no one will ever marry me. It's a real problem.

A girl who can't find someone to take her to the Junior Dance at Theodor Herzl School is not a girl who's going to have men falling over themselves to marry her.

This is a fact and even when we don't like them facts have to be faced. Fourteen is fourteen. It isn't eight or nine years old and something that can be joked away. These days boys are looking at girls and girls are looking back except no one is looking in my direction which in the long run can be a very serious matter although on this occasion things don't turn out too badly.

If you can call Alvin Silverman a date in the end I get a date.

Long after I've given up hope, out of the blue Alvin turns up at our house. He knocks at the door. He asks my mother if he can see me and when I ask why all of a sudden he wants to make an appointment when he can see me any day of the week free of charge he says how would I like him for a dance partner.

No one is ever going to mistake Alvin for Paul Newman but I'm not exactly in a position to be fussy so I say yes and why not and it's fine with me.

That's what I say to him.

To God I say a big thank you because He knows what was worrying me and now I don't have to worry about it any more. If I want the world to know no boy is interested in me I will put an advert in the *Star* newspaper. I don't need people to find this out because I'm the only girl at Theodor Herzl sitting home on the night of the dance.

Mrs Silverman made Alvin do it. What I don't know is how she managed it or how Alvin got to be the chosen one. For a woman with three sons to offer to pull out one of them is not such a big thing but I don't think the Silverman boys were fighting over who would have the pleasure of being my date.

Their mother may have made them pull straws. Alvin may have been chosen because he's the youngest and the other two are always shouting him down. His mother may even have offered him money to do it.

But in the end Alvin arrives on our doorstep in what I know is his brother Joey's suit because I saw Joey wearing it at his bar mitzvah. He has a corsage of frangipani in his hand and no one could be more happy to see him than I am.

When Alvin arrives at seven o'clock I'm in my room, sitting on my bed waiting while my mother tells him she'll have a look and see if I'm ready which is a big joke.

I started getting ready at three o'clock in the afternoon. By five o'clock I was as ready as I'm ever going to be and then I had to wait. This is how you do things on dates.

I have a lovely dress. My hair is teased so much it stands out like a pineapple and if my date or anyone else takes me out on the dance floor thanks to Wellatex it will be like dancing with a porcupine.

Our front room is full of friends and family to witness the great event of my first date. These are people who see us every day but if you could see the way they carry on you'd never think so.

When Alvin steps inside and I come out of my room to show what I look like in my new outfit they all scream and shout and say how fine we look and how grown-up we suddenly are. Alvin is a prince. I look like a queen and people are saying we make a wonderful couple.

They carry on as if the rabbi is going to come walking through the door any minute and my father and his friends are going to find a nice *chuppah* sitting around somewhere 'just in case' and Alvin and I are going to get married there and then which one look at Alvin's face will tell you is not very likely to happen.

When we get to the dance everyone's greeting everyone else and no one says anything about Alvin and me. Not a single word. They don't need to. It's no secret Alvin lives in the same neighbourhood as me. Everyone knows Ruth Silverman and Sadie are best friends. They never go anywhere without each other and our families have known each other for years.

People who don't live here think everyone in Johannesburg is made of money although I don't think anyone could make this mistake about us.

It's no disgrace not to be rich but it's no great honour either. Which is about the only thing you can say about it.

We don't live in Houghton or Parktown where the houses and gardens are so big you need a map to find your way around. We don't even live in Johannesburg

36

itself. We live in Germiston which is on the old mining part of the Reef. The part that has small houses with tin roofs and sits almost right on top of a native location.

People aren't fighting with each other to have houses here. Here people fight to do well enough so they can get out and go on to better things.

All that's between us and the native shanties is the old mineworkings and the dump and a barbed-wire fence that used to be there when the mine was still working and a stretch of red veld and a stream in between.

You couldn't forget the mine even if you wanted to. Our street is even named after it. If you stand outside and look up the road you can see the minehead sticking out of the ground. It's still there even though the gold's worked out and it's all closed up these days.

Anyone who was going anywhere packed up when there were no more pickings to be had, except our family which is one of the ones who stayed behind.

Our house once belonged to my grandfather. My mother and Sadie grew up here which doesn't mean we're here for sentimental reasons. You wouldn't have to push us too hard before we'd be willing to make a change.

In my mother's day there were plenty of families around here to be friends with. Now it's different and it's different because we're Jews. I'm not talking cruel or unkind or anti-Semitic. All I'm saying is 'different'.

If you were a Jew who lived in our street your parents could call you Sean or Craig or Tracey, you'd still never have any problem with an identity crisis. Where we live it's easy. Our house is the Jewish Woman's House. I'm the Jewish Woman's Daughter and Sadie is the Jewish Woman's Sister.

We are who we are and we don't take it as an insult when someone says it out loud. We don't mind but we do notice.

'Be polite,' my mother says. 'Polite is enough. You say good-morning and good-afternoon and answer if anyone asks you a question but that's where you draw the line.'

So I go up and down the road saying good-morning and good-afternoon and answering when anyone asks me a question and I make my friends at Theodor Herzl School or at *shul*.

My mother loves *shul*. She's there twice a week. You have to take either a train or two buses to get there and everything costs money but you couldn't keep her away even if you tried. Where we live in Germiston she may be the Jewish Woman but when she gets to Waverley she's the Queen of the Waverley *shul*. She spends so much time there you'd think she had shares in the building and was keeping an eye on her investment.

'If you're looking out for friends look out for someone at   *shul*,' she says. 'And stop this nonsense about living in Germiston. If someone really likes you they wouldn't care less where you live.'

My mother thinks because I go to Theodor Herzl which is a Jewish school where I can be with other Jews we'll all be friends and stick together and help each other for the rest of our lives but in some ways Jews are just like anyone else. Waverley likes Waverley and Houghton likes Houghton and Germiston is left to carry on the best way it can.

'Plenty of those nowadays hot-shot Theodor Herzl families started out here,' my mother says. 'I can give you names. So can Sadie, and if you don't believe us next *shabbas* you can ask Aunty Fanny.'

I can ask Aunty Fanny until I'm blue in the face, it isn't going to help me at all. I still have a friend and potential husband problem. It's not just where I live, it's also to do with the way I look.

'There's nothing wrong with the way you look,' my mother says.

If I had ten cents for every time my mother and Sadie tell me what a beautiful girl I am I'd be a rich woman but even so no one is ever going to mistake me for a beauty queen.

Every time I suggest I could use a little help from maybe Gossard or Helena Rubinstein my mother says a girl of fourteen doesn't need to look like a woman of twenty-five.

'You'll make yourself ridiculous,' she says. 'You look the way you look. Maybe you'll grow out of it, maybe you won't. Nothing's going to change in five minutes. If you're looking for something to do you should sit down with a good book.'

Sadie isn't like this.

Every day she goes out powdered and painted and looking beautiful, hoping this will be the day she catches the eye of someone who isn't just anyone and her troubles will all be over and there's no reason why it shouldn't happen.

Sadie's beautiful. Her hair's red. Her skin's like milk. She has very slender ankles and lovely hands and eyes as green as bottle glass and it's a pleasure just to look at her.

'It doesn't matter how pretty a woman is,' my mother says. 'Good men don't grow on trees. You have to go out and look for them. It's no good standing still hoping they'll come to you. Life doesn't work like this.'

Sadie is more than willing to look but so far no one has looked back. At least not in the way that counts.

When you're a poor girl who works behind Muller's music-shop counter for a living and live with your sister and brother-in-law in not exactly the ritziest spot in town, it doesn't matter how pretty you are, men aren't fighting their way to your doorstep.

'She dreams too big,' my mother says. 'That's the trouble. All I ask is I should live long enough to see with my own eyes a man my sister thinks is good enough for her.'

My mother isn't the only one who asks this. We don't say it out loud but that's how we all feel.

You don't know everything about a family in the first five minutes after you walk in the door, especially if you arrive in the middle of the night when half the house is asleep.

I don't know what Min's mother told her or how interested she really is in us or how much she knows. I suppose she knows about Davey. Not even someone like Mrs Delaney would expect a person to come and live in a house where such a sick boy is and not even mention it to them.

We don't broadcast around the town about my brother which isn't because we're ashamed of him. It's because people don't understand.

Davey has something that's wrong with his endocrine system. He's been like this since he was born so we've had plenty of time to get used to it.

What other people see, all they're really interested in, is that he's enormously fat. It's hard for him even to stand up and when he is on his feet he can move a little but only a very little and very slowly.

People think it's a terrible thing having a brother like Davey. They don't say it out straight though.

'A special child.' 'God's gift.' 'Gentle as a lamb.' 'A heart of gold.' That's what they say and they can say as much as they like what a sweet boy Davey is and how you can't help but love him. The face tells the secret and what they really think is in their eyes. Life's hard enough. Who in their right mind would want a boy who'll never be able to look after himself properly or do anything really important with his life?

The difference between them and us is that we're the ones who have Davey and he means the world to us and we don't mind.

You can forgive my mother a lot of things if you know how hard she works with Davey. He's the reason why despite being a clever woman she can only do a part-time job three or four mornings a week. Her full-time job is Davey and because of his needs he takes almost all our money as well.

We all love him but when he has bad nights my mother is the one he calls for. She's the one who gets up out of her bed and goes to sit up with him.

When you stay at our house you get used to lights being switched on in the middle of the night and the sound of people moving around. You get used to the whispering. If it's very bad my mother will sit by Davey and hold his hand and sing little baby songs to him in Yiddish.

'*Rozinkes mit Mendelins*', she sings, and 'The Kid That Was Bought For Two *Zuzim*'.

She sings softly so the rest of us can get a good night's rest and won't be disturbed. If you have to get up in the night to go to the bathroom and you go past Davey's room you can see her sitting by his bed. I think she would sit in the dark if she could but Davey can be afraid of the dark sometimes. He likes the light, so the night-light spills like water on the bedclothes and shines through my mother's hair.

Davey's fat is hidden under the covers and he looks just the same as any other person. All you see is his round face on the white pillow and the dark curls of his hair and his hand as small as a baby's in my mother's and my mother's voice singing the songs her mother used to sing to her and to Sadie.

Now he's more grown-up but when the pain is bad he still cries. Only now he thinks he's almost a man and when he cries he's ashamed so he turns his face to the wall because he doesn't want us to see.

These aren't things I talk about at Theodor Herzl. No one else I know has a brother like Davey and no one's really interested in a boy they don't even know.

So there's no one there who would understand.

But I can't keep Davey a secret from Min.

It should be easy. 'This is my brother, Davey.' That's all I have to say. Except it isn't so simple and there's more to it than that.

My first problem is when I should do it. Should it be sooner or should it be later? I decide sooner is better and on that very first morning, as soon as we're awake and out of our beds I say by the way I don't know if she knows but I happen to have a brother and I take her to see him.

We go into his room and he's already awake and tidy for the day and sitting enormous on his bed with a mountain of white pillows behind him to keep him up so his head stays up straight and he can breathe properly.

He's wearing blue pyjamas with long sleeves. Compared with the rest of him his hands are very small and they're side by side on the turned-down piece of sheet in front of him.

We try with Davey but nothing ever fits him properly. In the end everything stretches. Even the biggest sizes. Eventually things begin to pop. Zips do it. So do seams even after Ruth Silverman has double-stitched them on her fancy Singer sewing machine to keep them secure. Pyjama-jacket buttons do it too.

It isn't his fault. It's just that Davey asks too much of them and although they try their best they can never quite manage it.

'This is the girl I told you about,' I say.

Davey may be sick and not able to get around much but he likes to know things just the same as anyone else does. He doesn't like to be left out and everything I know I pass on to him. So Min may not know very much about Davey but he knows just what there is to know about her.

He doesn't see many strangers because seeing new people and showing himself to them makes him shy. He can always see what they think about him. He can see it in their eyes and it makes him sad. There's not very much he can do about the way he is and he wouldn't upset anybody for the world but this is how he feels with every new person he meets.

Only I don't think he feels it with Min.

I don't know what it is about her. You look at her and she looks like every other girl. Her hair hangs down her back in a thick plait. Her clean shorts and her shirt still have iron marks bent into them the way things have when you iron them wet and don't let them air properly. Her feet are bare and she walks soft and sure into Davey's room as if it's a room she walks into every day of her life.

She goes right up to him and sits down on a corner of the bed and talks to him as if he's an old friend.

'I like your room, Davey,' she says. 'You can see the garden from here.'

You can. That's why this room is Davey's and no one else's. From his bed he can see the beans nudging up to the tomatoes and the tomatoes glowing on their trellis and the Slippery Jack grapes by the fence and the gardening shed and my father's old striped deckchair where he likes to stretch out with a book when his gardening work is done.

'I suppose you can hear birds too,' Min says. 'I know everything there is to know about birds. There are lots of birds where I come from. More birds than anywhere else in the world. I could teach you or perhaps you can teach me. Perhaps you know more than I do and then we can teach each other.'

You would never think such a silent girl could suddenly have so much to say. There are words in Min and there are more than words. She sees through the skin and the fat and bone and all the insides of Davey that struggle so hard and do their best just to keep him going and keep him with us. She looks at

43

our Davey and sees what we see which is the beauty of Davey shining out of his eyes.

What Davey sees when he looks at Min is someone who will know him for himself as he really is and maybe even be his friend.

MIN

The Marigold Moment

1960

I had a brother too. His name was Justin but he's dead now. He died in Addington Hospital in Durban.

Things happened after that and nothing was ever the same again.

We don't talk about him any more. It isn't as if he did anything disgraceful or unnatural or anything like that. It's just that my mother says she can't bear to hear his name mentioned. It upsets her too much.

What upsets me is how you can let someone go alone into that long silence and not even allow them to leave their name behind and I say his name over and over again all the time but only to myself and not so anyone can hear. Just for the pleasure of being able to speak it again and thinking about how things used to be.

My mother says I can think what I like. There's nothing she can do about that but when it comes to my brother she prefers it if I keep my thoughts to myself.

Which is what I would have done anyway.

You have to be careful what you tell my mother and I am.

She lied when she told the Woolfs I'd never been to a proper big city before. These days she likes to forget it but in the long days of Justin's dying we stayed with my Grandfather Campbell in Durban so we could be close to the hospital. Grandfather Campbell invited us. My mother, my father and me. He said he'd be happy to have us but it was a very funny visit.

His house is as big as a cathedral.

My mother has never been invited here before and my father never talks about it much and it's much bigger and far grander than anything she expected.

My mother hates aeroplanes and won't fly so we drive and get out of the car stiff and tired and the house is enormous with a long driveway and six big pillars in the front.

'Come on,' my father says.

My mother isn't sure. I don't know why but I can feel she would rather go back than forward except it's too late for that now.

We walk up the front steps. With every step we take the house gets bigger and my mother seems to shrink and for the whole of our visit she can't go back to being how she was before and she's unhappy.

She says the servants creep around like ghosts in white turbans. She complains they give her funny looks.

'What kind of funny looks?' my father wants to know.

She says they're the kind of disrespectful looks servants give when they know too much.

'It's your imagination,' he says.

Most of the servants have been in this house since my father was a boy and grew up here and they're really happy to see him back. They keep coming up

46

close to him as if they want to touch him to make sure he's quite real.

My mother hates it.

'I've never seen such badly trained, disrespectful staff in my life,' she says. 'If there's one thing that's worse than trying to make a decent servant out of a kaffir it's trying to do anything at all with a coolie. Don't pay any attention to them. It'll only make them worse.'

I'm not paying attention to them. I have other things on my mind.

I can't believe my brother will die and be somewhere I'm not and not want me there with him.

When I was small he sometimes used to tease me. To play the fool, when we were alone out in the bush he'd walk away from me and pretend to leave me behind. I really believed he'd do it and it used to make me cry even though he always came back to fetch me.

Later it was different. He still left me but I knew he'd come back. All I had to do was wait until he did and there was no need for tears.

I can't believe he will die with his eyes closed and tubes in his arms and his head shaved in this strange place on a thin white bed listening to the sound outside his window and pretending the sea is the grass of our flatlands which is our place in this world and the place we belong.

Except Justin is never going back to the flatlands. It has all been explained to me and my father has told me so himself. There's no hope for Justin. No matter how much we want him to stay he's going to die and leave us and when he does he'll have to stay here and be buried in the family plot with all the other Campbells to keep him company.

I didn't know our family had a plot. Justin didn't know either but there's a lot of talk about it these days.

Lately I've been looking a lot at graveyards. There are graveyards all over Durban. I've never seen so many graveyards in my life as I have here but I still don't understand them.

Every day on our way to the hospital our car goes right past one. It's old and tired and has small headstones like crooked grey teeth. Sometimes there are circles of marigolds draped over them so you can't see the writing on them.

Marigolds are beautiful flowers. They seem to carry the sun in their hearts. They're so bright it hurts your eyes just to look at them but even so it's a sad place and every time we pass it I ask myself a question.

God has all of space. He has room and room to spare. How can we believe he would want us to lie in such narrow graves?

FRIEDA

Life on the Street

1964

This Saturday is Min's first day in Johannesburg. I'm excused *shul* on account of her being here and I'm going out earlier than usual and she's coming with me so she can have a look at our neighbourhood. Not that there's much to see. At least not in my opinion.

On Saturday women who work all week and don't have enough money to have maids are on their stoeps shaking out mats and blankets and although it's early there are already children playing out on the pavement where they're out of everyone's way and not underfoot.

There are people everywhere and you have to watch where you go. Friday is payday for most people in our part of the world. On Saturday there are fat ladies with their husbands' pay packets burning in their pockets and it's not only white people who are out.

The natives go out too, men and women in their raggedy clothes with their barefoot children running behind them and all of them keeping to the outside of the pavement where they're not in anyone's way.

When the cars come past close they have to push a little way in for safety's sake but when the cars are gone they're back in the street again or in the gutter. They have to watch out and be quick. If they don't jump quickly enough people shout, 'Stupid kaffir!' out of their cars and sometimes they blow their hooters. 'Want to get yourselves killed?'

That's their business not ours even though it's hard on natives because they've got nowhere else to go. They can't be on the pavements with us or they'd get pushed and shoved and told not to act so white or be so uppity and if they go in the street they take their life in their hands.

It's like that everywhere and you get used to it but you'd think Min had never seen such a thing in her life. She stops right in her tracks to look as if she can't believe her eyes.

I like to know what's going on just as much as anyone else but this isn't the way I'd find out.

When I'm out I do what my mother does, I keep my eyes down. I mind my own business to keep myself out of trouble. I haven't got time to stop and stare. In any case what's to see? The cars hoot and there's shouting and the natives jump and scream to their children to jump too. We're all used to it by now.

It's nothing new. You can come any Saturday and look as much as you want but if Min carries on standing stock-still right where she is with her eyes sticking out and her mouth hanging open all that will happen is that people will get fed up with her. She may even be knocked over herself because all she'll be is in the way.

Being out in the Saturday rush isn't really a place for girls by themselves which is why, on ordinary Saturdays, I don't mind sitting quietly in *shul* between my mother and Sadie and missing it all. When you're out it's every man for himself and everyone's in a hurry and women who have men with them can push along the pavements much harder than we can.

It doesn't worry me. It's something you learn when you live in town. When people push you, you say, 'Excuse me' and push right back. This is what I do and people round our way are used to the Jewish Woman's Daughter. They can push and shove as much as they like. They know I can push my way with the best and Min is right behind me in her old jeans and top and looking at absolutely everything.

You can see who lives in town and who's just come in from the country.

'Haven't you ever seen a black person in your life before?' I want to know. 'Don't stare like that.'

I take hold of Min's hand and pull her along. 'They're not doing anyone any harm. They need to do their shopping just the same as anyone else does.'

Mostly they go right down the main street to one of the Indian shops near the end of the town down by the bus station. These shops started life as Mine Concession Stores. That was their grand and proper name and what they used to be called. Now like everything else around here they've come down in the world and we call them kaffir shops.

Things are cheaper there and you can buy little-bit, little-bit, depending how much money you've got, and that's where the natives shop but sometimes they stop at Silverman's on Saturdays when only the non-*kosher* shop is open and the blockman is in charge.

They go to the fly-screen door at the back of the shop and they stand there till someone notices them and throws the door open and asks what they want. Then they ask for cow bones and chicken heads and feet.

They'd never go to the front where they can put the real customers off by being so many of them. They know if they wait out in the yard by the back door where the ice trucks from the slaughterhouse make their deliveries eventually someone will take notice of them.

You can see them there every Saturday sitting around waiting for the door to open and the big trays of bones to be taken out. It isn't every shop they hang around like this but they don't mind waiting at Silverman's.

The blockman knows that as far as the Silvermans are concerned natives are customers and their money is as good as anyone else's. At Silverman's a customer, black or white, *kosher* or non-*kosher*, gets good quality at a fair price and that must be why the natives keep coming back week after week and are willing to sit there patiently waiting for the blockman to decide he's ready to help them because sometimes they sit for a very long time.

'Stop staring,' I tell Min. 'They're human beings the same as we are. If you leave them alone they won't hurt you.'

I don't know what they teach a person out in the wilds but at our house we have respect for other people. We know what it's like to be pushed around. We haven't forgotten what happened to us and we never will.

We don't stare at poor raggedy people who no one seems to want around. Other people can look as hard as they like. We've learnt our lesson and had our turn. Today it's them. Tomorrow it might be us again.

'Never mind all the other things they teach you at *cheder*,' my father says. 'If you've learnt that lesson and understand it, you've learnt a big lesson in life.'

I'm curious about Min.

My father carried in the big trunk with the MISS MINNIE CAMPBELL label on it but the only things Min cares about are in the old suitcase she carried into the house herself.

I can open the cupboard whenever I like and I do. I hold her dresses against myself and turn and twirl in front of the mirror and for a few seconds be so beautiful in fine clothes that if I open my mouth I'll probably talk with a rich girl's twang.

All this is fine with her. She doesn't mind at all. What she cares about is in her old bashed-up box suitcase and what I want is to see what's in it that's so special. I'm curious. I can't help it. So, because she's so nice about the clothes I ask if she minds if I take a look inside the other suitcase as well. She can only say no and if she does how much worse off can I be?

'Let me see,' I say.

'It's nothing,' she says.

'If it's nothing then let me see anyway and I'll decide for myself.'

It doesn't really matter what's inside her case but suddenly it's important and I'm taking it personally and thinking maybe my Jewishness has something to do with it. Maybe Min doesn't like Jews. Maybe she doesn't trust us. How would I know? We all heard what Mr Delaney said and the way he said it.

I'm wondering if this is the way it is and if for all the time she's here we're going to have to live with this thing between us.

She looks as if there's nothing in the world that could make her give up her suitcase and then suddenly she changes her mind and she picks it up and hands it to me.

'You can look if you like,' she says. 'But don't blame me for what you see. I told you it's nothing.'

I have the case in my hand. I want to open it and have a good long look. Yet now I can I don't want to any more and I'm sorry I made such a big thing about it in the first place. I asked for too much and Min had no choice but to say I could look if I liked.

She's sitting on her bed looking at me with her

see-everything eyes. Her legs are stretched out in front of her, heels down on the floor.

'You can't see if you don't open it,' she says. 'So, open it. I said you could.'

As if she was the Queen of Egypt and I was her Jewish slave.

Not that I'm going to let that worry me. Not when I've got a personal invitation to see what I want to see for myself. So I open it and what's to see?

'What are these things?'

A man's hairbrush with soft white bristles and a silver back. Small square cufflinks. A white silk scarf with tasselled fringes. A wooden top with a metal tip to spin it on and a grey piece of string wound around it. Old photographs held together with knicker elastic tied in a knot. A Jock of the Bushveld book and a bracelet made out of something that looks like strands of black wire.

'And this?' I say.

'It's elephant hair,' Min says. 'For good luck.'

Thank you very much. How lucky can a person be when they're no longer among us and all their remains fit into a small child's suitcase and even then there's plenty of room to spare?

There's a penknife made of mother-of-pearl with a hidden-away blade with a little dent in it so you can pull it in and out and a little stick with a sharpened end and a glass jar filled with marbles, all colours of the rainbow. Some plain and some beautiful ones with a burst of colour in the centre.

I take the marble-jar out first and set it down next to the case because this is what makes it weigh such a ton. Then I take out the bundle of photographs, some in frames and some not.

'Is this you?'

'My dogs,' she says. 'I had to leave them behind when we left where we lived before.'

She's in the middle of the dogs with bare feet and

shorts and a big smile. Standing behind her with his hand on her shoulders is a tall man who I know is her father who's dead and next to her a boy taller than she is with the same face as hers and the same lick of hair down to his eyebrows and a big boy's grin.

It's a subject I'm not supposed to bring up unless she mentions it first and I won't. I'm not such a *klotz*. If I asked her and we talked about it what good would it do? What would I have to say to her?

How can you imagine such a thing if it's never happened to you and how can you explain it to someone else if it has? Where would the words come from?

So we sit together in silence and things that belonged to two people now dead lie on the white cotton bedspread between us and the old cardboard case with the crayon scratchings on its open lid stands empty.

I touch the hairbrush with my hand. I give it a little stroke and Min doesn't pull it away.

Is this mentioning it?

I pick the penknife up and lift it in my hand, feeling the weight of it, letting the light slide over the mother-of-pearl just for an outing after being in the dark for so long.

I never mention any names out loud or anything. If this is the way they do things then this is their way and I'm quite happy out of politeness to keep it that way.

We're different and we all have our way of doing things. Saying nothing is also a way of saying something and a friendship doesn't always need words. Sometimes it can begin in silence.

MIN

A Special Birthday

1959

It's my brother's birthday. What he wants more than
anything else is a pearl-handled penknife. I don't
know why. It has something to do with a game
boys play. They call it '*mesgooi*', which is knife-
throwing.

You hold the knife by the handle and then you twist
it off your hand into the sand. You can do it from your
elbow, from your shoulder, from your chest or using
different fingers. The knife has to spin and hit the
ground and the one who throws it in the most unusual
way is the winner.

Justin doesn't usually do well with presents because
his birthday is quite near Christmas but this year I
think he'll get what he wants. Mainly because he's
dying.

He's thirteen years old and although this birthday is
a victory we pretend everything is the same as ever
and we do the things we always do on birthdays as if
nothing's changed.

There's a chocolate cake with creamy icing and candles pushed into it by my mother.

'Baby rubbish,' Justin says.

'We'll have them, thank you very much,' my mother says. 'We always have them. We'll have them again this year just like we always do.'

'Let's not have them,' I say.

Candles are for wishing. We know what we wish for Justin and it isn't going to happen.

These birthday candles are just a big waste of time. All they do is blaze away for a few seconds, just long enough to remind us that the things most worth having don't last very long.

'I don't recall asking for your opinion,' my mother says.

She's gone to a lot of trouble about the candles. She kept them in the fridge all summer to stop them melting and nothing is going to stop her lighting them now.

She's wearing a dress with flowers on it and her hair is pinned on top of her head but my mother is different these days. She cries in her bedroom with the door closed. Her eyes are red and swollen up and she smells of gin but tonight she's putting on a good show.

'We must have a photograph,' she says. 'Be quick. Stand by the cake while the candles are still alight.'

She's standing in front of us with my father's pre-war flash camera wavering in her hand.

'Stand closer,' she says.

I can feel my brother's arm warm against my shoulder.

'Smile,' my mother says.

Her red mouth goes open and closed and she makes a pretend smile to show how it's done. All we can see are teeth underneath and her high forehead above and the twist of her hair on top of that. The rest of her face is hidden behind the camera and when the flash comes it's so quick and bright it catches us by surprise. If we weren't who we are it would make us afraid.

Where we live there are still some old black people who won't have their photographs taken. To them it's terrible magic. They say to take your photograph is to take a piece of your soul away from you but we're white children and don't believe rubbish like that. Our father is a doctor and a scientist and even though we're out here in the bush we're being turned into educated people.

This is the job of our schoolmaster, Mr Morefe. Because of him we know about science and mathematics. We have biology classes walking with him out in the bush and my father does his bit too. Every month a big box of books, my father's standing order from Adams and Company, West Street, Durban, arrives for us.

'The whole world inside one cardboard box,' my father says. 'Just think about it. We don't need to move an inch to find the world. It comes right here to us.'

He's the first to touch the books fresh and new when they come in. He looks at them and runs his fingers over their bindings. He flicks through the pages and smells the newness of them as if it was the sweetest perfume in the world and then he hands them over first to Justin and then to me so we can do the same.

'Ask, look, read, ask me and I will direct you,' Mr Morefe says. 'If there's something you don't know you have no excuse for not being able to find out about it for yourselves. All you have to do is ask, look, read and ask me.' We are asking him things all the time and he is always there, waiting and ready with all the time in the world to give us an answer.

We are lucky to have Mr Morefe and my father. We know much more than the old people ever did but all the same when I look at Justin and think about what my father said about how little there is we can do for him it makes me wonder, with all our knowledge, exactly how much it is we really know at all.

This year Justin's birthday falls on a Tuesday which is Father Ignatius's chess night.

'Not tonight,' my mother says. 'We don't want any outsiders.'

My father doesn't agree. He wants Father Ignatius there just the same as he always is.

We aren't religious. When we were small we said our prayers, Gentle Jesus meek and mild and God bless Mummy and Daddy and Grandfather Campbell, but we outgrew them. If Father Ignatius knows this he doesn't mention it. Perhaps it's because we're not Catholic and he isn't actually responsible for us so it doesn't really matter to him all that much and he's still our friend.

At the very moment my mother is at her most cross Father Ignatius is walking down the path to our house. He's carrying a torch in his hand that will light his way back through the night. So we can see he's come to stay for a while.

He stops at the garden gate just like he always does. He says it's to give a few words of encouragement to Justin's dog. We know the real reason is that although it isn't a very long walk what he really stops for is to catch his breath.

He smokes too much and he won't stop and when he's alone in the evening he likes the whisky bottle for company but this is his business and nothing to do with us. Sometimes, these days, I think the only time my father is really happy is when Tuesday night comes around and he sees Father Ignatius coming down our path with his torch in his hands ready for the weekly chess challenge.

At the supper table, after the lamb has been carved

and my father has poured wine, Father Ignatius speaks about Justin.

He doesn't stand up or anything. He doesn't act as if he's thought about it at all. He just tags it on after he's said grace which is not what is usual at our house but something we do when he's there.

'I really don't know why we bother,' my mother says behind his back. 'There's no need to put on an act for him.'

'Out of respect for his belief,' my father says.

Justin and I don't mind. We quite like it.

When Father Ignatius says may the Lord make us truly thankful it sounds as if it's Justin he's talking about and not just the lamb we're having for supper and the strawberry ice-cream for afterwards.

He says Justin is leaving being a boy behind and it's the right time for us to consider what a fine boy he's been.

Justin fidgets.

My father leans back in his chair so his face is in the dark and we can't see it. My mother's face is red and shiny as if the reflection of the birthday candles is still on it. It floats in and out of her yellow-gold hair in the wavy light from the outside generator. Her hands are thin and she has to fold them so they hold on to each other to keep them still.

Father Ignatius looks the same as he always does. His face is filled with deep lines like dry river courses and his hair is grey and springy like the kitchen steel wool Grace uses to clean the pots.

Justin who has lately pleased everyone when his exam results from the white examiners came through the post is trying to look as if he doesn't know how much we love him and how we all feel.

Perhaps so much love is hard to bear.

We sit there and our door stands open to the night. There's a big moon floating around in the sky outside. The crickets sing and the guineafowl settling down to sleep make their noise like the screech of ungreased wagon wheels.

No matter what my father tells me or what all the doctors and specialists in the world might say I don't believe my brother will leave me even though my father has taken me aside and talked to me about it.

'We can hope,' he says. 'But we must also be prepared.'

I am prepared.

'Love is stronger than death.' I've heard Father Ignatius say so and I believe I love my brother so much he won't leave me.

I don't think I got it wrong. As long as I keep loving Justin, as long as my love is strong enough, he won't go. He'll be here for me for ever. It's up to me. Just as long as I keep loving him enough.

'Let's take hands,' Father Ignatius says and we do and I look at Justin but he doesn't look back.

I think Father Ignatius will say: 'Let us pray.'

Sometimes he does, but he doesn't tonight. He doesn't say anything at all. We sit there with our eyes wide open and our hands knitted together and when the moment is gone it's gone for ever.

FRIEDA

Chicken Feet and Giblets

1964

Although Alvin Silverman is not exactly what you'd call my boyfriend I decided to let Min have a look at him and I thought maybe I'd ask her what she thinks of him or maybe I won't. First I'd have to take a look at her face when she sees him.

If it was up to me I would have taken her that first Saturday but there's no point going to Silverman's on Saturdays because none of them are there.

They're all of them in *shul* with their parents and the *kosher* side of the shop which Mr Silverman runs himself is closed down and shut up just like it always is from Friday early closing until Monday morning.

So I have to keep my little surprise to myself and wait a whole week until Friday afternoon comes around again.

On Friday it's my job to pick up our meat order before the shop closes. You can have meat delivered but it costs more and anyway the walk is good for us.

On Friday afternoons there's always a big rush for

weekend meat at Silverman's *kosher* shop and the Silverman boys help out.

What I wanted was to walk into Silverman's and show off my new friend but now she's actually here I'm not so sure I want to do it any more. The reason is how she looks.

I don't mean her face which is not bad as faces go. I mean her clothes. If she'd been there to see it I don't think my mother would have let Min out on the street and especially not into Silverman's looking the way she does.

It needn't be like this. She has the most beautiful clothes you've ever seen. A suitcase full of them and the suitcase labelled with her name on it. MISS MINNIE CAMPBELL. As if she was going cruising on the *Queen Elizabeth*. I would give my right arm to be so grand and take it all for granted the way she does.

The first time, when I asked if I could see her clothes before she packed them away, she pulled them out of her suitcase and threw them down on the bed and they lay there in a big pile and most of them still had their price tags on them.

'If you like them you can have them,' she said. 'They're yours and you're welcome to them.'

All she wants to wear are her old shorts and her boy's shirt and those terrible tyre tackies.

Maybe that's what they wear in the bush but it's not the kind of thing white people wear up the High Street when they go shopping and I don't know what to do about it and Sadie isn't much help.

'We all have to put clothes on our backs in the morning,' Sadie says. 'When you've got so many things to choose from why shouldn't it be something nice?'

'Those clothes were bought by my mother's husband,' Min says.

From this we're supposed to understand everything and excuse us if we don't.

'I never asked for them. I don't need them and I won't wear them. If I don't suit you the way I am then you'll have to leave me behind because what I'm wearing is all I have that actually belongs to me.'

She doesn't bother to think about me. I'm the one who has to walk out in my own neighbourhood with a girl who wants to look the way she does.

When we get to Silverman's Alvin is there.

He says: 'Hi, Frieda!'

This is because his mother's watching but I say, 'Hi!' back anyway.

'Hello, Mrs Silverman,' I say. 'This is Min who's staying with us for the holidays.'

Ruth Silverman sits on a stool behind the till the same as she sits every day keeping her eye on everything and taking in the money.

When she sees me she says: 'Ask Alvin what he's got special for you,' and at the same time she's talking to me she's saying thank you to a customer and the till is tinkling and the till drawer is sliding backwards and forwards and money is changing hands.

'I brought biscuits for you, Mrs Silverman,' I say. They're sitting in my basket in greaseproof paper. 'Sadie said to give them to you.'

Every Saturday Sadie sends something, biscuits, a banana loaf and sometimes fruit cake, and Mrs Silverman slips something into the basket free of charge and special for Sadie like some nice chicken's feet or giblets or big bones for the soup pot and it's not any old feet or bones. They come from the special separate section inside the big shop where the *kosher* meat is kept which Mr Silverman supplies and delivers to Jewish families all over town.

It's the *kosher* business that Mr Silverman built up his reputation on. The High Street business is his bread and butter. The *kosher* trade is the jam. When the Silvermans come over on Sunday evening for a walk to our house and a cup of lemon tea that's what Isaac Silverman tells my father. That's how I know.

People much more important than us who you never see around the streets of Germiston take their business to Mr Silverman. Reuben Lazar who's got more money than the rest of us put together buys there too. Twice a week Silverman's delivery van goes to his house to deliver. He wouldn't give his business to any other shop. This is because Silverman's give quality and a man like Mr Lazar knows quality when he sees it.

When I get to the front of the queue Alvin Silverman sees me and waves his butcher's knife.

I smile but I look at him and I wonder what I always wonder when I see him these days since the dance.

Here I am and here is Alvin. One day soon I'm going on the market and as far as a husband is concerned Alvin seems to be the kind of boy everyone thinks is first prize. Which puts Alvin in the position to be choosy which is not exactly the same place you could put me.

The Silverman boys are what they are right now and forever helping out in their father's shop, but one of these days they're going to be doctors and lawyers or have businesses of their own and then we won't see them for dust but it still doesn't answer the question.

How come Alvin can be so picky and everyone thinks it's fine and I can't? It doesn't seem right to me.

For all I know Alvin may do well in life. He may be all set to go very far which, whichever way you look at it, can't hurt me because although I don't think he's the man for me, one day when he's famous, I won't mind telling people he was my first real date.

On Saturday afternoons as soon as the worst heat of the day is over Sadie goes to the cemetery at Brixton.

'Why anyone would want to spend every Saturday in a cemetery beats me,' my father says.

Sadie's always been fond of going to Brixton. She used to go once a month, maybe twice. Now it's every Saturday.

'It's unnatural,' my father says. 'Why doesn't she take a friend and go to the pictures like other people do? Wouldn't Ruth go with her if she asked her? Why don't you go? Have an outing. See a bit of life.'

My mother will always stick up for Sadie.

'There aren't many young people who respect the dead the way Sadie does,' she says.

'I don't have an argument about honouring the dead,' my father says. 'All I'm saying is every Saturday out to Brixton is too much. Sadie's still a young woman. She should be doing other things. I think someone should tell her this.'

Someone has. My mother has. She's told her that very day. 'You may be my own sister,' she says. 'That doesn't mean I understand you.'

Sadie's sitting on the edge of the bed in the big front bedroom where my mother and father sleep. Her feet are bare and her dressing gown is thrown any-old-how over her shoulders. You can see the lace petticoat sticking out from underneath. Her hair is loose and flaming all around her head and my mother is bending over and looking in a dressing-table drawer for her best white silk blouse.

'It's in the top drawer on the right-hand side,' Sadie says and my mother finds it and pulls it out and hands it over.

'Here you are,' she says. 'Take it and you're welcome and wear it in good health but I still don't understand. The more you explain the less I understand.'

'Perhaps it's the weather,' Sadie says.

'I'm beginning to think that for a change maybe Aaron's right. This running backwards and forwards to Brixton is not a natural thing.'

'Am I doing anyone any harm?' Sadie says.

My mother can't say yes so she doesn't say anything but she doesn't have to. Between sisters there's no need for words to be wasted.

'What's there to worry about then?' Sadie says.

'You should be worrying about the living, not the dead,' says my mother. 'You know the best way to please the dead? Have a good life. That's all anyone asks of you. That's what Aaron says and he's quite right.'

'Aaron's always right when he's saying what you want to hear.'

'So? For a change I agree with him. Is it such a terrible thing for a woman to agree with her own husband?'

'You don't have to worry about me. I know what I'm doing.'

'You're not going to find what you're looking for at Brixton cemetery,' my mother says. 'To find what you're looking for you need to get on a bus and take a ride into town.'

We all know what Sadie's looking for. No one needs to say it out loud.

'You should go and sit for a while in the Jacaranda Garden. Order a coffee or maybe a nice glass of soda. It needn't cost you a week's wages. You don't have to eat anything. Get a seat by the window so people can see you. Who knows who you might bump into there?'

'Who knows?' Sadie says but you can see she's not really interested.

'Listen to me, Seidela,' says my mother. 'Just for a change take a piece of advice from your sister. To find a nice man you must go where men are. Six feet under the ground is no good to anyone. Believe me.'

'I believe you,' Sadie says.

Maybe she does and maybe she doesn't but she's still going to do what she wants to do anyway. The bus that goes past Brixton leaves at four o'clock and it's half-past three now and the dead may be in no hurry but Sadie is. She's already looking at her watch.

In the late afternoon the storms roll in from the veld. You can feel them coming. You can hear the rumble and smell the rain in the air long before the water arrives.

The sky gets dark and people get restless. The air is like a thick, heavy blanket wrapped tight around the world. It traps you in but you can't throw it off.

People on the street are in a hurry to get to shelter before the rain comes. Hadedas screech away in pairs and it's a sad sound and when the rain comes it comes in torrents.

Then just as quick as it started it's over. The sun comes out and before you've turned around the water has turned to steam and all the edges of the world are soft and you can smell the ground.

Saturday after the rain is the time my father and mother spend together with Davey. His room gets tidied and they wash him nice and clean and get him ready for bed.

When this is done it's time for my father to get togged up to go out to the Starlight Room or wherever else he has a job going so he can play his saxophone and be paid for it and we can have bread on our table.

This is the time no one worries about me and what I do. If I want to ask something this is when I slip it in.

'Can I take Min to the river? I want to show her.'

We call it a river although it's only a stream really. It comes gushing down after the rain but by the time the sun goes down there's no river left except a few muddy puddles and the holes where the Flat Anna frogs call from. So you have to be quick.

My mother thinks the river's not the safest place in the world but today she's in a good mood so she says we can go.

'If we want to get the best place we have to hurry,' I say.

We're both in rubber sandals because of the wet and although mine are a more decent kind of sandal we're walking fast and both of us are squidging rubber on the wet ground.

'I thought we were going to see a river,' Min says.

'We are,' I say and I won't say anything else.

To get where we're going you have to go through the hole in the fence and then across some open ground. You can hear the river splashing over the ridges of rock and the mine dump is big behind us. We haven't even come to the first corner before we see it. When you stand at the bottom it looks like a mountain.

It isn't exactly beautiful but when the sun comes out and you close your eyes against it you can see all kinds of colours in mine-dump sand. You can see mauve and pink and the dusty glint of gold.

Usually I go right past but this is Min's first time here and she stops at the bottom and looks up. She looks at it as if it's marvellous.

'Do you climb it?' she wants to know.

'People do,' I say.

The local children do but not me and it's nothing to do with being too grown-up for it. It's just that making a sled out of a cardboard box, climbing to the top then sliding down as fast as lightning is not my idea of a good time and never has been.

'Have you ever actually done it?' Min wants to know.

It's no good lying.

'If I wanted to I would,' I say. 'Except what's the point? You climb up, you can nearly kill yourself getting to the top and then when you get there there's nothing much to see.'

It's not the kind of thing I've ever done or ever would do and why should I start now? At my age. With other things on my mind. What for?

'If I climb up will you climb with me or are you scared?' Min says.

She's standing at the bottom with her hands on her hips and looking up and you can see that in her mind she's already on her way. She's thinking how high it is, how fast she can do it and how long will it take.

What I'm thinking is that this is not what I want to do and I'll be a big fool if I let her talk me into it.

'I don't mind climbing,' I say. 'Lots of people have climbed this dump. I can do it any day I like. I'm not in the mood for it today. That's all.'

'You do what you like then,' she says. 'I'm going to do it.'

We'll look such fools. We're too old. If anyone saw us they'd fall over laughing. They'd probably hand out tickets and charge a fee so other people could see us too. Making spectacles of ourselves. Acting like kids.

Maybe Min doesn't know it yet but this part of our life is behind us. We don't need it back. Very soon we won't be able to have it back even if we wanted to no matter how hard we tried.

'Don't look like that,' she says. 'I'm going up and it won't take long and when I come down we'll do whatever you want to do.'

'I don't know what you want to do this for,' I say. 'There's nothing to see.'

'Then come with me and show me nothing,' she says. 'How will I know for myself unless I've seen it?'

She sounds like me which is exactly how she wants to sound so I'll hear her and remember something I once said to her, and so I learn something else about Min. She's not the kind of girl who forgets and so although it's against my better judgement and I hate this kind of thing I say I'll do it. Which is a big mistake.

Min is a much stronger climber than I am. I keep

having to stop to get my breath and all I see are the backs of Min's legs going higher and higher. I feel hot and I feel foolish and I know I shouldn't be here.

Wet dune dust is awful. It pulls at your muscles and you have to pull back whether you like it or not otherwise you'd fall over and the sand smells like wet wool jerseys which isn't the nicest smell in the world.

If there's anything else in this life that's more of a waste of time than this I'd like to know what it is. Even Min has to stop half-way to catch her breath.

'It's not so bad, is it?' she says.

She puts her hand on my shoulder and makes me turn around. 'Look down,' she says.

Who am I to argue? If look down is what I have to do then I'll look down.

We're much higher than I thought. From where we are the sound rises up and although Min doesn't know it she's actually done us a favour because from here we can hear what we've come to hear and we'll hear it much more clearly than we ever could from the ground.

I sit with my legs stretched out flat under the flared skirt of my summer dress and my arms behind me and my hands dug into the sand and down below the whole world is spread out. You can see the tops of gum trees and the roofs of houses.

Herc houses are small and all in straight rows. They're old-time miners' houses with bow fronts and red stoeps and green corrugated-iron roofs for the hail to bounce off and gardens that stretch out behind them.

From where we are we can see right across to the other side of the river where the location is. The blue smoke from the natives' supper fires curls up and makes the air smell funny and tickles our noses while we sit and wait.

'What are we waiting for?' Min says.

'You'll know when we hear it,' I say. 'It doesn't happen just when you want it to. It happens when it's ready. We have to sit still and wait for it.'

I don't think anyone could be so glad to sit down as I am.

I like Min. She may not have much to say for herself and I don't know how she feels about me but I feel sorry for her. Her father is dead and so is her brother. Her mother is how she is but Min has been kind to Davey.

I don't know exactly why but I feel I would like to give her something. Except I don't have all that much to offer and then a little something comes into my mind that I think she would like to know about. Not the usual kind of thing but something I think Min will like because she isn't used to towns and I think she misses the country. The sky is pink and purple over our heads the way it is after rain and my ears are almost flapping in the wind with wanting to hear what I've come to hear and then I do.

'What is it?' Min says.

'You're from the bush,' I say. 'You're supposed to know. Just listen.'

It comes again and then again and Min's face lights up like the sun. She knows what it is and I know she knows because it's the long low roar of a lion and once you hear it you never forget it.

I don't know if it counts as a good deed but what is a 'good deed' anyway? Does it need a proper name and to come with a certificate signed by a rabbi to make it all *kosher* and make us both happy?

'Don't go back and say you never had some surprises here,' I say. 'No one ever believes there are lions right in the middle of Germiston but there are.'

'Where are they?' Min says.

'One day I'll take you and show you but not now.'

I stand up and brush the damp dust off my skirt.

I've done my good deed and still have to get down off the dump and in my opinion that's more than enough for one day.

We're walking along and almost home and we see my father coming the other way and it's getting dark fast. He's wearing the evening suit he wears to work. He's walking to the corner to wait for the lift that takes him to the Starlight Room. In his hand he's carrying his saxophone case. I know him by his walk and his white shirt gleams towards us.

When he sees us he says: 'You better get moving. Sadie's back and your mother will send out a search party for you if you're not there in five minutes.'

Min and I walk on together and my father stands where he is on the pavement watching us. I turn back once to wave and then I do it again. I keep on doing it all the way to our gate.

Our house stands open to the late evening. The shutters are flung wide, the curtains are drawn back and the inside light is shining out. It's warm in the street and the night noises are starting but that isn't the reason I'm not ready to go in.

I want to watch the last of my father. I want to see him go all the way down the road as far as the corner held safe in my sight until I can't see him any more. I don't know why but I feel funny and goosebumpy about it and a little bit cold.

Min leans back against the warm wall and watches me watching my father, waiting for him to get as far as the corner and not moving until he disappears.

When he's gone I'm the one who speaks and it isn't my father I speak about. I don't really know why but I want to change the subject.

'Do you know Mr Pagel?' I say. 'Have you heard of him? Have you ever heard about Pagel's Circus?'

She shakes her head, she hasn't.

'Old Mr Pagel lives in a big house on the other side

of the dump and all his old lions that are too old to work any more live there with him.'

They're old and tired and their teeth are blunt. They wouldn't want to hurt anyone. All they want is to be left alone in a nice place where they're cared for and can be lions in their own way which has nothing to do with a zoo or the bush.

These poor lions wouldn't know the bush if they landed right in the middle of it. They'd be dead in five minutes because of not being able to look after themselves any more and out of loneliness for the life they once knew in showbusiness.

It was my father who took me to hear the lions in the first place. He thinks they should be allowed to see out their days just where they are.

It's a stupid thing but it's not something you'll find anywhere else. We may not have much in Germiston but this is something we have we can truly say belongs to us. I thought it would make Min happy to be in on the secret but I don't think it did because that night after we'd gone to bed and the light had been switched off she turned her back on me and lay with her face to the wall and cried.

MIN

Girl With a Breaking Heart

1960

I've become fascinated with the business of being alive. It looks much easier than it is. Because of this I've started to look at people differently. My father for example.

His arms and neck aren't the arms and neck of a town person. They're burnt brown by the sun. His muscles are hard lumps under the skin, exposed for anyone to look at. When I look at him I see his heart beating in his neck, pumping blood around his body, keeping him alive.

It's incredible and amazing that for some people living seems so easy.

I'm fascinated by my own heartbeats and my breath going in and out all by itself with no help from me.

I lie face-down in the bath and hold my breath for as long as I can but I always roll over and come up gasping for air, lying on my back like a landed fish on the riverbank with its gills flapping and mouth gaping.

It's when I'm lying there with my eyes shut against the light and my chest hurting with the way I'm trying to catch my breath again that I think of my plan. Something I haven't told anyone and don't intend to. Except for Justin.

Usually Justin and I make plans together. This one is all my own but I plan to tell him anyway when the time is right.

I don't care what other people say. I know he can hear me. I visit him every day. I sit by his bed and I talk to him all the time. Sometimes, most of the time, my mother and father are there too and doctors and nurses come and go but I'm the only one who talks the way I do. I'm the only one who knows the things he's really interested in.

I tell him what it's like staying with Grandfather Campbell. I call him the 'mad old bugger'. There's no one there to hear me and Justin knows who I mean. It's what we used to call him to ourselves at home.

I tell how clever he is with languages. He calls the salt and pepper 'condiments'. He speaks to the servants in Zulu or in Hindi. He pours Bay Rum all over himself before he goes out for his afternoon drive. He eats lamb chops every day and I think the jewel in his driver's turban is real and if it is, I think it's a ruby. Very big and red as blood.

'Tell her for God's sake to be quiet,' my mother says.

'He can't hear you,' says my father and I feel his arm go around my shoulder but that's not what I want so I shake myself free.

'He's in a coma,' my mother says. As if I haven't been told that at least a hundred times.

'You know how sick Justin is,' my mother says. 'But you insist on ignoring it and making life difficult for all of us. As if it isn't hard enough already.'

All I see here are white doctors and white nurses and no one else but white doctors and white nurses and what I know, what I've learnt in our village, is that white doctors don't know everything. Not even my father does and he's the first to admit it.

So I talk to my brother and my mother tells me to stop my mumbling but I won't. The nurses say it doesn't do any harm and I keep on doing it.

I know, even if no one else does, why my brother doesn't answer me and why he keeps his eyes closed all the time. I know because it's exactly the same thing I would do myself.

I would lie quite still waiting for night when it was quiet and I could hear the sound of the Durban sea and pretend it was the wind whispering its secrets through the grass of our flatlands.

FRIEDA

The Small Space Between Us

1964

I lie in my bed and Min lies in the dark with her face tight against the wall but even so I can hear her crying and I hope my taking her to hear the lions has nothing to do with it.

It's very hard to know what to say to a girl who speaks as little as Min does.

'Are you all right?' I say.

When she doesn't answer I say the very next thing that comes into my head.

'I can come in with you if you want. If it'll make you feel better.'

When Davey was small whenever he was crying and afraid this is what we did and he never minded. Even when he got bigger and space was scarce we still did it. We made our own space and it was worth it because even though we were squashed together once he could feel me right up close to him it made him feel better.

'I'm not asleep,' I say. 'I don't mind. If it'll make you feel better I don't mind.'

I suppose there are things you say in the summer dark you will never say under the light of the sun but what difference can it make when a person's heart is breaking?

What would be nice is if she would answer me or even just move over to let me in but she doesn't. All she does is keep on crying.

So, on the one hand I suppose out of good manners I should keep quiet; but on the other hand this is my room too and I think this entitles me to some say.

'I hate you to cry like this,' I say. 'Really I do.'

I'm sitting up in bed, the sheet's thrown back. My bare legs are swung out and my feet are on the floor. Min has a pillow over her head. Maybe she thinks it will muffle out the noise, in which case she's made a big mistake because it's not the kind of noise you can get rid of so easily.

The room is bright with night light and except for the two of us our house sleeps. Outside and all around it's the most peaceful night anyone could wish for. The whole wide world is fast asleep and peace pours in through the window.

In this business of Min's breaking heart there are just the two of us.

I am bare legs and nightgown standing on the floor in the small space between our beds. Min is curled up and crying. All you can see is her long, thin body made into a curve and the hand holding the pillow against her face and she's crying as if she's the last person left in the world and everything else is lost. Which doesn't make sense. Why cry like this when there's someone else in the room standing right next to your bed and asking and willing to help you?

'Is it because I'm Jewish you won't let me come in with you?' I say. 'Is that the reason why? If you've got something against it, you can say so if you like. I won't mind.'

Which isn't actually true and also not the kind of

thing I'd ever say out loud in daytime but I'm saying it now because this is what I feel.

'Would it be different if I wasn't? All I want to do is help you. If I wasn't Jewish, would I be able to help you then?'

'It isn't that,' Min says. 'That's got nothing to do with it.'

She moves over and sits up. She pulls the pillow into her lap and puts both her hands palm-up against her face as if she's trying to push back all the pain and I sit down next to her and reach out and put my arms around her.

I've never been so close to another girl before. At Theodor Herzl we don't do very much of this. At *shul* all the women are kissing each other all the time but all anyone gets for their trouble is the smell of expensive scent and sometimes a lipstick blot on the cheek.

I'm not very good at it. I can feel Min's shoulder-blades under the palms of my hands. Her skin is warm under her pyjamas and there's a scent like soap and lemons in her hair. I hold her tight against me. My arms go right around her and I can feel all her top-quality ivory bones pressed against me.

It's funny about Min and me sitting held tight together in the dark like this. She's not a Jew and I am. All our lives people tell us we're different. I've been told it and I'm sure she's been told it too. Now I know we're not so different at all.

I hold her close and when she cries, even though I have nothing to cry about, I cry too. I do it because it's the only thing I can do and when I ask myself why I who have so much to be grateful for am doing such a thing there's an answer for this too.

It's because I have a father too and a brother I happen to love.

*   *   *

Beauty works for us. She used to live across the river and walk to work with her friends. Now she has to come by train and bus.

On Monday mornings you can hear the maids coming. If you look out of the window all you see are the colours of their headscarves and berets bobbing along the road.

We have Beauty so my mother can go out three mornings a week to work in the archive down at the *shul* and help Rabbi Weisz out as a secretary.

It's not every girl who'll look after a house with five people and take care of a boy like Davey. We could live without Beauty but life wouldn't be the same.

At *shul* people always say to watch out for the *shvartzers*.

'Be careful, Miriam. That's all we're saying.'

This is what the *shul* women say even though they all have maids themselves. They're always saying what a nuisance they are and how if they could they'd live without them.

Which is something I'd like to see.

Their maids are their life. These women spend their whole time running after their maids. In the day they have to check up to see things have been properly done. In the evening when the girls leave they have to check their shopping bags to see nothing's walking out of the house with them and on its way to the location.

My mother hasn't got time for this. Beauty may need her job with us but we need her as well and anyway she doesn't carry a shopping bag. She brings her overall neatly folded up in a piece of brown paper and everything she ever needs is tied up in a piece of cloth and pushed down her bust bodice and that's where it stays.

We all give our maids food. What they love is samp and beans. Even a fancy food shop like Thrupp's has a special maids' section where the madams and masters can buy samp and beans for their maids. When we're at home and Beauty's cooking the whole house smells of her food. Even if you're at the bottom of the garden you can smell it and know that Beauty's somewhere not too far away.

She has all her own things in our house and she keeps them in a separate part of the cupboard in the same place as her packet of sugar and her tea. No one we know would allow a maid or any black person to eat out of their house or to use their things. Everything is always separate. It's a little bit like keeping *kosher* but different.

The *shul* women have terrible stories they say they saw in the newspaper. Stories about maids who use the toilet and bath when the madam's not there and dress up in the madam's clothes and entertain their boyfriends on the madam's best china.

It's never happened to us.

'Don't be so certain,' Ruth Silverman says. 'Who knows what goes on when a back is turned? There's always a first time.'

We haven't had a first time yet but if there is one, even though we need her, we would have to let Beauty go because there is no such thing as a second time.

If there is I've never heard of it.

I don't know what Beauty thinks about Min but I know what Min thinks about her. She can't get enough of her. Wherever Beauty goes Min is only one step behind.

'Let's walk as far as the park,' I say.

'We can go later,' she says.

'We can go down to the river and sit there for a while if you like.'

'You go,' she says.

I get fed up with it. She may not want to be here but nor do I. I don't want to spend my whole summer listening to *Tea With Mr Green* on the radio. I want to be on Durban Beach lying under a sun umbrella looking at the world through cats-eye sunglasses and sipping Coke float through a straw and if I was sure no one I know was looking I would even think about eating a *trayf* hamburger at the Hamburger Hut.

All Min wants is to be everywhere after Beauty.

When Beauty's doing the washing Min's face is at the bathroom door. When she's hanging it out in the yard Min is sitting on the back stoep. The book on her lap is closed and she's watching Beauty as if she's never seen a maid hanging out washing before.

You've seen it once, you've seen it. One person's shirts and skirts and underpants are just the same as anyone else's. She forgets she's here to visit me and I'm the one she's supposed to be talking to and keeping entertained.

In the end even Beauty can't stand it any more. She puts the washbucket down and comes over and stands huge in front of Min and clicks and clacks in Native. Then she asks Min in plain English if there's something wrong. Is there something she wants to know? Has she got something on her mind and if there is would she like to say what it is?

As it turns out there is something on her mind and she does want to say it and she says it right out loud. *Click-clack* she goes to Beauty, right back in Native, and I slam closed the magazine I'm reading and think: This is a nice surprise and thank you for telling me first.

It's the kind of thing a person likes to know. It's like being able to play the piano or sing. It makes you look at someone in a different way and I'm not the only one who thinks so.

Beauty opens her mouth and then she puts her hand over it and not a single sound more comes out and I sit where I am with my *Fair Lady* magazine on my lap and think how things will be different at our house this summer.

No more secrets from the master and madam which all by itself could be worth gold to some people whose names I could mention. Everyone wants to know what their maid says about them when she thinks they don't understand. If there were any *shul* women left who weren't at the seaside and they knew what I'd just heard they'd be standing in line to invite Min over.

Min's talking and Beauty's nodding and when Min's finished Beauty shakes her head and starts to laugh and that's not a thing that happens every day either. Maids don't usually laugh at madams. Not even young ones.

'What's so funny?' I say and I'm not very nice when I say it. It's not so great being the one who's left out. I'm the one who lives here and it would be nice if someone would take some notice of me for a change.

'Nothing's funny,' Min says. 'I was just talking to Beauty.'

'I can see that much for myself.'

'Then what's all the fuss about?' Min wants to know. 'There are hardly any white people where I live. Everyone speaks Zulu to everyone else so I do too.'

She can't understand why no one in town does or why I find it so interesting that I have to tell my whole family about it and they find it interesting too.

'The black people who live here would like you far better if you did.'

'I'm sure they would,' my father says.

This is what he thinks too and maybe he was going to say more but he doesn't because even before his mouth is open all he gets for his trouble is a look from my mother.

'What makes you think the natives don't like us?' Sadie says.

She doesn't mean to but Min sounds exactly like the *shul* women who are always telling us the natives hate

84

us. One day they're going to come and murder us in our beds and we can be as good to them as we like, that's all we can expect for a thank-you.

Six million it took for some of us to learn a lesson and still not everyone's learnt it. When you're not wanted somewhere you should be packing your bags and getting out of the country. What we should be doing is waving a very long goodbye to Johannesburg and the bush and the blacks.

But we don't talk about these things in our house and never at the dinner table because we mind our own business. What blacks feel is their affair. What other whites feel is their own business. What Jews feel we discuss with each other but not in front of a non-Jew who happens to be staying under our roof.

Min can bring her bush ways and her bush talk with her. Her politics she will have to leave right outside the door.

Later that night while we're lying around on our beds reading it's a different story.

'Why do you think the natives don't like us?' I say.

It's a question I've wanted to ask for quite a long time but it's hard to get an answer in a house where we don't usually talk about such a subject.

'I've only been here for five minutes,' Min says. 'How would I know? For all I know maybe they like you very much and think the sun shines out of you.'

'If that's what you think why can't you just say so?'

She has her back to me. She's brushing her hair, pulling at the damp bath-steam knots and tugging with her hairbrush to get them out.

'What's the point of our having secrets?' I say. 'Especially stupid ones? If I ask a straight question why can't you give me a straight answer?'

'There's no secret,' she says.

She's shining with cleanness the way very blond people do. Her hair is brushed. It's in a big bunch held together at the back of her neck with an elastic band.

Her shoulders are like a coat-hanger on either side of her shorty pyjama top and her bony brown legs are sticking out.

You can see what Beauty thinks is so funny. Even tanned brown Madam Min with all the click-clacks locked inside her is the whitest girl you ever saw.

'I asked you a question. Will it kill you to give me an answer?'

'How can they like you?' she says.

'And what's that supposed to mean?'

'All it means is maybe you should think about it. Next time you go out just open your eyes.'

I do go out with my eyes open and if there's anything to be seen I don't miss it. Anyone who knows me will tell you that.

'I suppose it's politics.'

'If that's what you want to call it,' she says.

Then she lies down on top of her bed and puts a pillow behind her back and holds a book up in front of her and starts to read it and after that what is there to say?

MIN

The Great Silence

1960

The graveyard plot where all the Campbells go is in
the white cemetery near Umlazi. It's surrounded by
sugar-cane fields. There's frangipani and hibiscus; the
smell of gardenia and jasmine is in the air and Indian
women with red marks between their eyebrows and
fingernails stained orange with henna keep the graves
tidy.

They move like yellow and red and green birds and
their saris are flecked with gold thread. They shimmer
in the light and they begin very early in the morning
before the heat is up.

There's an open place to park outside the cemetery.
Enough for even the biggest funeral and a sign that
says NO HAWKERS because the general opinion is
that Durban Indians have no shame. They'll take ad-
vantage of any situation to trade and once you allow
them in there'll be no end. Flowers, which would be
all right in themselves, will give way to fruit and fruit
to iced drink and chips and ice-cream and all the

rubbish that comes in their wake and the place will look like a 'coolie bazaar' and no one wants that. So it's not allowed.

Only the Indian women are allowed and behind the closed gates they sway gracefully in their saris and bend to their task of keeping the graves weeded and watered and sweeping away fallen leaves and blossoms and they move easily on their bare brown feet and you'd think they were moving to some music that we can't hear.

There's a marble angel with outstretched wings and lidless eyes that gazes up at the sky. She's very young for an angel, not much older than Justin and me, and she looks unhappy. Under her feet there's a big head-stone with a long list of names on it and that's where my mother keeps her eyes fixed.

She doesn't look at the coffin with Justin inside it. Not even once. When it's lowered into the ground Grandfather Campbell puts his arm around her and my father stands to one side of them alone and no one takes any notice of me at all.

Since Justin died I haven't said a word. Not a single word. Everyone thinks I'm talking to someone else and no one has noticed I'm not and that suits me just fine.

I know my mother will notice eventually but it's a long time before she does and when she does it doesn't please her.

'She's doing it on purpose,' she says and she looks at me with fire in her eyes. 'First she couldn't keep quiet. She talked and talked and drove us all half mad.'

The funeral is over and we're driving home. Just at this moment when my father most yearns for the freedom of flight with the birds far below and all of eternity around we're driving because my mother hates flying and we have a very long way to go and for most of it the road is not good.

'Does she know you and I had to go to the hospital

separately without her just to have some peace?' my mother says. She's in the front seat next to my father. I'm in the back and she pulls herself around hard so she can look at me. 'You didn't know that, did you?' she says. 'Even when we explained to you that he couldn't hear us any more, you wouldn't listen.' She won't say his name. It isn't a hard-and-fast rule yet but it's already begun. 'You're so stubborn,' she says. 'You always know better. You always want your own way.'

When my mother cries her eyes are two white lakes with a small blue fish swimming at the centre of each. Tiny, angry fish that seem in danger of being washed away.

'Now you have nothing to say,' she says. 'We can't get a word out of you.'

She looks straight ahead in front of her and on either side of us the square green fields that lead to our mountain and the pass that winds down to our house speed by. She doesn't seem to care that every mile that passes leaves Justin further and further behind, alone in the ground with only the sad angel for company.

'Playing dumb,' my mother says. To my father, not to me. 'Carrying that ridiculous twig of wood with her everywhere. What for? Why, for God's sake? It's quite beyond me.'

Then it's my father's turn. She turns on him in a flash.

'I'm going back with you now but I'm not going to stay,' she says. 'You can do as you please but there are limits to what you can expect from me and I've reached them.'

She turns her head to the side and when the light is right I can see her image swimming against the glass of the window.

'Stop crying, Julia,' my father says. 'It's not going to get us anywhere.'

'It's her,' she says, meaning me, as if my name has been taken away along with Justin's. 'She's doing this on purpose. This not-talking business. She's doing it because she wants attention and I won't give her any. I'm all used up. I haven't got any to give.'

The silence is not as I expected. It is a large place and dark. I wonder what exactly it is I've come upon and if it's the same place Justin is now.

FRIEDA

The Man Who Came to Dinner

1964

It's just before Christmas and Coronation Avenue is at its best. Every house has a necklace of pink and blue Christmas roses around the bow-front of its stoep.

'I have something to tell you, Miriam,' Sadie says. 'Something good. A surprise.'

'What surprise?' my mother says.

'I've invited a friend for *shabbas* Friday,' Sadie says. 'A gentleman friend. Just as long as it's all right with you. That's what I told him. "I'd like you to come," I said. "But first I'll have to ask my sister." '

'What are you talking about, "all right"?' my mother says. 'This is your home. You ask who you like here. Where else should you invite your friends? Don't talk to me about all right.'

'Is it someone we know?' I say.

'Not exactly,' Sadie says.

'Then who is it?'

My mother waves me to be quiet.

91

'Give Sadie a chance to finish,' she says. 'If she can't get a word in how can she tell us who her friend is?'

'I've been wanting to tell you,' Sadie says. 'But you know how it is, first I wanted to be sure if he'd say yes.'

It's too hot to sleep. What's nice is to sit in the dark in the old cane chairs on the back stoep and drink Russian tea and watch the small night insects flying round and round in the beam of light from the kitchen.

'Does your friend have a name?' my mother wants to know.

It's no good pretending. The air's so full of excitement you can cut it with a knife. Sadie inviting a man home at all, never mind to take *shabbas* with us, is not an everyday thing and this is not the end of her surprises.

'It's Mr Reuben Lazar I've invited,' she says. 'I asked him if he'd like to have *shabbas* with us on Friday and he said thank you for the invitation and he's very pleased to accept.'

My mother can just about stay still in her chair. Reuben Lazar is one of the richest men in Johannesburg. For all we know he may be one of the richest men in the world.

'How do you know Reuben Lazar?' my mother says. 'You never said anything to me.'

'Until today, there was nothing to say. I met him at Brixton and he's very polite and for a long time we just greeted. I didn't even know who he was.'

In Johannesburg no deal is made, no deal is even thought about if Mr Reuben Lazar doesn't know about it and isn't consulted but to us there is something even more important about him than this. What's really important is that Reuben Lazar is a widower.

'He lost his wife three years ago,' Sadie says. 'Every Saturday he's at Brixton. I've never known him to

92

miss a Saturday. Not even one. He must have been a wonderful husband to his late wife.'

What she means is that if Reuben Lazar has been a wonderful husband to one wife he can maybe, if God sees fit to bless us, be a wonderful husband to another one. My mother can hardly believe our good fortune.

'What exactly did he say?' she says. 'What did he say when you invited him here?'

'He said it would be his pleasure,' Sadie says.

'You'll wear your best,' my mother says.

My father's out at early-afternoon rehearsal at the Starlight Room and she hasn't waited for him to come home. She and Beauty have poor Davey in the bath and out of the bath and dressed and sitting quietly long before we leave for *shul*.

These days Min sits with Davey on Friday while we're at *shul* so our family can all go together but on the night of the Great *Shabbas* Supper Beauty is here to help out. She does it for a favour but not entirely out of love because she also gets extra money plus train and bus fare back to the township.

'Wear your blue Hanukkah dress,' my mother says. 'And just for a change Min can look like a lady as well. She'll do it as a favour to us.'

We never bring up the question of the cupboard full of clothes Min won't wear. They're all there hanging on their shop hangers. All brand new with their price tags still on them.

The few old things she squeezed into the bottom of her suitcase when her mother wasn't looking are the only things anyone ever sees her in. They're off her back and into the wash then back on her back again. My mother and Sadie have given up begging and pleading and reasoning with her to every now and then go out on the street looking like a decent person for a change.

'The pink party dress is the nicest one,' my mother says.

She's been into the cupboard and run her hand over all Min's clothes, moving them aside one after the other like someone shopping at Anstey's or The Belfast or some other very nice shop.

The dress is pale pink nylon with full puff sleeves. It has a blue satin sash around the waist and there are flat blue party pumps to go with it. The price ticket is still on it and I can name ten girls at Theodor Herzl who would kill to have a dress like this in their cupboards never mind on their backs.

'Such a dress!' my mother says. 'A quality dress like this. It's a shame you can't wear the price on the outside so everyone can see.'

'If you like it so much Frieda can wear it,' Min says.

'You'll wear it,' my mother says. 'You'll wear it to please me because I'm asking you to.'

Min has never gone up against my mother before and if you know her the way I do you can see my mother isn't in the mood for an argument. Not with a girl my age who's a visitor in our house. Not on this night of nights.

The dress is set out on Min's bed and with it underwear with real lace edging and a nice suspender belt and nylon stockings still in their packet. The blue shoes are on the floor sticking out from under the bed. All the dress needs is a girl inside it and everyone will be happy.

'Put it on,' my mother says but Min won't budge.

My mother's in the doorway and Min is standing between the beds in her bare feet and shorts like she always is.

'No, I won't,' she says.

'Yes, you will,' says my mother.

I think there's going to be an argument which just goes to show how much I know because instead of standing her ground like she always does Min does the last thing in the world I expect. She looks at my mother. Her eyes fill with tears and she starts to cry. Which makes my mother even crosser.

'Over a dress?' she says and she shakes her head and throws her hands up into the air. 'Such a big *farible* over such a small thing?'

She turns to me and asks me if by any chance I happen to know what makes Min carry on like this but I don't. All I can say is it's just the way she is. When she cries she cries her heart out and there's nothing I or anyone else can say that can make it any better. It won't do any good even to try.

I don't know now why we were so worried about Reuben Lazar. He's not very tall. He has pink skin that shines like a baby's and thick silvery waves of hair. He's beautifully dressed in a quality suit and a nice striped shirt and he smells of cologne. He's come straight from *shul*.

'In a Cadillac, if you don't mind,' says my mother who is just about ready to *platz* from excitement.

'New out of the box,' says Sadie.

She may say Mr Lazar is only out on approval and they're still making up their minds about whether or not they suit each other but you can see the way the wind's blowing.

We waited a long time for this gentleman caller but when he eventually arrived Sadie didn't let us down and he was worth the wait.

He can't praise my mother and Sadie enough. He hasn't even sat down at the table and already everything is wonderful in his eyes.

'Just wait until we eat,' my mother says. 'Sadie's a wonderful cook.'

Then just in case he's deaf and maybe hasn't heard Aunty Fanny chips in.

'Not only a good cook but so beautiful. Our Seidela is an angel. In every way an angel.'

Sadie looks down and won't look at Mr Lazar because she knows what they're doing and so does he.

'Frieda's a great help in the kitchen,' Sadie says. 'She's the one who's the good cook in the family.'

Just to change the subject she tells all the things I can do. It's all right to talk about me. I'm not the one being pushed in Mr Lazar's direction. No one needs to be embarrassed when I'm the subject of conversation.

'I can see your mother and your aunt are bringing you up in a proper way,' he says.

He means in a proper Jewish way. What I'd like to know is what other way there is in a house like ours but I don't say so.

Sadie's offering a bowl of water and a linen towel around so we can wash our hands before we settle down to the business of *shabbas* and my mother and Sadie shouldn't have worried so much. Mr Lazar can see for himself the way we are.

He may have come a long way in life but when you get right down to it he's just the same as everyone else. Money didn't fall like manna from heaven into his lap. He started out somewhere just like we all do. He may be living in a palace these days but you can see he knows houses like ours and families like ours as well. I think he knew before he walked in our door what he should expect but he came anyway and he won't go home disappointed.

The table is beautiful. The sun has gone down and the candles are lit. Two for the sabbath and one pair each for Sadie and me who are both in our separate ways daughters of this same house.

There's Cape salmon flown in fresh that morning sitting on a serving plate on the table and potato *latkes* and a beautiful salad, all colours of the rainbow, every piece of it picked by my father from his own vegetable garden at the back of our house.

There's apple for apple *tzimmes* simmering at the

back of the stove and the smell of cinnamon is in the air.

On the sideboard there's fruit and a silver dish of *teiglach* to take with our coffee. The two white loaves of *challa* which we call *kitke* are in front of us waiting to be broken and Min is sitting next to me in her beautiful pink dress and her eyes are a bit red which is the only sign of the terrible *farible* of such a little while ago and it's only a dress after all.

You can see she isn't Jewish but she looks very pretty. She acts politely like a real lady and Mr Lazar who we have no objection to impressing can see for himself that even when it comes to a guest we know good quality when it comes our way and would only offer him our best.

My father's at the head of the table and the *kitkes* are next to him. Mr Lazar is in the seat of honour on his right hand and Davey is there too, sitting quietly in his special place where he has plenty of room, and we're all ready and our eyes are on my mother.

Her head is bowed and her hair is covered with *Bubbe* Rochel's white lace. Her long fingers light the candles and I see their light and hear her voice reciting the blessing and welcoming the sabbath. First in Hebrew, then in English.

She bows her head and makes three long sweeps with her arms and her voice is low and sweet as she welcomes the sabbath right inside our house. Then she spreads her hands over her face and prays.

Then there's quiet while those who are no longer with us fly over and look down and see each of us who are left sitting in our place among the living.

'Blessed art Thou, O Lord our God, King of the Universe who createst the fruit of the vine,' says my father.

My mother looks at Sadie and Sadie with her hair like fire in the candlelight looks back and something strange happens to me. I see my mother and

97

Sadie with their faces turned towards each other in the red-yellow flicker of the candles and I know it's *shabbas* but suddenly I understand what it's really about and it's about us and people like us.

It's as if my grandmother, the late *Bubbe* Rochel Wassermann, has paused in her travels through eternity just so she can give me 'knowing' because as the grandmother this is the gift she has to give to her grandchildren and she can choose the day and the occasion to give it.

My father looks at my mother.

'Her children rise up and call her blessed;
Her husband also, and he praiseth her.'

That's what is said and I like to hear it. I'm not always quite sure what men are here for but I know about women. I've seen it every Friday night for all of my life but tonight I see it again and I know for the very first time what it is I'm seeing and what I'm seeing is love.

It's the love of women like my mother and Sadie and late *Bubbe* Rochel that keeps us all together. It's always been like this. It always will be and nothing is ever going to change it.

MIN

Things That Are Important

1960

In the bush you learn the things you need to know which are not things that are held captive in the pages of any book. The things that are important are not the stories that are given to anyone to tell.

Only the storytellers have the magic and they choose what they want to tell and when.

Clear nights are the best when you can see the moon and the stars stud the sky. That's the time when people want to sit out and listen. Those are the nights of the best stories and the best stories are always the stories of a life's journey because every one is different but in every one there is something that is the same.

If you listen you learn about life and you learn about death and if you listen hard enough and you understand in time you can learn all there is to know.

I've listened and what I've learnt is that it's a bad thing for a man to die far from the place where he belongs.

This is a great fear, this fear of dying in a foreign place where the grey mist offers up her hands to the grey sky and they hold fast together and become one large greyness in order to confuse the spirit.

How can a man find his way home when he can't see the sun in the sky or the moon at night or feel the earth beneath his feet?

Who, in that place where no birds sing, will take a man back to the place where he belongs? If no one comes to guide him, how will he find the home kraal and come to rest among his own people?

How, among strangers who do not know the spirit of the special river and mountain where he was born and where he belongs, can a man with no one to guide him ever find his place again?

This yearning for the home kraal is a terrible thing.

It's more fiery than love. It's stronger than death and we all know about it.

Its story is there among all the other stories and songs of the bush. If someone who is yours, bone of your bone, blood of your blood, dies in a faraway place it is up to you to bring him home and when you set out on such a journey nothing will stand in your way.

The lion and elephant and crocodile will let you pass and the sun and moon will light your way.

'I will come for you.'

That is the promise we give each other while we are living and it's the most important promise we can give.

'When you hear me coming because we are bone of the same bone and blood of the same blood you will know me and not be afraid.'

We know how it will be. It's in the stories and we've been told. First it will be soft like the wings of the morning and then like the thunder that rolls in over the veld and you, the beloved, waiting alone where you are in that place we are not allowed to know, will feel joy in your heart because you know us. We are your people and we have come to take you home.

I know what I must do. I know how it's done. All who live here know how and it sounds such a difficult thing but it's not. Not if the will is strong enough.

There's the catching of the departing spirit which can only be done in the branch of a buffalo thorn tree. No other tree has the magic and to catch it is not such a hard thing. All you do is pass the branch over the body the person once lived in. The rest the spirit will do quick and eager by itself because in death as in life we all want to go home.

It is only after this that it becomes difficult.

For a man to take hold of another man's spirit is a great impudence and a very great responsibility because until he has done what must be done he must carry this burden of his brother's spirit and there is no heavier burden in the world.

What can be a heavier load than this? What do we know of another man's spirit until we've carried it on our own shoulders? What do we know of ourselves until we've been tested with such a burden and carried it as far as we must?

This is what my teacher Mr Morefe told me and when he did Justin was still here with me to hear it too. He told us this and one thing more. Once this task is undertaken there is no turning back.

To get to our village there's a pass that zigzags high up through the air and as you go up higher the air gets thinner and thinner so that if the road climbed only two inches more you'd be floating around weightless inside your car the way astronauts do.

'You have such an imagination,' my mother used to say to Justin. 'The most fanciful imagination of any boy I ever knew.'

I wonder what's happened to Justin's imagination

now? If I'd asked him perhaps he would have left it behind for me.

Perhaps he has.

God Helps Me Pass. It says so on the name board that stands at the highest point on the pass. God helps us. Father Ignatius says so too even though my mother never wants to hear him say it.

We are just we three in the car and we're going home.

'There's never been a serious accident on this pass,' my father says to no one in particular, just for something to say, and the words come out tired and bruised and in a funny way.

Perhaps He does help us but while He's doing it He's neglecting His actual job because people driving along country roads drive like maniacs and die like flies. There are little piles of stones in their memory all along the way and sometimes bunches of flowers or dead wreaths but not here.

I don't really mind dying any more now that I know about it except I can't die now because I still have my job to do.

When that's finished I can do what I like.

'For God's sake put her out of the car,' my mother says. 'If that's what she wants just let her go.'

The car is a black Ford Prefect, sugar-coated with the dust of our journey. Our suitcases are secured on the roof with a piece of rope, tested by my father, pulled this way and that to be sure it will hold.

There's a canvas water-bottle tied to the front fender because sometimes we stop and drink the flat bitter water made cold by evaporation and when we've drunk my mother holds the bottle to her face and presses it against her arms to cool them and holds it under arms folded across her chest against her heart, cooling it even more, nursing the water-bottle as if it was a child.

Some people travel at night on foot and in coolness under the great canopy of the sky with all the stars in heaven to chart their way. But not my father. He weighs up the relief of the coolness of night travelling against its dangers. At night bewildered animals wander into the road and are trapped by the wavering beams of car headlights.

At night our eyes deceive us. Things are not as they appear to be and my father decides to travel by day so we will reach the flatlands that lead to our village in the late afternoon.

I'm not certain.

I hold the branch carefully. I have carried it all the way here, ashamed by my lack of faith in believing my brother cannot manage without me but even more afraid of his need.

My branch is a young branch but no longer pliant. It shows the small bumps and gnarls of what it would have become if I hadn't picked it. I asked a gardener at Grandfather Campbell's house if it would grow again if I planted it. He held it in his hands and took a careful look at it but he shook his head.

'No,' he said. 'It's too late.'

I curve my fingers around it. It's familiar to my touch. It has become part of me and I'm reluctant to let it go but at the same time I'm embarrassed about it and ashamed of myself for believing in native stories and so I lie. We do that these days. We lied a lot about Justin, saying perhaps some terrible mistake had been made and he would get well. We pretended some new drug might come along just in time to save him.

Even my father.

We spent a lot of time reminding ourselves that doctors make mistakes every day. All it shows is that the more you lie the easier it gets and nothing changes.

The branch is Y-shaped and looks like a sling. The shape of a bird snare which has proven its mettle at trapping the unsuspecting. It's the shape of any boy's toy. I think that's why it escaped my mother's attention because usually she doesn't miss anything.

My parents are wrapped in their own thoughts. The road is uneven and their bodies sway with the rhythm of the car, taken over by it as if, since Justin died, there's no life left in them either.

I feel responsible, as if I'm the only one awake in a sleeping house and I pass the moments focusing sharply on the branch so that the world outside blurs.

We used to sing. 'Ten Green Bottles', 'Old Mac-Donald', 'She'll Be Coming Round the Mountain'. We used to play I Spy. I spy with my little eye something beginning with J and J is for Julia, my mother's name.

We used to look for lazy tortoises and call out to my father to stop the car so we could move them out of the road and save their lives. We used to vie to be the first to see the small round top of our mountain. Sometimes we asked my father to stop the car and let us out so we could go the last part of the way home on foot by ourselves.

'Let her go if that's what she wants,' my mother says. 'I've had enough. I don't read sign-language. I hate this stupid game of hers. It's childish and ridiculous and I want her to stop it. When we get home either she behaves properly or she doesn't come home at all. I mean it. That's how I feel. Just don't bother to come home at all. I've had enough of her. I've had just about all I can take.'

MIN

My Mother and Me

1960

My mother's face is a moon floating in the open window of the car, framed in black. Her words clash with the *chug-chug* of the idling engine and the sound of the handbrake being released. Then she winds the window up and her face disappears.

I find myself face to face with a ghost girl but she's taken away by the car and I'm left behind listening to the sound of the engine as it fades away, watching the lashed luggage swaying on the roof as the car is swallowed up in the shimmering heat-haze.

I watch the car shrink down to dinky-car smallness and hear the silence that comes as the fly-speck car rounds the curve of the hill and disappears from sight.

It's purple. The colour of kings' blood. The time brother sun and sister moon float side by side in the sky. It's the best time. The bush, alive and mysterious, sighs to rest. The small night insects float upwards. They spangle heaven like millions of tiny stars and the world is tucked under the soft down of the sky and the air smells of grass and sun.

I must be swift on sandalled feet and make my way home before the long twilight catches me and my voice which has been trapped since the moment Justin left this world jumps free and in the stillness it sings aloud the songs of our childhood, swooping and diving with freedom and joy.

I sing of Kokkie Lobben.

My father, who's in love with words, made up these songs for us so we would always remember where we came from, that although the little robin is an English bird and we're singing the same songs English children sing we are children of Africa and must never forget where we belong.

'YennisZwile, YennisZwile, Kokkie Lobben?'

That's what we used to sing. That's what I sing now and the sun sinks down sulking and the old lady that lives in the moon starts her climb up the black ladder of the sky carrying the stars in a big sack on her back.

You can see our village from above. Even late at night its fires glow and there's a steady stream of lemon generator light from the few houses where white people live. Father Ignatius's church and school and the hospital that was once a monastery are drawn on the sky in neat dark lines. You can see the silent upside-down teacup that is the church bell.

Silent night. Holy night.

I sing of our Christmas tree with its presents and my father offering sweet wine which we're allowed just this once and on special occasions only and my mother putting nuts and raisins into a bowl.

A herd boy brings the cattle in and I sing their names softly, not for their ears but because we know them moving heavily through the grass with their tick birds weaving in the air above them, bending delicately to ask right into their ears whether they have seen Ndiepe, the little herd boy who is lost for ever although they will keep on searching for him till the end of time.

I smell the sweet musk smell of them and the birds rise up to roost with a slow flap of wings and a black eagle soars and catches the last of the sun's rays pink and gold under its wings and the branch is light in my hand and I walk fast now because the story of our small time together is coming to an end and it comes out in hard breaths.

You're supposed to tell all of a life and leave nothing out so that everything may be taken into the next world but I can think of no more to tell and I think I may have forgotten things.

Happy birthday to you and may the Lord make us truly thankful. I had forgotten. I said nothing about the stone angel.

The things I can't remember are stuck in my chest and hurt me and when I stop to breathe the whole world is rising upwards on the last silver eddying heat-haze and above it the small night insects drift and I'm at the door of our house and home and my job is almost done and something in me rises upwards too.

'What now?' my mother says. 'What for heaven's sake is she doing now?'

My mother's standing on the stoep. The generator light from the front door pours over her and she glows like an angel. Her hand is on her hip. My father is handing the unlashed luggage to our servants. Grace and Isaiah. Christian souls who belong not to us but to Father Ignatius and to God in a way that we do not.

'You said you wanted her to talk,' my father said. 'She's doing what you want.'

'She's talking gibberish,' says my mother.

To the servants she says: 'Unpack only the small things. That's all. I'm not staying. I can't face it. I can't face it for another day. Not for one second longer. For God's sake, Thomas, what is she doing?'

My father knows. I can see it in his eyes. He bends towards me and I shrink from him. I shrink from a man who has never touched me with anything but kindness.

I hold the branch against myself and my father knows.

I, who am lately so fascinated with life, feel the whole of myself pumping with it and I'm ashamed because my brother and I always shared equally. There was never one of us who had when the other did not. Except this time.

My father's eyes are soft as dogs' eyes. He has to go down on his haunches to look at me and be level and even then I won't look at him because I'm afraid of what he might tell me.

'It isn't true,' he says. 'It doesn't work like that. If you'd asked me I would have told you.'

'What is it?' my mother says.

'It's nothing,' my father says. 'It's a legend. That's all. An African legend. A story. They learn it at school. You know how impressionable children are.'

'Give me that,' my mother says. She steps out of the light. 'Give it to me.'

She takes my brother from me with a hand swift and sly as a snake and the wild, free thing that is my voice leaps out of my body screaming.

'For God's sake, Julia,' my father says. 'Give it back to her. It's harmless enough. It's a legend. That's all. It's a story. She believes she has Justin's soul in the buffalo thorn branch. She wants to bring it home and bury it somewhere here and put it to rest in some special place. That's all.'

I am outside myself still screaming when my mother hits me hard.

'How dare you?' she says.

She has me by my collar. I want to look at her but

my eyes are closed. She hits me again and she can hit me for ever for all I care. I welcome the pain.

'Fucking white kaffir,' she screams. 'That's all you are. A fucking white kaffir girl.'

I can taste the iodine taste of blood in my mouth and it is more beautiful to me than water on a hot day.

When we were small we sat by the river above the place where the women wash, where the water is clear and ice cold, and we cut our wrists with a penknife made clean with the fire from a match.

'Suck the blood,' Justin says. 'To make it come out.'

He holds out his wrist and I see a thin thread of his blood like red cotton on the white inside of his wrist where the rivers of his veins run blue.

'It doesn't hurt at all.'

I wouldn't care if it did. I would do anything Justin asked me. I offer my wrist up to be cut and he cuts it and then we sit wrist to wrist on the riverbank while our blood flows together and we watch the cold water of the river flow by swift, sure, unhesitating and clear as glass and we ask no questions about where it goes.

'Our blood's joined now,' Justin says. 'It doesn't matter if you're a girl. It makes us blood brothers.' He's very serious about it. 'It's for ever,' he says. 'You must remember that. It's for ever.'

'For God's sake, Julia,' my father says. 'Leave the child alone. It's enough.'

It is enough. It is enough and more than enough and at last it's over and after that there is silence because that's how it is. You may not speak to anyone still in this world until the job is done and I am not yet done because my mother has taken the branch from me and will not let me finish.

FRIEDA

We Make an Occasion

1964

We don't celebrate Christmas at our house. Hanukkah is as far as we go.

We can easily give Christmas a miss but we can't ignore it. How can we, when everyone else makes such a big thing out of it?

At Christmas you can't put your foot in a shop without Father Christmas asking you what it is you'd like for a present. I used to feel a fool saying nothing, thanks all the same, because I happen to be a non-Christian and a Jew.

Even if we don't join in we've got nothing against it. Live and let live. That's what we say.

The middle of town is decorated. Every shop window is dolled up to the nines and there are lights up and down Eloff Street just like there are every year.

When Davey was small and not so fat we used to get dressed up and go into town on the tram to see the lights for ourselves. Then he got sick and I outgrew the whole thing and we stopped going but this year it's going to be different.

Through Sadie Mr Lazar has made us an offer. He will be happy to take Davey and Min and me into town to see the lights and because his car is so big all of us will easily fit in. He said would we like to do this and we said yes.

'Now you'll have something interesting to write to your mother,' my mother tells Min. 'You can tell her thanks to Mr Reuben Lazar, whose name maybe she knows, you drove right down the middle of Eloff Street in a Cadillac motor car. It's not every girl who can say that.'

I think at last my mother's satisfied. God forbid Mrs Delaney should think she wasn't getting her money's worth the day she decided to send her daughter to stay with Aaron Woolf and his family.

Picture postcards come for Min almost every day and my mother makes a big fuss of them.

'They're so beautiful, you should stick them up on the wall next to your bed,' my mother says.

'I'll think about it,' Min says.

I know she won't do it. A postcard you hardly bother to look at is not a postcard that's going to find its way on to a wall. Where they'll end up is shoved any-old-how into a drawer and never looked at again. I know this and my mother knows it too but that doesn't stop her trying.

It's not just because Julia was once her friend. It's because Julia is a mother and Min is her daughter and no matter what Min may think in her heart of hearts there's no such thing as a bad mother. Not where we come from anyway.

I don't think Min's interested in her mother at all. Julia is never going to hear anything about the Cadillac car or the Eloff Street lights or any of the other things we do.

'A funny kind of child,' my mother says to Sadie.

111

'A funny kind of mother,' says Sadie, but then she never had much time for Julia in the first place.

The one thing we're all agreed on is that it isn't right for someone to be among strangers for a special festival.

'Everyone likes to be with their own family at such a time. How would you like to be on your own at Pesach or Hanukkah?'

This year because of Min my mother and Sadie have decided we'll do a little something at Christmas. We'll have turkey with stuffing and a Christmas pudding with five-cent pieces inside it and mince pies made with *schmalz*. After all, what harm can it do?

'We'll make an Occasion,' Sadie says.

She's in a good mood these days. The Cadillac car is forever outside our house, sometimes with Reuben behind the wheel and sometimes his driver. Things are going well and we're hoping for big news soon.

'Reuben Lazar is a lovely man,' my mother says. 'Such a man isn't going to come past twice in a row. You should hang on to him.'

Reuben's been a lovely man from the first minute his Cadillac car drove up and stopped at our front door.

'He can be the loveliest man in the world,' my father says. 'It doesn't make him one day younger and he's still too old for Sadie.' Which is not what my mother wants to hear.

My mother and Aunty Fanny say it won't be very long before Mr Lazar starts talking serious business and sets a date with Sadie.

'Then the diamonds will start coming in,' Aunty Fanny says. 'You see if I'm not right.'

My father hates this kind of talk. He thinks Aunty Fanny's beginning to sound like a *yenta*.

'All she talks about is Reuben Lazar's money. Morning, noon and night she's counting the days till Sadie can get her hands on it.'

'Can I help it if the man who wants to marry my sister happens to be a rich man?'

'You should ask first if he's a good man,' my father says. 'Maybe this is something you and your sister should think about.'

My mother isn't in the mood for a *yeshiva* debate. She knows what she knows about life.

'You could at least act as if you're a little bit happy for Sadie. Sometimes I look at you, I feel I don't know you any more.'

It's all this talk about money. My father doesn't think it's proper. He doesn't like it and it's putting him off the whole thing.

Christmas and New Year are a busy time for my father. There's plenty of work. Sometimes he plays with one band one night and fills in with another the next. Just whenever he's needed.

He has practice sessions during the day and when he's not practising or playing he's going through his sheet music looking for new tunes to make people happy. When he finishes he's tired and not always in the best mood. Then he has to shower and do a quick change so he can go out and play his saxophone with the band.

Christmas seems to put people in the mood for dancing and having a good time. I don't know why but we're not complaining. Why should we? It's good for business.

My father plays the Starlight Room on a Saturday night but at Christmas time and until after New Year he can play every other night of the week too if he wants and sometimes he does. He takes what he's offered because the money's good.

We're all pleased about that even though it means we don't see very much of him. What we see is him and his saxophone case disappearing round about six o'clock. When we go to bed he's gone. When we

113

wake up in the morning he's back again.

I have a magical father. Now you see him, now you don't. I like the times you see him better.

My poor father. He never thought he'd live to see the day we celebrated Christmas in our home. The whole idea makes him shake his head and smile but he understands. God forbid we should have a guest under our roof and not treat her in the right way.

'So, I'll take a piece of turkey and some pudding,' he says. 'It won't kill me. It's not such a terrible thing.'

He'll be there. We all will and Aunty Fanny and Reuben too. Reuben's contributing the turkey. He's arranged with Silverman's to send over the biggest one they can lay their hands on.

You think finding a *kosher* turkey's an easy thing? I can tell you for nothing it isn't as easy as it sounds. At Christmas the turkey business is booming and people are not too worried about what Jews can eat and what they can't eat. Still, if you're as good a customer as Reuben is someone like Isaac Silverman can always make an arrangement and by Christmas Day we're all ready.

Sadie has put as much trouble into our *kosher* Christmas as she ever does for Pesach or Rosh Hashanah. When Min wakes up on Christmas morning there are presents in star-and-reindeer wrapping paper just waiting for her to open them and the turkey is already sitting on a baking tray inside the oven.

'Merry Christmas,' we all say and it sounds so funny coming out of our mouths my father makes a joke of it and says *mazel tov* as well. 'Just so we cover all our options.'

Sadie finds a crêpe-paper crown and puts it on Min's head and we all sit around while she opens her presents and there are presents from all of us.

A book about historic Johannesburg from my mother and father. Goya Black Rose perfume from Sadie because the day comes when you suddenly realize you're not a little girl any more and that's the day when you can forget about Palmolive soap all by itself and you need a little bit extra.

There's a small Dairy Box and a paper fan with yellow and orange flowers from Aunty Fanny. There are two nice handkerchiefs from Davey, and Reuben has given a box of writing paper with envelopes to match which Sadie chose for him.

My present is right at the bottom of the pile. I put it there because I wanted her to save it till last.

I hope she doesn't think I'm a fool.

My mother said a pen for writing on Reuben's nice writing paper would be nice and maybe if I gave her one it would put her in the mood to use it for writing a few lines to her mother every now and then. Sadie said soap or talcum powder to go with the Black Rose. Aunty Fanny said chocolates are always welcome and a good choice.

But Ruth Silverman had the best idea of all and it was her own special friendship with Sadie that gave it to her.

'Friends should give something you can keep always,' she said. 'Something to keep for a memory.'

I know Ruth once gave Sadie a gold-plated brooch in the shape of a forget-me-not bow and Sadie really likes it. She slaps it on just about every outfit she wears as if it was real gold.

The brooch is nice but I have an even better idea for Min. What I get is an autograph album from CNA. Every page a different colour, pale pink and lemon and blue and green, and a nice cover of pink plastic with *Autographs* in gold flowing writing on the front.

I was very excited about it when I was busy buying it. When I showed it to Ruth Silverman to get her opinion she said she thought it was the perfect thing and in exactly the right spirit. But when at last I saw it in Min's hands with the wrapping paper pulled off and lying in a little ball at her feet I had second thoughts and decided perhaps it wasn't such a good idea after all.

Autograph albums are big fashion here but from the look on Min's face it seems as if the fashion hasn't found its way into the bundu yet because she's looking at her present as if she's never seen anything like it in her life before. She's holding it in her two hands as if she thinks I found it and bought it on some other planet.

'It's so if you meet any famous people they should sign their names in it for you,' Sadie says.

Which just goes to show how much she knows. You don't have to hang around waiting for Cliff Richard or Pat Boone to come along. In the mean time you get your friends to write in your book so afterwards you can look at what they say and remember them and sometimes the things they write are really funny although they don't have to be. You can write what you like.

'Open it,' I say. 'I've written something inside it for you.'

I may just as well tell her what to expect because she's soon going to see for herself anyway and there's nothing I can do about it.

When I wrote what I wrote it seemed like a good idea except now that Min's about to read it for herself I'm not so sure.

She opens up the book and smooths down the page in that ever-so-careful, everything-must-be-exactly-right way she has and all you see is her bent head and the gold swing of her hair and the book in her hands and her eyes looking down and the smiling brown curves of her eyelashes.

You'd never think a person with a private education could take so long to read such a few words.

'You can tear it out if you don't like it,' I say.

'I like it just fine,' Min says.

'If you pull out that page and the page at the back of

it as well it won't make any difference to the book,' I
say. 'No one will even notice.'

'I don't want to,' Min says.

'Why don't you read out to us what Frieda's written
in your book?' my mother says.

'Because it's rubbish,' I say.

'No, it isn't,' says Min and it doesn't seem to matter
to her that I'm the one who wrote what she's reading
and can say anything I like about it, she gives me one
of her looks as if I don't know what I'm talking about.

'You don't have to make a whole big thing out of it,'
I say. 'If you're going to read it then read it and get it
over with.'

'Fine,' she says, and she does and her voice is clear
and light and the words I chose dance out of her
mouth and into the air where everyone can hear them.

> 'Friendship is a golden chain
> That binds two friends together
> And if that chain we do not break
> We shall be friends for ever.'

There they are stamped on the air for everyone to
hear and the way she says them makes them sound
different to me and nicer and when she's finished she
looks at me and she smiles and I smile back and then
it's smiles all round and I'm glad I did what I did.

Then she closes the book and puts it down next to
her on the chair half tucked under the top of her thigh
as if she thinks someone will take it away from her.
Which is stupid because the book is hers and meant
for her and nobody else would want it.

There's a present from Min's mother too. A fortune
in money. Twenty-five English pounds with the
Queen's head on them and a Christmas card (not to be
opened until 25 December) with snow and robins.

'That's a lot of money,' my mother says.

'I suppose so,' says Min.

117

I don't think it's breaking her heart that her mother isn't here. She has her Christmas money and her other presents and the sun shining outside. What her mother has is snow and another country and Mr Delaney for company. If you asked me I think I could say who Min would think is the one who's best off.

'What are you going to spend your money on?' I say.

I've never had twenty-five English pounds in my life. I've never even had twenty-five rand. Not of my own, all together in my hand at one time, unless I was going to pay something for my mother, but I don't begrudge Min a single cent. I only ask what she's going to spend it on because this is the kind of thing I like to know.

'I've got plans,' she says.

'What plans?'

'Wait and see,' she says and that's all she'll say.

That's one thing about Min. If she makes up her mind to keep something to herself there is nothing and no one in this world that can get a single word out of her.

FRIEDA

Twenty-five Pounds

1964

The sun pours down on Christmas Day. The church bells ring and our neighbours and their visitors are in and out of their cars or walking up and down the road in their new clothes and the whole world smells of baking and cooking.

It's strange to be the same as everyone else and have a turkey in the oven and the waste-paper basket full of Christmas wrapping paper. It's funny to be sitting out on the front stoep drinking cold drinks and waiting for our lunch guests to arrive.

It's only one day. It can never change anything in a major way. Still, I can imagine the kind of talk that'll be going on at our neighbours' houses.

'These days the mad Jews down the road are celebrating Christmas,' they'll say. 'What next? Goodness knows what the world's coming to.'

The maids are working overtime and for the first time ever Beauty is working at our house to help out with the celebration of Min's Christmas.

The buses are slow on Christmas Day so we don't know when she'll get here but we know she's definitely coming and Min is in and out of the house running down to look over the gate. She can't wait to see Beauty coming down the road with her red beret on her head and her nice clean overall wrapped up in its same old piece of brown paper.

When Min sees her she goes running off down the street to meet her which is not how anyone else behaves towards a maid. Maids are maids and madams are madams. That's the way it is and that's the way it always will be. Nothing's ever going to change it. Not unless the whole world changes and that's never going to happen.

I know she doesn't like the idea but Min is going to be a madam one day. Even if she doesn't want to be she still has to do it. It doesn't matter how they do things in the bush. You can live in the bush as much as you like. It doesn't make any difference because you're still a white person and there isn't any other way.

Min says she'll never do it. It's stupid and she hates it and she'll be friends with who she likes just like she is at home and she'll never change her mind and will be like this as long as she lives until the day she dies.

Except the world doesn't work like this. I've tried to tell her but she won't listen. If she doesn't change her mind someone will change it for her.

I used to think she carried on like this because she and Beauty are two *goyim* together in a Jewish home. Now I'm not so sure. I think what she wants is for Beauty to be her friend, not just on Christmas Day but for every other day of the year and if this is so then it's sad because I know it can't happen.

They walk down the last bit of road click-clacking together and I suppose the neighbours will have something to say about this too. I'm sure she's telling about her Christmas surprises but when they get closer to the gate I can see it's more than this.

They stop and Min's giving Beauty something and Beauty's giving it back and there's more talking and Min is talking more than anyone else and Beauty is shaking her head no and when she comes into the house Beauty doesn't even put her things down. She goes straight to my mother.

She has one of Min's Christmas envelopes in her hands. The expensive ones Sadie bought with Mr Lazar's money which we thought Min could use for letters to her mother.

'Miss Min gave me this,' Beauty says and she hands the envelope over to my mother.

It's torn open so you can see she's had a look inside and she knows what's there and it's money and my mother takes the money out and it's all Min's Christmas money from her mother.

'Miss Min says I must take it,' Beauty says. 'But it's too much and I think you must keep it for her.'

Girls like Beauty always worry about things like this. If someone like Min does something like this, even if the money is hers to give and someone like Beauty takes it, you can be sure the next thing will be that she's accused of stealing.

It's not a nice thing to be thinking about at Christmas but that's the way things work. It doesn't matter if Beauty's never been caught stealing anything in her life, if something like this happens she could find herself in very big trouble and while all this is going on Min is furiously angry.

'That money's mine to do what I like with,' she says. 'I want Beauty to have it.'

My mother stands with the money in her hand and Beauty is in her red beret and you can see she doesn't know what to do. She's hot from the walk from the bus stop and there are beads of sweat on her face. The open envelope with all the pound notes inside it is in my mother's hands and twenty-five pounds is a lot of money in anyone's language and you can see my mother doesn't know what to do either. Then my father steps in and makes up their minds for them.

'If Miss Min wants you to have it then you must take it,' he says.

He takes the envelope from my mother and pushes the money back inside it. Then he picks up Beauty's tough old hand and puts the envelope into it.

'Merry Christmas,' he says.

Beauty's hanging on to the envelope and Min's full of smiles and I look at them both and think what I think quite a lot. Why is Min forever doing things that nobody else would even think about?

Reuben wonders that too.

'What for?' he says. 'Money's so easy to come by these days, you can just give it away? You think they appreciate it? Tomorrow she'll be back for more.'

'Min's young,' Sadie says. 'She'll find out.'

At least that's true. We all find out things about people as we go along. For example we've found out something about Reuben and that is that nothing's ever for nothing as far as he's concerned. There has to be something in it for him, otherwise he's not interested.

While I'm standing there thinking and making up my mind how I feel about all these things there's suddenly the sound of singing from the street.

'Let's go outside and see what's going on,' my mother says and she shows with her hands towards the front door.

I think maybe she's thinking the same thing I am and isn't too sorry something has come up to take her mind off it.

When we step out we see the whole road is outside enjoying the show. The men have glasses in their hands. The children are hanging on to Christmas toys.

The women are out of their kitchens still in their aprons.

The natives, our neighbours from the location across the river, have come to sing to us for Christmas. They're standing neat and tidy in the street with grown-ups behind and children in front and if my father depended on them for business we'd be in big trouble because they're their own music.

They don't need a piano or an orchestra. They sing with all their voices joined together to make one big voice and there's something in their singing that keeps you standing right where you are.

We don't really belong.

Between Christmas and natives there isn't really much place for us but we're used to this by now so although we don't move off our stoep it feels as if we're squeezing in and we listen anyway.

We're all there. My father and mother and Davey in his big chair at the side of the stoep and Reuben and Sadie and Beauty and Min and me. On every stoep there's a maid out with an overall on and an apron on top of it and some with half-washed dishes and dishtowels still in their hands.

When the natives sing like this at Christmas people throw money for a thank-you. Not big money, just small change, and the money falls on the singers like bronze and silver hail and they pick the coins up off the street and it's nice because it means they'll have something for Christmas too.

'Thank you, boss,' they say. 'Thank you, madam.'

'Give something, Aaron,' my mother says.

'I'll give something too,' says Sadie and she stands up to go inside to look for her purse.

We're not even looking at him but the big question is if Reuben who has the most will be willing to give also.

'I'm not the one with twenty-five pounds,' he says and he shows with his head towards Beauty. 'If they're not even willing to give to their own they're not going to get anything from me.'

My father's money goes spinning up into the air with all the rest and tinkles down on to the street just beyond our gate but Reuben doesn't move an inch.

'Reuben's right,' Sadie says. Her face is flushed but she sits down again and Reuben leans across and takes her hand and my father looks at my mother and my mother looks away.

MIN

The Time of Great Silence

1962

In our bush house we had very few things and money
was not a thing that worried us very much.

When we had to move to town in the time after
Justin left us, some or other shop delivery van was
always drawing up outside the house we rented and
something new would be offloaded at our gate.

'After all we're not poor,' my mother says. 'Your
father's rich as Croesus. Very few people these days
live the way he does.'

There are big wooden boxes and out of them come
smaller wooden boxes with beautiful lacquered lids
and jam-packed with silver. Crystal glasses and vases
come buried deep in sawdust and when you reach in
for them they come out wrapped in white tissue
paper. There are porcelain cups you can see through
when you hold them up to the light and white plates
rimmed with midnight blue and decorated with gold
leaf.

'And there's more coming,' my mother says

triumphantly and my father listens and says nothing at all. 'I'm tired, so very tired, living the way we've been and you never wanting to spend a cent on anything that wasn't black and begging. I must have been mad to put up with it.'

She won't allow the house servants to unpack the boxes.

'Kaffirs smash up everything they lay their hands on,' she says. 'If I let them loose half these things will be smashed to smithereens before we've even had five minutes' use out of them.'

She puts on a maid's apron, one that's never been worn before, taken from the servants' cupboard and still in its packet, and she unpacks these things herself and when eventually she's finished and our living room is filled with all things we never knew were so important my mother stands in the middle of them in her apron flushed and smiling and telling us that at last she's happy and what is there for either my father or me to say to that?

Not that anyone expects me to say anything because I don't talk. Not any more.

'You can if you want to,' my mother says.

It isn't true.

'You're doing it to punish us,' she says. 'Except you're not as smart as you think you are because you can only hurt someone if they care what you do.'

I know my mother doesn't care about me. She can hardly bear to look at me. Her main concern is that 'after this business', no matter how good my marks have been, St Anne's won't take me.

'I wouldn't if I was them,' she says. 'All your junior schooling in some half-baked kaffir school with a coon for a teacher and now this. St Anne's is not a mental institution. The kind of tricks you play won't go down well in a place like that.'

I have a special doctor. Her name is Marion Davis and we've had to move to Pietermaritzburg so we can be close to her. My father agreed. He said we could stay for as long as it takes for her to make me well.

He did it because he had no choice and neither did my mother. She wanted to leave our village and never have to go back and in the end she got her wish but only as far as Pietermaritzburg and not in the way she wanted it.

'It's not what you'd call Johannesburg is it?' she says.

Pietermaritzburg may be pretty much the backwoods but even so it's too big for my father. He's found a locum to take his place but he misses his patients and he misses his clinic. It's me who's taken something he loves away from him but there's nothing I can do about it.

My mother's busy making new friends even though she says she wonders who'd ever want to come and visit people like us. Not while we are as we are and seem determined to make no effort to put our bush ways aside.

Where else have you heard of white people who go in through the back door of a house or drink water straight from the kitchen tap out of any old cup, even the same chipped ones the servants drink from?

My mother has found two servants and dressed them in the terrible uniform town servants are supposed to wear. For 'everyday' Patience has overalls and a headscarf to match and a big floral tie-around apron. For 'best' she has a black overall covered by a small white apron edged with *broderie anglaise* and a starched cap to put on her head.

When my mother starts asking people to supper this is what Patience has to wear. I would have thought she'd rather die than wear it but she does and before guests arrive she has to stand in front of my mother for inspection to make sure everything is just perfect.

Josias has khaki shorts and shirt for 'ordinary' and

'everyday', and white longs and a shirt and a red sash over the shoulder for best.

These people who work for us have never known a white man like my father. When we first came he addressed them politely in Zulu but they won't talk Zulu back.

'You only embarrass them,' my mother says. 'They're not impressed with you. Surely you can see that?'

My father and I are the two biggest embarrassments in the world to my mother especially the way she is these days. She doesn't wear slacks and sandals and men's shirts any more. Nowadays she has Berkshire stockings with seams that snake up the back of her legs and new friends prepared to put up with us so they can listen to her stories and make her laugh even though they feel awkward in front of my father.

My mother is finding herself and I am in her way and so she really hates me now. She said as much to my doctor.

'She's a wicked, vengeful girl,' she says. 'She's always been like this. She's very good at getting her own way. When she wants something and doesn't get it she blackmails until she does.'

'Minnie's suffered severe trauma,' Dr Davis says. 'That's what we're dealing with here and different people experience trauma in different ways.'

My mother and Dr Davis don't have much time for each other. That's easy to see.

My father's the one who understands the silence. Not only because he's a doctor himself but also because lately he's become a quiet kind of man himself.

MIN

The Storyteller

1962

My father is the one who talks to the doctor. My mother says she's said all she has to say. If my father thinks any of it is of any interest to my doctor he's at liberty to tell her. She has no interest in doing so herself.

She's taken up tennis and plays bridge twice a week. 'I'm still young,' she says. 'I have to pick up the pieces and get on with my life.'

That's the way things are between them.

My father goes in his own direction except on Wednesday and Saturday afternoons because those are the days my mother entertains her new friends. Then he has to be home by the time the houseboy wheels the drinks trolley out on to the veranda because women and servants don't offer sundowners to guests. This is a man's job and my father seems to do it willingly enough.

'You mustn't mind Tom and his strange ideas,' my mother says apologetically, as if anyone does. They take his drinks, ice cubes floating, lemon slices abob, and no one minds Tom. They don't pay any attention to him at all.

It's my mother who's the main attraction. She's the one people pay attention to. She has a big audience these days and they hang on to every word she says and one of them hangs just a little bit harder than any of the others and his name is Mr Gerald Delaney.

My mother has a reputation for being an amusing storyteller. Her stories are about our life in the bush and the way she tells it it was the funniest life anyone could ever imagine. Telling about it can always be relied on to make people laugh.

'You can't believe what it was like,' she says. 'Even the name of the place we lived is unpronounceable and we were living like savages. I gave up on Tom. My God, I thought, he's going to go bush-happy and what's to become of me then?'

She has a way of talking, in small rushes with a flutter of her hands in between and a vivid way of using her eyes. She flashes them all around the circle drawing everyone in on the joke and all her words are carried on a never-ending ripple of laughter.

She's a good storyteller. She knows how to take hold of an audience. She knows what to tell and what to hold back and when to pause and when it's time to rush on to the story's end and when she talks the people we once called our friends become in her telling of them capering savages, imbecilic childlike natives, and when the story reaches its end Gerald Delaney laughs louder and longer than anyone else.

'It's a crime,' he says. 'A pearl like you being buried in the heart of the bundu.' And for this he gets a smile. 'Mind you,' he says. 'If I was your husband I'd also be tempted to hide you away and keep you all for myself. I wouldn't want you getting into any mischief.'

For this the smile gets even bigger.

'Bottoms up,' he says and he holds up his glass in a toast to my mother.

'Bottoms up,' everyone says because these days this is the fashion in Pietermaritzburg and this is where we live now and my father sits quietly with his drink on the table next to him and doesn't say anything until long after the last of the guests have made their way home. Then it's his turn to speak.

'Why do you do it, Julia?' he wants to know.

It's late and at last we're alone and the house is quiet. My father is showered in gold from an overhead lamp. His book, unopened, is on his lap. He sits very still. His shirtsleeves are pulled up, held in place by expanding silver bands. His hands, brown from summer sun, are laid flat on the book so the cover lies hidden beneath them. I can't see his eyes.

'I asked you a question,' he says. Then he waits and for a long time she doesn't answer.

She moves around the room touching her things. Touching them lightly with her hand. Her feet in their high-heeled shoes *tip-tap* on the bits of floor that aren't covered by carpet and it sounds as if she's dancing.

'I do it because it's amusing this way,' she says. 'It makes people laugh. I do it because the truth is just too bloody awful to bear retelling.'

MIN

We Know About You

1962

There's been a protest march in the township. There's a funny feeling in the air and everyone except my mother seems affected by it. Things are really bad. In the beginning my mother had a lot to say but then my father stopped her with a single sentence.

'Other women's sons die too, you know,' he says.

She says it's the cruellest thing she ever heard.

'But just the kind of thing I'd expect you to say,' she says. 'It's so exactly like you.'

After that she said she couldn't care less what the trouble was about. They could kill each other off until no one was left. As long as the servants pitched up for work she didn't want to hear about it because she simply wasn't interested.

A fourteen-year-old township boy has been taken away for questioning. The police came at three o'clock in the morning and pulled him out of bed. The whole township heard. Those living closest to his house heard the roar of the van, the banging on the door and his mother and grandmother screaming and crying and the policemen shouting.

News of it went from neighbour to neighbour.

Townships sprawl all over the place. Sometimes it can take almost an hour to walk from one end to the other but when you know your way around you find out they aren't really as big as they seem to be. When something happens it doesn't take long before everyone knows and from that moment on everyone is involved.

This was three months ago and nothing has been heard since.

Perhaps it's the city way.

In the country it's different. People treat each other differently. They defer to each other's opinion. When a local man of age and respectability approaches you and asks if he may discuss an important matter with you, you don't turn him away.

You put aside what you're doing. You invite him to sit down. You sit down with him. You allow some time to pass and then when the time and the feeling between you is right he'll tell you what's on his mind and you'll listen to him.

That's the way things are done.

If there is help to be given and you're able to give it, you will. That is why he has done you the honour of seeking your counsel. Otherwise he wouldn't have come in the first place.

It's not like that here. Here someone has gone to the trouble of giving what's going on a name and it's called incitement.

What the man who's in trouble wants is for the district magistrate to tell him the whereabouts of the boy taken on that night because he hasn't been heard of for three months. There's been no reason given and he's had no answer to all his enquiries and that's why my father and some others have intervened.

133

They walked into town. Peacefully. To the magistrate's office to ask for an answer. They walked three and four abreast. They made a long line that stretched almost all the way between the township and the town so that just for a moment those two places were very nearly linked and held together by this living line and my father was part of it and this is why the policemen come to our house.

There are two, standing on our doorstep. Plain clothes. That's how things are done. In the township they come in uniforms and armoured vehicles making as much noise as they like. To white houses they come in ordinary everyday clothes the same as anyone else might wear so no one seeing them is disturbed or upset.

One is old and one is young. The old one has a grey-flecked moustache and the young one has pink skin and crinkly blond hair. They ask Josias to call the master and my father sitting reading in the living room marks his place and puts his book down on a side table and gets ready.

He can hear what's being said at the front door but he waits where he is for Josias to call him and when he does his eyes are large and white with brown circles of consternation at their centre.

'Don't be afraid,' my father says. 'There's nothing to be afraid of. This is nothing to do with you. It's me they want to see and you can tell them to come in here and I'll be happy to see them and you can show them the way.'

So this is what Josias does and everyone greets and introduces themselves and the younger one comes straight to the point.

'You know what this is about,' he says.

'I think I do,' my father says and my mother, who's in the small sitting room next door, says: 'What is it, Tom? Who's arrived? Don't get caught up in anything. I'll need you soon to pour drinks.'

She says it lightly in the voice she uses for guests but today she's not important and no one takes any notice of her.

'May we sit?' the older one asks.

'Certainly,' my father says and shows the chairs and the sofa but he doesn't sit himself and so in the end no one else does either. It's not that kind of visit.

To me he says: 'If you don't mind I'd like you to stay in the room, Minnie. These two gentlemen are policemen and I think it's important for you to hear what they have to say.'

The younger one looks at the older one and the older one shrugs. 'It's an unofficial visit,' he says.

Even so it's exciting because my father has asked me to stay and he isn't a man who does things without reasons so I sidle into a corner, suddenly grown-up, excited, uncertain, instantly forgotten.

'Is this you?' the young one wants to know.

A photograph slides out of a big brown envelope. It goes carefully from one policeman to the other and then to my father who takes it and hands it back with a nod of his head and barely a glance down at what it is they've given him to see.

'Are you quite sure?' the young one says. 'This is very important. Take your time and study the photograph carefully. Take as much time as you need. We need you to be quite sure.'

He hands the photograph back to my father and my father nods again and hands it back again and this time he doesn't even bother to look down.

'Do you know these men?' the older one asks.

'Certainly,' my father says. 'Here you see us all together.'

'How long have you known them?' the young one says.

'Since we first came here,' my father says. 'Almost five months ago now.'

The young one takes out a notebook and begins writing in it.

'It's not official,' the older one says. 'It's important to keep everything straight. That's all.'

My father's face is like stone.

'Have another look,' the older says.

The picture is offered again and my father takes it again.

'The one in the middle?' the young one says.

'I believe he's a schoolteacher,' my father says. Then he hands the picture back.

I haven't seen these pictures. I don't know these men my father knows. I wonder if the schoolteacher is anything like Mr Morefe but I can't ask. What they have to show they'd never show me.

My father's mouth is one long set line.

'You're a doctor,' the old one says. 'You work at a bush clinic in Zululand. We have it all here.'

The young one takes the envelope the pictures were taken from and draws it half-way down and wriggles something out of it and inside there is a file tied with pink tape. He doesn't offer to show it but it's as if just by doing it he says, Look at me, and, I'm nobody's fool.

'Maybe people are different there,' the old one says. 'Perhaps where you were before you could get away with things you can't get away with in town.'

The old one moves forward and the young one moves back. It's as if they're attached to each other with invisible wires the way puppets are, so when one moves so must the other and I don't take my eyes off them for a minute. I don't mind the younger one. The older one is the one I don't like. He has sharp eyes and a sad-sounding voice and I don't trust him.

'When you and your friends set out on this so-called protest march to the magistrate's office, did you think the police were asleep?' he says. 'Did you imagine you'd be allowed to do as you please? Didn't it occur to you that we would intervene? That it's our job to do so?'

'We had a simple question,' my father says. 'We had a right to ask it and to expect an answer. That's what we went for and it's all that we wanted.'

'People don't like the idea of white men stirring up blacks,' the old one says. 'In the end it sets white people against each other and there's no need for that when a quiet word between educated people will do just as well.'

'I see,' my father says. 'Is that what we are?'

It seems to me that these words all by themselves are worse than any protest placard waving in the wind because they certainly make the old one cross. There's an ugly red blood welt rising underneath the skin just above the white collar of his shirt.

'There's nothing you can tell me about blacks,' he says. 'I grew up with them. If you want what's best for them don't try and lead them into protest. The city is no place for them. They belong on the land. Just turn them back where they came from.'

Then he gives my father a long, hard look and shows with his head to the younger one that he's ready to go.

'Good-evening, Dr Campbell,' he says. 'I'm sorry to have disturbed you. Please apologize to your wife for the intrusion.'

Josias is always good at knowing when guests are ready to leave. Usually he's at his post like magic, ready to open the door, but not tonight. Tonight, for the first time I can remember, he isn't there so our visitors open the door for themselves. They let themselves out and close the door quietly behind them.

My mother, in a red dress, stands in the hallway and as they leave the policemen touch their hats to her.

137

FRIEDA

May and September

1964

'I'll never get married,' Min says. 'Never in a million years.'

It's what she always says. I don't know why she's so against it.

'Yes, you will,' I say.

I'm beginning to take up where Sadie left off.

'Not even fifteen years old yet and already an expert on marriage,' my father says.

I should be. There's been plenty of talk about marriage at our house and these days there's even more than usual because at last Reuben has asked Sadie to marry him.

After *shabbas* one Friday he asked if he could speak to my father. We knew what it was about because my father is Sadie's only male relative.

'The sooner the better,' is what he says straight out to my father. 'A man my age has to think this way. Provided you don't have any objections to having me for a brother-in-law.'

138

This is what we hear later and when my mother hears it she puts her hand palm-flat over her heart as if it will jump right out of her chest with happiness.

'Objections?' she says. 'What objections could anyone have to getting a man like Reuben Lazar for a brother-in-law?'

'He's too old for Sadie,' says my father but no one takes any notice of him any more. In the matter of Reuben Lazar my mother and Sadie stopped listening to my father a long time ago.

May and September. What difference does it make? Sadie loves him and he can't keep his eyes off her. He's given her an emerald the size of Zoo Lake for an engagement ring and a pair of earrings to match and Min thinks we've all gone mad.

We've had these kinds of talks before and it's always the same. Min knows a lot about a lot of things but she doesn't really know anything that counts.

'We'll both find boys and get married,' I say. 'What else do you think you're going to do with your life?'

'I've got plans,' she says.

She may have but I've got news for her. When the time comes her mother will find some poor boy and push him Min's way. Her mother's very good at finding husbands. We don't need anyone to tell us that, but if you try saying this to her she nearly goes mad although I can't see what's so terrible about it.

My mother tried to explain it to her.

'When a man like Reuben says a thing like this what we're hearing is that Sadie is a very lucky woman. She'll be well taken care of for the rest of her life and we couldn't wish for more for her,' my mother says.

Then my father chips in and that doesn't help at all.

'Cheap show,' he says. 'When Miriam and I got married we could fit the whole wedding party into one picture and no one was complaining. It was good enough.'

'I didn't marry one of the richest men in the country,' my mother says.

In a way it's a fight but what the fight is really about is who's going to pay for the wedding. Reuben has a big wedding in mind, no short-cuts and no expense spared. Anything to make his Seidela happy.

'It wasn't us who asked him to pay for the wedding,' my mother says. 'He offered and if he wants to, for Sadie's sake, I think we should let him do it.'

'Sadie. Sadie. All I hear about is Sadie. You're so busy about Sadie you don't stop even for one minute to think how this makes me look?'

We want everyone to be happy and the wedding to be a happy occasion. The way things are going it doesn't look as if it will be. My father's attitude, his crossness and his hangdog expressions are a big cause of worry.

'I'll speak to him,' Sadie says. 'Maybe it will be better coming from me.'

'You'll say nothing,' says my mother. 'Reuben says it will be his pleasure to pay and who are we to deny him? Aaron will have to accept it and in the end he will. You'll see. He'll do it for your sake.'

It's going to be Sadie's day and one of the things we're celebrating is that Sadie is putting Coronation Avenue behind her and going into a new life.

'She's going to have only the best from now on,' my mother says. 'She may as well get used to it.'

One thing you can say about Sadie. She waited for a long time to get what she got but in the end it was worth it because she walked away with first prize.

The summer rolls on and our life along with it and Min's time with us is coming to an end. One of these days her mother and Mr Delaney will come back from overseas and fetch her to take her home. She won't even be here for Sadie's wedding.

'Even if I was here and invited I wouldn't come anyway,' she says.

She says it's because weddings are a big waste of time but I think it's because in a house where a family is taking sides it's hard to stay out of things and her side is not with my mother and Sadie or me it's with my father but all the same it's funny to think of our family having an Occasion and Min not being there.

'Do you think we'll never see each other again then, once you've gone home?' I say.

'I don't know,' she says.

Min always looks facts in the face no matter how hard they are. She never tries to say anything that could make things even just a little better. She's like this but I'm not. I didn't mind telling her that I miss her already and she hasn't even gone yet.

'It's because we're friends,' she says.

Which I don't need Min to tell me. I've already worked it out for myself. Hearing her say it doesn't make me feel any better about her leaving or facing the fact that maybe unless we're very lucky we may never see each other again.

I feel very down in the mouth when I think about it but then at last something happens and things change again and I feel better.

I thought she'd forgotten all about our walk up the mine dump but on her last night Min says we should go there again. Out of the blue she's decided the mine dump is her favourite thing of all the things she's done here and she wants to go back there one last time.

'I'll come,' I say. 'But I'm not climbing up anywhere. You can if you like. You can go right to the top if that's what you want to do. I'll wait on the ground for you.'

'All right then,' she says. 'Not the mine dump. Let's go by the river. I've got something to show you.'

141

I say OK because we have to have our last walk somewhere and the river's as good as anywhere else even though all you see is river and open ground and the half-torn-down barbed-wire fence and the location shanties beyond all wrapped up in their soft blue blanket of evening smoke.

But we go there anyway and the shadow of the mine dump creeps over us and although they're a long way away and can't see us we can see the natives going home from work and they look like stick figures that someone drew against the orange sky. It's hard to believe they're real people at all.

We can see the women swaying slow because of the babies tied like humps to their backs and the loads on their heads and the heavy carrier bags in their hands and their skirts fanned out like black fans around their legs.

The afternoon thunderstorm has come and gone.

The evening cooking fires have begun to burn and everything is soft with smoke and even where we are we can smell the wet smell of summer wood trying its best to burn and it snakes up our noses and makes our eyes sting.

We sit with our legs dangling down and our sandals on the ground next to us and our bare feet hanging loose over the dying river. Our faces are turned to the sun and we half close our eyes against the sun-dazzle and also because the world looks better this way.

All I can see is a half-world through the bar of my own eyelashes and the sun washes over me, ironing my clothes and me inside them and making my head spin.

'Look at this,' Min says.

Out of her pocket she takes the mother-of-pearl, sharp-as-a-razor penknife and pulls it open.

'Look at what?' I say.

'I want to show you something. Unless you're afraid, that is?'

142

'What's there to be afraid of?'

There's one thing Min and I know about each other by now. She's the one who's never afraid of anything and I'm not. I will turn away from something and she will march towards it. Nothing frightens her.

'What am I supposed to be looking at?' I say.

'I'll show you,' she says.

She takes a handkerchief out of her pocket and spreads it out on the ground. She puts the open penknife down on it, then she takes out a small book of matches and strikes one.

'We have to clean it first,' she says.

This is what always surprises me about her. How does she know these things? Between the bush and her expensive boarding school, she's learnt to do some pretty crazy things and it's very nice to know how to do things but what good is knowing what she knows going to be to her in later life?

She lifts the blade of the knife into the fire and lets the flame lick it clean.

'That's it,' she says. 'Now it's clean.'

'And now what?'

'Watch me.'

She puts out her hand and turns it palm up so the white wrist side shows and you can see her veins under her skin and then she picks up the knife.

'I'll show you,' she says.

With a quick stroke while I nearly have a heart attack and before I can stop her she runs the blade light across her wrist. It's so light she barely touches the skin at all and all that's left behind is a thin thread of blood and we both look at it as if we've never seen blood in our lives before.

'Now you,' she says. 'You needn't do it yourself. I'll do it if you like. It doesn't hurt.'

'What for?'

'Hold out your hand and I'll show you.'

This is another thing Min and I know about each

other by now. She can make me do things I'd never do by myself.

'One, two, three and it's all over,' she says.

So is life if you want to look at it that way and if the knife happens to slip but even so I hold out my wrist and it's quick and it stings and I look at the blood seeping out and it doesn't hurt at all.

'Now we put our wrists together and mix our blood,' Min says. 'Then we'll be friends for ever. Or are you afraid?'

Why should I be afraid? Why should it even worry me? You get a funny friend like Min and you do what you have to do. I don't even think twice about it and it's done and I sit there with a little bead of blood sliding down my wrist.

'Now we have to rub our blood together,' she says. 'So we won't forget one another and always remember.'

It's not because I'm afraid I hesitate. The trouble is I thought we would be friends for ever anyway but if doing it this way makes her feel any better it's no problem to me and who am I to stand in her way?

I put my wrist against hers and we rub our wrists together and make pink-orange blood patterns on our skin.

'You can't go back on it now,' she says.

Which is fine with me because I don't want to.

BOOK TWO

Life Happens

1968–1976

FRIEDA

The Bar Mitzvah Boy

1968

Hazel Friedman is my friend these days.

'You see,' my mother says. 'All this nonsense about nobody liking you. Hazel likes you. Hazel's a very nice friend for you. What more do you want?'

My mother knows Hazel's mother from *shul*. The Friedmans are bigwigs in the retail clothing business. They've got a whole chain of shops called Mr Bellini because in a high street clothing business like Mr Friedman's Italian is better for business.

I've known Hazel since the first day I started at Theodor Herzl but she was busy with her own life then, she had her own friends and never used to look in my direction. When Sadie married Reuben things changed.

'It's your imagination,' my mother says.

My mother thinks Hazel's the bee's knees but I think she'd change her mind if she knew what Hazel was saying behind her back about the one big thing my mother goes on and on about these days which is Davey's *bar mitzvah*.

'Your family aren't really thinking about a *bar mitzvah* for your brother Davey, are they?' Hazel says.

One thing about Hazel. She has opinions about just about everything and she doesn't mind letting you know what they are. When Hazel's around if you want to be heard you have to learn to speak up for yourself.

'Why shouldn't Davey have a *bar mitzvah* the same as anyone else?'

Maybe being around Hazel so much has rubbed off on me because these days when I've got something to say I say it straight away and get it off my chest and when I ask her what her objections are to Davey being *bar mitzvah* she raises her eyebrows as if she can't believe she's going to have to waste her breath telling me something I should already know.

'I asked a question,' I say. 'I'd like an answer.'

'He won't be able to do all the things a *bar mitzvah* boy's supposed to do, that's why,' she says. 'You can't just make up your mind a boy should be *bar mitzvah* and that's the end of the story.'

'We didn't just make up our minds. We talked to Rabbi Weisz.'

I don't want to fight with Hazel but I will if I have to.

'If Davey really is going to be *bar mitzvah* and my father and my brother Raymond hear about it they'll fall on their backs.'

Maybe I should keep my mouth shut but I ask her why something as simple as Davey's *bar mitzvah* should come as such a surprise to her family.

'Because it probably shouldn't be allowed,' she says.

The way Hazel goes on you'd think being allowed to wear stockings and patent-leather Baby Louis shoes and go to four-to-sixteen age-restriction films makes you an expert on everything.

'I know Davey's your brother but even you have to admit he isn't exactly a genius.'

'Nor is your brother Raymond. But he was *bar mitzvah* last year and no one said anything about it and Davey will be *bar mitzvah* too and if anyone has anything to say they can talk to Rabbi Weisz and if that isn't good enough they can talk to me.'

Raymond Friedman is the stupidest boy who ever walked this earth and beside him my brother Davey shines like a light.

I don't make a big show of it but I judge people according to how they treat Davey. Min isn't here any more but she never forgets him and whenever she writes and tells me how things are at St Anne's or on Mr Delaney's farm where she has to go in the holidays she always puts in something special for Davey, sometimes a few lines and sometimes a funny picture, and once she sent him some red and black lucky beans.

She always ends her letters the same way.

'Give my regards to Mr and Mrs Pagel,' she says.

'There must be some kind of mix-up,' says my mother when I show her my letters. 'You don't even know the Pagels.'

I don't know if Min will be able to be at Davey's *bar mitzvah*. I don't even know if she knows what *bar mitzvah* is but she says if Davey is having an Occasion she will do her best to be part of it. So I can see she hasn't forgotten her time with the Woolfs altogether and will do her best to be there.

I told her about the *bar mitzvah* being on or maybe not on all depending on what Rabbi Weisz decides but also on Davey's health. On that score we've been lucky because Davey is well lately. He's the best he's been for a long time. He's so well he doesn't sit stuck in the corner of the stoep any more. Every afternoon Beauty helps him get ready and takes him walking down the street so he can see a little bit of the world and they stroll along slowly together arm in arm.

The two of them are becoming quite a sight going up and down Coronation Avenue and our neighbours are getting used to Rabbi Weisz as well and his small car sitting outside the gate.

He comes to explain to Davey all the things he needs to know to be a good Jew and because it's Davey it takes a little longer than it would with other boys and my father apologizes for the time it takes the rabbi to come all the way over to our house to give Davey his special lessons but Rabbi Weisz doesn't seem to mind.

'There are rewards, Aaron,' he says. 'David is a willing listener. He doesn't look for excuses to get out of classes. I should be so fortunate with all my students.'

It may take longer but Rabbi Weisz says to Davey what he says to all the *bar mitzvah* boys.

'All you should remember, David, is that you must be the very best person you can be. Once you get that right it's easy. People will look to you and see how you live your life and if what they see is a good man, that will automatically make you a good Jew.'

'It should be so easy for everyone,' my father says.

'No one says it's easy, Aaron,' Rabbi Weisz says. 'What we say is that we should do our best. That's all any of us can do.'

I think Davey isn't the only one the rabbi's visits have an effect on. My father doesn't run to *shul* twice a week the way my mother does but his own special-occasion *tallis* which his father gave him is out of its tissue paper for this occasion because everyone who knows Davey will be in *shul* on that day, even Aunty Fanny who's coming by taxi from the Sol and Sheila Zuckerman Retirement Home.

'God only knows what for,' Sadie says. 'I told her a hundred times Reuben and I will drive by to pick her up.'

'At her age you don't have so much left,' says my father. 'What Fanny has is her independence and maybe that's something she'd like to hang on to for a little while longer.'

There'll be a party at our house. Nothing fancy and nothing catered. My mother and Sadie and I will be preparing the food and my father's friends will be getting together to make a little music and on top of it all there's been a phone call, long-distance, from Mrs Delaney.

Our telephone hasn't been with us for such a long time and long-distance isn't something we get every day so my mother is shouting down the telephone because she thinks people who are so far away won't hear if you don't shout.

In between shouting she puts her hand over the mouthpiece and waves to me to get my attention then she points to the phone with her forefinger to show important news is coming over the line.

'Min says she'd like to be there,' is what her mother's saying to mine. 'I've got some shopping to do and I've twisted Gerald's arm and moved things around a little bit and it looks as if we're going to manage to do it.'

Also there's the question of Min's university acceptance interview for the next year.

She's the cleverest girl in St Anne's and a straight-A student and no university in their right mind would turn her down but at Wits they like to have a little look at you for themselves so they know what they're getting before they sign you up.

Her mother wants to know if we can put her up again.

'I'd be so grateful if you could,' she says. 'The thing is I'm staying with people where Min wouldn't really fit in.'

'It will be our pleasure,' my mother says.

'Same arrangement as before?'

'Certainly not,' my mother says. 'This time Min is our guest and it will be our pleasure to have her.'

The word 'money' is never mentioned but we don't need Mrs Delaney's money any more. These days we can afford to be generous because we have Sadie and Sadie is married to Mr Reuben Lazar.

It's nice to have Min back and the first thing she does after she arrives is go and see Davey. We told him she was coming but I don't think he believed us. Not until he saw her with his own eyes.

She brought him a present which is like no present he's ever had in his life. It's a band that looks as if it's made out of layers of tough black string. She tells us it's a big-game hunter's band of elephant hair.

'We're not talking rabbits or wart-hog or *gemsbok* here,' she says. 'This comes from a bull elephant's tail.'

I know because I've seen it before. I saw it in her funny cardboard suitcase of really special things but I don't mention this and neither does she.

'They don't feel a thing when you pull the hair out but you have to be brave to go up to an elephant and give his tail a tug. So it's very strong magic. When you wear it nothing bad can ever happen to you.'

She picks up Davey's hand and slides the bangle around it and it's all too much for Davey. He thinks it's the most wonderful thing he's ever heard in his whole life.

FRIEDA

The Jewish Woman's Daughter

1968

In these days just before his *bar mitzvah* Davey still goes out walking with Beauty most days. They go slowly down the road and Davey looks at the world taking his time like he always does. Most days it's good and then one day it's not so good any more.

Some boys with bicycles start shouting after him.

'Fat boy,' they shout. 'What are you looking at, fat boy?'

They're ordinary boys but even ordinary boys can do terrible things.

'Fat pig,' the boys shout and Beauty holds Davey's hand tighter and pulls him close to her.

'Filthy Jewish pig,' they shout.

They puff out their faces and push out their stomachs which is supposed to show how fat Davey is. They take off his funny walk. They all take turns to do it. As each one does his take-off the ones looking on scream with laughter and wait their turn and the maids on the street see what's going on

153

but there's nothing they can do about it.

The boys are fourteen or fifteen years old and white. What young white masters do is not the maids' business and they can't tell them to stop. If they do it will only get them into trouble and shouted at as well. That's something maids learn very quickly.

At that time of day there's no one in a street like Coronation Avenue who can stop them. These boys can do exactly what they like and they know it.

One of them picks up a windfall kaffir-plum from one of the trees that grow all down the side of the road and throws it hard at Davey and the others all join in and it's a great game. They take aim and put all their weight behind each throw. Kaffir-plums are small but they're hard as stones. If you get hit by one you know all about it.

Min and I are walking down the street together and as we turn the corner this is what we walk into. We see the boys. We hear them shouting and we see Davey. He's standing still looking at them. He doesn't even try to move away.

There's a lot of Davey especially when he's standing still like this and most of the kaffir-plums hit him and only a few miss but he doesn't cry out or even lift up his hands to protect himself.

Beauty is trying to stand in front of him to shield him but he's too big and the kaffir-plums are coming hard and fast and falling down like hail and Min and I are right into the street and half-way down it but the boys are enjoying themselves so much they don't even see us.

I know I should do something but I don't know what to do. It's my brother who's in trouble and the best I can do is stand where I am with my hands over my mouth and even while I'm standing there I know I'm not very much good to anyone and no help at all.

Min's different.

She bends down and picks up a handful of some

154

windfall plums of her own. She takes one in her right hand and flips it up and down a few times to see how heavy it is. Then she takes aim and throws it. She throws it just as hard as she can and she's a strong girl with a good eye and if she wants she can throw better and harder than any boy can.

The kaffir-plum hits a boy on the side of his bare leg and he spins around and yelps like a dog from the way it hurts.

'Don't just stand there,' Min says. 'Throw back at them.'

She takes aim and throws another plum hard and then another and by this time the boys have forgotten all about Davey. All their attention is on Min now and on me except it's no good looking at me because we don't do violence. I don't say it out loud but it's what my father taught me.

'It's not a sign of weakness to refuse to commit violence,' he says. 'It's a sign of strength.'

I can hear it in my head. It says so somewhere in the Talmud and I'd like to believe it because my heart is beating like a drum and I can't see myself standing in the road throwing plums hard as stones at hooligans.

'Pick some up off the ground and throw them.'

Min is bent down and picking away and I can see her face red and cross and upside-down looking at me from under her elbow but if you gave me a million pounds I couldn't bend down or pick up a plum. If those kaffir-plums really were stones and my brother was being stoned to death right in front of my eyes I couldn't do it.

'Stop that,' Min says shouting at the boys and the way she says it makes the throwers stop in their tracks.

They stand as if they've been frozen and while they're standing like that Min takes another plum and throws it as hard as she can and the boys stand where they are looking at her as if she's just arrived from outer space except for the biggest boy who's a bit braver than the others.

'You a Jew-lover or something?' he says.

'You leave him alone,' Min says.

'We were only having some fun,' the main boy says. 'A kaffir-plum never killed anyone.'

Min's strong. She takes another plum, aims it at the main boy and throws it hard with all her might and it hits him like a rocket so he screams out with pain.

'Are you mad or something?' one of the boys shouts out. 'You could have thrown his eye out.'

'A kaffir-plum never killed anyone,' she says. 'You said so yourself. How do you like it when someone throws one at you?'

She marches right up to the hurt one and looks at the big red lump on top of his eye.

'You're mad,' he says but he moves backwards.

'You leave him alone and let him go home,' Min says.

Before the boy can find an answer Mrs Ross from number 37 is out on the street.

'What's going on here?' she says. 'My maid came in to call me. She said there were white children outside brawling in the street.'

'It's nothing,' the main boy says.

'If it's nothing what happened to your face?'

She looks at all the boys one at a time and they get a sulky look but no one's saying anything.

'You just take your bikes and get away from here,' she says. 'Decent people live in this street. You go and make trouble on your own side of the road.'

Then she turns around and looks at Min, red and cross with her hair all over the place and her hand full of kaffir-plums clenched in a fist around them.

'And who are you?' she says.

The boys have their bicycles up and are wheeling them away and Mrs Ross has her hands on her hips and she's waiting for Min to answer but I answer for her only you'd never say it was me speaking.

Some people don't like Jews. You hear about this kind of thing all your life. You say you know it happens but you don't. Not until it happens to you.

'I asked you a question,' Mrs Ross says. 'I'm waiting for an answer. Who are you and where do you spring from?'

Min is ready to answer but she doesn't have to because I answer for her. In all of my life I'll never forget our Davey with kaffir-plums falling down like hail and the look on his face and the pain in his eyes.

'She's the Jew-lover from number 18,' I say.

My mother would have a fit if she heard me. I can't believe myself that I would ever say such a thing. It's that look on Davey's face that gives me the courage to say it and now I've said it and it's not enough. I still have something more and I say that too.

'Just in case you didn't know,' I say, 'I'm the Jewish Woman's Daughter and this is my friend Miss Minnie Campbell from Natal and she's staying at our house.'

Davey's *bar mitzvah* is a great event.

He has a new suit, specially tailored, hanging in his cupboard and his magic elephant bracelet on his wrist which he shows to everyone including Rabbi Weisz who he also told about its magical powers.

When she heard it my mother nearly had a heart attack but Rabbi Weisz never said anything at all. He looked at it politely and asked where Davey got it. He never even mentioned that it was a strange thing to see round a Jewish boy's wrist on the eve of his *bar mitzvah*.

'What did you expect?' my father says. 'You think Rabbi Weisz is new in the world? You think he doesn't know anything about life that something so small should be such a big shock to him? He's seen bigger things than this believe me and he's still here to tell the story.'

Sadie and I are in the kitchen planning and making shopping lists and cooking and it really is like old times and I remember why it is I like cooking so much. It's because when I stand in a kitchen and cook I know exactly what I'm doing.

You don't have to act smart with a side of salmon, and a fowl, *kosher* or otherwise, isn't interested where you have your hair done or shop for your clothes and that suits me.

We're in the Coronation Avenue kitchen wrapped in clouds of white apron and cooking our hearts out. I don't know if doing this will ever make up to Davey for what I didn't do when he really needed me but I'm doing my best and cooking as if my life depended on it.

We're giving a tea and then a cold buffet.

There'll be apple strudel and sour cherry tart, baked cheesecake and home-made beesting and almond tarts and biscuits. Everything made by Sadie and me. Every single biscuit and *petit four* iced by hand and no two just the same.

My father has been popping in and out to see how we're getting on. We can feel his hand coming out from behind us having a little piece of this and a little taste of that. We're so busy with what we're doing we don't even look up.

'Thrupp's will be closing down their business when they hear you're back in the kitchen, Seidela,' my father says.

Our kitchen is steamed up. My face is boiling and my feet hurt as if I've been wearing shoes that are too small for me. My hair's frizzing all over my head with heat. I'm mixing cakes on one side and on the other side Sadie's tipping freshly baked ones light as air out of their baking dishes. Beauty's red beret is moving up and down. The washing-up water is steaming in the sink and it slip-slops around with the way Beauty's washing and you can smell the soap.

Cheesecake is cooling on the table and Sadie's rolling Swiss roll in damp white cloths and apricot jam is squeezing out of the edges and it really is like old times. There's *lox* and bagels, smoked salmon and pumpernickel bread.

It's fish only. Only the freshest fish flown up from the coast and the finest herring. Every single kind you can think of. Danish and pickled and mustard and even ordinary everyday and Sadie and I are chopping away and our hands smell to high heaven. There's nothing you can do that will ever get the smell out. Once it's there, it's there to stay. It's the same with the horseradish. Sometimes it's like grating concrete but we grate it anyway.

Bubbe Rochel's cloth is on the table and my mother's plates and cups and knives and forks are set out and ready. I don't think our table has ever seen so much food in all its life. I keep going out of the room and then going back into it again just for the pleasure of looking at it once more. When you see a thing like this what does it matter if your hands smell of fish? You'll probably be able to smell the *bar mitzvah* boy's family all over the *shul* but everyone will know what it's about. No one will mind.

I ask myself why and I stand there in my white apron with the steam rising all around me and the answer comes to me like answers sometimes do.

No one will mind. How could anyone ever mind when it's the smell of our lives and who we are that we're talking about?

On the big day we're at *shul* early and dressed to the nines. My mother's in beige guipure lace with *Bubbe* Rochel's good opal brooch on her shoulder and I'm in my royal-blue shantung with the hat to match and we're up on the balcony with all the other women but we have a good view.

First my mother stands to the front and then Sadie. Then my mother pushes Min and me forward so we can look down and see what's going on downstairs.

I can see Reuben in his good place which he always has when he and Sadie come to our *shul*. He's not the tallest man there but his silver hair is sticking out from under his yarmulka and it's hard to miss him.

My father is next to Davey. His special *tallis* is around him and Davey's new one, a *bar mitzvah* gift from father to son, is over his shoulders. His head is bent down for the prayers and the sound of the men's voices drifts up to us through all the usual rustles of the *shul*.

When Davey was a little boy and still able to come with us to *shul* twice a week my father's everyday *tallis* used to cover them both. We didn't know then the problems Davey would have in his life. Today we know. This is what makes this not only such an Occasion but also a really Special Event.

When my mother and I look down from the women's section we see Davey's face looking up at us and I think he's looking up because he can feel me looking at him and when he does our eyes meet and in some funny place inside me I feel something strange.

I look at my brother and the years fall away and the fine new suit seems to vanish away and his bare skin and the fat that embeds him disappear with it. It's as if Davey is made out of nothing at all except light and air and shimmering through this I see his sweet face and on this great day he looks how he always looks inside which is not so different from everyone else. Which is how he always looks to me anyhow and how I will always remember him.

There will be no photographs to remind us because this is the sabbath but it makes no difference

160

because I have all the pictures I need in my mind and I will never forget a single minute of it.

Whenever I want I can see the *shul* garden and my mother *kvell*ing with pride outside on the steps and Sadie with her new crocodile bag pulled high up on her arm and Davey showing his elephant magic bracelet to anyone who will look at it and Aunty Fanny who may be old but isn't blind asking what that thing is Davey has on his wrist and Sadie telling her.

'He showed it to Rabbi Weisz,' Sadie says.

You have to bend down and shout loud if you want to be sure Aunty Fanny hears anything these days.

'Have you ever heard of a Jewish boy wearing such a thing on his *bar mitzvah* before?' Aunty Fanny wants to know.

'What harm is it?' my father says.

We're all together and there's no harm in anything this day. People come over and wish us *mazel tov* and it all gets too much for Ruth Silverman. She takes one look at Davey and bursts into tears.

The Silverman boys are there and they take turns to shake Davey by the hand and they call him David and wish him *mazel tov* too along with everyone else. My father puts his arm around my mother and pulls her up against him under the *tallis*.

'Behave yourself, Aaron,' she says.

There are jokes and remarks and we couldn't stop smiling if we tried and I will never need anything to remind me because I will always remember this day. It stands out like gold in my memory.

I remember it for the joy of it and the day it was but most especially I remember it because it was the last time we were all together like this because not so very long afterwards my father died.

FRIEDA

Getting to Know Grief

1968

People say my father 'dropped down dead' but it wasn't like that. He didn't 'drop' anywhere. He went out one afternoon to see how his vegetables were getting along.

'There might be some tomatoes ready,' he said. 'If there are I'll bring them in for supper.'

Those were the last words he said to me.

When it got late and he didn't come in I went out to look for him and found him in his deck-chair at the bottom of the garden. His legs were stretched in front of him and his old gardening hat was pulled over his forehead just like it always is. A Raymond Chandler detective book with his glasses folded on top of it was on the ground next to him and his tomatoes that he was so proud of were all around him. Only they were living and he was dead.

'It's a good way to go,' people say but it isn't true. It may not be the worst way but when you're not ready

162

for it no way is a good way. At least not as far as the family's concerned.

My mother's lying down and Sadie puts her arms around me to try and make me feel better.

'Believe me, darling,' she says. 'It's a blessing. He must have felt not so good and sat down to have a little rest and the next thing it was over. He wouldn't have known a thing about it.'

I can feel her soft skin cheek to cheek against mine and smell her Ashes of Violets scent but she's crying so much when she says it you'd have to be a genius to work out how dying this way suddenly got to be such a good thing.

'When the time comes who needs to linger? Good people get taken fast.'

My mother doesn't agree. She can't get over a young man like my father sitting down to read a book and dying the way he did without so much as a word of warning. You'd think he'd done it on purpose and the way she's going on I don't think she'll ever find it in her heart to forgive him.

'Grief does funny things to people,' Sadie says.

I have to take her word for it. She may know all about it but grief is new to me even though I'm finding out about it fast.

It's grief that makes us close the curtains and turn the pictures to the wall. It makes us cover all the mirrors so we're spared the extra misery of having to look at ourselves when we're busy grieving. I know why we're not supposed to look. What I want to know is what difference it can possibly make?

I suppose I should have asked this a long time ago. I'm sure I did. I'm sure I asked and someone answered and I didn't bother to listen and now I don't remember and all because it didn't seem important then and now it does.

It's the kind of question I could have asked my

father. If he'd been spared he would have given me the best answer he could.

'What will happen if I take a look at myself?'

'Just don't do it,' Sadie says.

'Please, Frieda,' Mrs Silverman says. 'Stop this kind of talk. Your mother's upset enough already.'

'Why are you asking this now?' Sadie says. 'I thought you were a top *cheder* scholar? What did you learn all that time you spent in *cheder*? Didn't they teach you anything at all?'

They teach you a lot of things at *cheder*. What they don't teach you is how you'll feel when your father's there one day to answer all your questions and the next day he's taken away dead and all that's left of him is the hat he wears out in the garden and a pair of glasses.

I've never actually met Grief before this day and now it's among us as if we invited it in and made it an honoured guest in our house and now that I've seen it I don't like it very much.

'I can't see the point,' I say. 'Goys are allowed to look as much as they like and they aren't struck down dead or anything like that.' Not so far as I know.

'What *goyim* do is their own business,' Sadie says. 'It's got nothing to do with us.'

'If we're not going to be struck down or anything how much trouble can we find?'

Has God got so much time on His hands He hasn't got anything better to do than hang around heaven with eyes for nothing but Coronation Avenue just waiting to catch Frieda Woolf out? Will one look kill me? I don't think so.

On the third day of prayers while everyone is taking lemon tea and a slice of date loaf which Bella Goldman brought I make my excuses and go to the bathroom and close the door behind me.

In the bathroom is my father's shaving mirror which Sadie has put a white handkerchief over. It sits on the

164

flat lid of the washing machine and I sit on the closed top of the toilet and lean forward and reach out and take off the white hankie put there by my aunt out of tradition and respect then I stand up and look down right into the mirror but what's to see? I'm still there the same as ever and I can't believe I'm the first Jewish girl in recorded history ever to have done this.

I look away and then I look again. I do it a few times but it's always the same. Every time I look I'll still be there but my father won't. He'll never look in this mirror again because he's gone for ever and when I think this and realize what it means I sit down on the cold tiled bathroom floor with the mirror in my hands and my heart hurts so much I can't get myself up again and Sadie has to come banging on the door looking for me and calling out my name.

'Frieda? Are you in there? What's going on? What's keeping you so long?' she says. 'People are asking about you. Are you all right?'

If I had an answer I would have given it to her but my tongue's thick in my mouth and my throat hurts and I can't say anything at all.

'Open the door this instant,' Sadie says. 'I don't care what you're doing. You're making everyone frightened.'

I'm sitting on the floor with my head on my knees. My knees are held together by me holding on to them with my arms wrapped around them and I would have opened the door if I could but I couldn't and it wasn't locked anyway.

'What's the matter?' Sadie says.

Once she opens the door she can see for herself.

The uncovered mirror is on the floor next to me and the hankie that covered it is on the Formica lid of the washing machine just where I left it and Sadie doesn't mention anything about any of this.

'Your mother will miss you in a minute,' she says.

'Rabbi Weisz is just leaving and would like to say goodbye to you.'

I don't want to see anything ever again but when I turn my head a little bit to the side I can smell violets and I know from the sound of her voice that she understands.

'Come on,' she says. 'Give me your hand and I'll help you up.'

I get up without her help and without even an answer but when she puts her arms around me I don't turn away. You have to see Grief sometime and now I have. I know what it is and I've learnt my lesson. From now on I think I'll stick with the rules.

FRIEDA

Looking for Mr Right

1973

Once he was in our family Reuben told us some
things about himself that other people didn't know
and didn't like to ask about. Things concerning his
late son.

He had a son named Nathan who passed away a
young man and a grandson called Lenny who lives in
London who he visits once or twice a year.

You'd think now that he has his Seidela and more
money than one man could spend in three lifetimes
Reuben would be a happy man but he isn't because at
the bottom of it all he's just like the rest of us.

What he wants most in life is the one thing he can't
have and that is the pleasure of having seen his
grandson growing up in front of his eyes and having
him close by him in these later years. This is the one
and only last thing he needs to bring real *naches* into
his life.

Sadie's often told us this. 'People always look at
Reuben and think he has everything,' she says. 'But if

God ever took it into His head to do Reuben a real favour this is what it would be.'

My mother understands. 'As you get along in life you want your own flesh and blood around you,' she says. 'You want to know that after you're gone there's something that's going to be left behind.'

We all talk a lot about Lenny but no one talks very much about his mother. Her name never crosses Reuben's lips. Once someone made a mistake and said it out loud in front of him and he spat three times and said it was an offence to his ears and he never wanted to hear it again, that was the end of that.

'He blames her for Pearl's death,' Sadie says.

It isn't as if she took out a revolver and shot the late Pearl through the heart or anything like that but why go to the trouble? There are other ways of killing a Jewish wife and mother. We all know that.

'Her heart was broken,' Sadie says. 'It broke on the day that terrible woman got her claws into Nathan.'

Nathan drowned. We all know the story and when it comes to the part when Sadie tells how the telephone call came to Reuben to say his only child was dead she pulls out a handkerchief and wipes her eyes and all you see are the late Pearl's diamonds on her fingers going backwards and forwards and the white lace of her handkerchief.

'If that woman he married had stayed in her own house like a decent woman should, it would never have happened.' This is my mother's opinion. She's heard the story before and has her own ideas about it.

Nathan and his wife were running around Europe, here, there and everywhere, having a good time and throwing Reuben's money around as if it was water when it happened.

The phone call came long-distance from France.

'She knew where to telephone when there was a tragedy. Millionaires and film stars were all she was interested in but come a tragedy she picks up the telephone and she phones Reuben. Suddenly she knows what his telephone number is.'

This was not a new story in our house and when he was still alive to hear it it nearly drove my father crazy.

'Reuben is Nathan's father, who else should she telephone?' he used to say.

He needn't have wasted his time. No one is going to spoil a good story with common sense.

It happened in two seconds flat. One minute they're sitting on the beach with all their ritzy friends around them having the time of their lives and the next minute Nathan's gone.

'Did she try and stop him going into the water? Of course she didn't. What did she care? "Go," she says. "Enjoy yourself," and the next thing he's stone dead and drowned.'

A heart attack. That's what the doctor said afterwards but how can you ever rely on doctors to give you the full story? That's my mother's view. Especially as the doctor happened to be a foreigner.

Sadie believes the doctor.

'I wouldn't be surprised,' she says. 'All that running around. Stuffing himself full of *trayf* and dancing around to her tune, day and night, night and day, trying to keep her happy. How long can a man last who lives a life like this?'

Ruth Silverman found out from someone who used to know them that Reuben's daughter-in-law is called Maud but out of respect for Reuben and to be on the safe side my mother and Sadie call her the She-Wolf From Shepherd's Bush because that's where she comes from.

'She may be a Jew,' Sadie says. 'But there are Jews and Jews. Being a Jew doesn't stop a person being a gold-digger. Otherwise why make such a big secret of it and run off to a registry office?'

Nathan married in a hurry and didn't tell his

mother and the She-Wolf went right along with it and if she had any objections to things being done hole-in-the-corner and not in the proper way no one we knew ever heard about them.

'You think London's so far away they don't know about Reuben Lazar?' Sadie says. 'You think she didn't know that when people talk about Reuben having a few shillings it's not *bubkes* we're talking about?'

'Anything to get the ring on her finger,' my mother says. 'She knew Pearl would put a stop to it if she found out.'

Pearl had her own plans for Nathan and they didn't include some girl from Shepherd's Bush no one had ever heard of. Ruth Silverman found this out too.

'The sun may have shone out of Nathan as far as she was concerned but there comes a time when a mother puts her foot down.'

One minute Nathan was in London and supposed to be learning the garment-wholesaling business. The next minute he was on the telephone telling his father about the jewel he'd got hold of and married and while he was speaking every word that came out of his mouth was breaking his mother's heart.

'You have to feel for Pearl Lazar,' my mother says. 'It's a terrible thing for a son to do to a mother.'

Personally I used to feel quite sorry for the She-Wolf. No matter what anyone says I've seen photos of the late Natie Lazar and even painted in and touched up I don't think she was the one who got first prize. Never mind all his father's money.

Then when he died the way he did people who didn't even know her put the blame on her. Except me. I never said anything out loud but I felt for her. If you ask me she was young and silly and didn't have much sense where men were concerned which taken by itself is not a crime.

I didn't have much sense myself in the days when Sadie was pushing Alvin Silverman in my direction.

I'd like to say things got better when I got older but this isn't the way it worked out.

I'm not blaming anyone. It isn't as if Sadie didn't do her best for me. There isn't a single Jewish boy in Johannesburg who wasn't some time or the other pushed in my direction thanks to Sadie's efforts. I don't know what she told them about me but believe me Sadie has her talents. If she wanted to she could sell ice to an Eskimo.

She could get boys who wouldn't know me if they fell over me in the street to phone up for a date and even to come as far as the front door and after that it was up to me and I was always willing to try.

Except there was always a catch and some of Sadie's princes came in very strange shapes and sizes.

It isn't as if I didn't do my part but there are limits to what you can do with certain raw material. You can be squeezed into Gossard and squashed into shoes and Helena Rubinsteined up to the eyeballs. You can be as ready and willing as a girl can ever be in her whole life. You still don't know what you're going to find on the other side of your door when date time comes around or what you're going to think of it or what it's going to think of you.

Reuben looks at things differently. He looks at me and sees an ordinary kind of girl who his wife can't find a husband for and to him this is not such a big problem as it seems to Sadie because as far as Reuben's concerned I have a talent and sometimes having a talent can be even better than having a husband.

When you choose a husband you can never be sure what you land up with. If you're a good cook like I am and hard-working, with proper backing and advice you can open a delicatessen shop and turn your talent into cash in the bank.

'If she doesn't get married is it so terrible?' Reuben wants to know. 'When it comes to business I know what I'm talking about and I'm telling you that for a small percentage I could be prepared to back her and if you do it right such a shop could turn out to be a goldmine.'

'Stop talking goldmine,' Sadie says. 'She doesn't need a goldmine. Who's interested in a goldmine? What she needs is a nice boy and a home of her own.'

Except by now I'm realizing nice boys don't grow on trees and maybe the shop idea isn't such a bad idea after all.

I'm thinking what a long wait Sadie had before she found Reuben standing in front of the late Pearl's grave in the Brixton cemetery and as far as I'm concerned I'm facing the facts which are that a nice little delicatessen shop backed by Reuben is going to be far easier to come by than a husband.

To get a shop I need Reuben to open his chequebook and some advice from his accountant. To get a husband it looks to me as if what I need is a miracle; and then everything changes again and along comes Lenny Lazar to pay a little visit to his grandfather.

He's handsome. He's nice. He's got plenty to say for himself and he's smart. He's got a full head of hair on his head and it's all his own and on top of this he has all his own teeth which is more than you can say for some of the men who've been pushed in my direction. He's dressed retail in a nice pair of slacks and a cashmere sweater. He has matched luggage and lots of it so it looks as if he's come to stay for a while and he has a nice smile.

He is, also, thank God, Jewish and if things can get any better I'd like to be the first one to hear about it.

I know one thing. Now I've met Lenny Lazar if he comes swimming past in my direction I'm going to throw out a net and grab hold of him with both hands and then I'm going to hold on to him just as hard as I can.

FRIEDA

Exactly Like Her Father

1974

It's no good talking to Min. She couldn't care less about love and Lenny Lazar. She thinks time is too precious to waste on men. There are other more important things to do with it. All she's interested in these days is finishing her medical degree and women taking over the world and what's going on in politics and getting herself in trouble.

While I've been at Bella Goldman's Cookery School working at making perfect Béarnaise sauce Min has been joining banned organizations and being arrested and taken away by the police. This is what university has done for her. This is why she has to leave Medical School Residence in a hurry and come and stay with us.

There's been a terrible fuss. She came so close to being expelled you could just about put a sliver of cotton between her and all her hopes of being a doctor. Every string that can be pulled to help her has been pulled. Her grandfather sent two lawyers and an advocate all the way from Durban to Johannesburg just to give her side of the story in words not exactly her own which Reuben worked out must have cost him a good few Big Ones.

You'd think Min would be grateful but she wasn't. She was furious. She has her own ideas. She has a voice. She can speak. Which, as my mother points out, is exactly what landed her in such big trouble in the first place.

We've never met Min's grandfather but someone must have given him our name so we've been dragged in on the act as well because she really is in desperate need of help.

Just so she can go to lectures and finish her finals and get her medical degree which otherwise would go down the drain Min has to have respectable people who'll take her in and be prepared to vouch for her good behaviour. The court says so.

We know what Min's like and how stubborn she can be. Only mad people would ever agree to such a thing. Even so, when the Durban advocate comes to our door and says who he is and what it's about we tell him he's come to the right house and invite him inside.

'We've known Min for a very long time,' my mother says. 'She's a good girl and life hasn't always been easy for her. You can tell her grandfather and the court and anyone else who wants to know that she can come and stay here with us. Our door is always open for her.'

So these days when Mrs Ross tries to find out our business from Beauty what she'll hear is that we're harbouring a dangerous political activist and she can decide for herself how she likes *that* idea.

Mrs Delaney has to be sent for and she comes in a hurry and she's furious.

'Well, Min,' she says. 'Here we are again. I hope you're pleased with yourself.'

The way she's carrying on you'd think Min had gone out and shot someone when all she's done is been in a student protest which isn't exactly a new thing. She's done it before. It's something she does whenever she gets a chance. It's something all the students do.

No more detention without trial. Academic Freedom. Open Universities. Abolish Job Reservation.

There are protests and marches and pamphlets being handed out on street corners every day in all weathers but that's as far as it goes. The students don't rush off looking for something to blow up and most of the time the police carry on as if they're nothing better than a big joke but that's only until they've had enough and decide the joke's gone far enough and is over.

'It's the last straw for Gerald,' Min's mother says. 'It hasn't been easy from the start. It's been a constant battle since we married. I sometimes wonder why he married me at all. Any sane man would think twice about taking on a woman with a daughter like Min in tow.'

She smokes and talks. She hardly looks at us and there really isn't very much for us to do except be there because she doesn't seem to need anyone to answer her. She stubs out one cigarette and lights another and under her smart cap of new-look silvery blond hair her bright pink mouth keeps moving up and down as though she's chewing gum.

'I don't know why you do these things,' she says.

She's speaking to Min but she acts as if she can hardly stand to look at her. All Min is worth to her mother is a snaky little flick of the eyes every now and then.

'Sometimes I think you act like this to spite me. To get back at me in some way and I ask myself what I've ever done to deserve it.'

'Everything isn't about you,' Min says. 'This isn't.'

'What's it about then? You resented my remarrying. I think you blame me because your father died. You've never stopped trying to hurt me. If this isn't what this is about, then what is it about? Tell me and at least give me the benefit of trying to understand.'

'It's nothing I'd expect you to understand,' Min says.

'Young people have their own ideas,' says my mother. 'Maybe you shouldn't worry so much. Children grow up. Things change when they get older.'

'These aren't her ideas,' her mother says. 'That's the trouble. I've been through all this before. What she's doing is trying to be exactly like her father. He was a kaffir-lover too.'

Min sits where she is with her mouth tight closed.

'I know we aren't supposed to speak ill of the dead but what's true is true. Tom was in love with kaffirs. That's what it was. It was love. You simply can't call it anything else. He couldn't do enough for them except of course he wasn't doing it for them at all. He was doing it for himself.'

'You're upset,' my mother says but it's no good. Once a woman like Mrs Delaney starts something like this and makes up her mind she's going to have her say it isn't so easy to put a stop to it.

'As if the blacks care. I told him that a million times. They'll grab everything they can but actually they hate us. They don't even try to hide it.'

She stubs out her cigarette in an old saucer I fetched from the kitchen and pushes it across the table as if she hates it now she's finished with it and it's nothing more than mess. It's her cigarette but somehow she acts as if the mess is our fault.

'He was always on call for coons. You'd think he was practising in Harley Street and they were the *crème de la crème*. They could send for him any time they liked. There were always filthy little piccaninnies hanging around our gate. Waiting for the big

176

white doctor. He loved that. It made him feel important.'

The tea tray is on the table in front of us with the teapot standing on it and the tea inside it unpoured. Min sits with her face turned to the window and these words, which none of us wants to hear, pour out of her mother's pink mouth and wash all around us and although we can't see them they're like an odour in the room.

'He was a war hero, you know. I thought I was marrying a hero but all I got was a kaffir-loving disaster.'

We don't want to know any of this but we don't know how to put a stop to it and then suddenly it's ended. Mrs Delaney stops and she smiles and it's over and everything is quiet again and my mother tells me I should pour the tea and the tea splashes cold and brown into the cups.

'We'll pay of course,' Mrs Delaney says.

'There's no need,' says my mother. 'For what's left of the year Min will continue her studies. She'll have the room that used to be Sadie's. It's right at the back of the house and nice and quiet. She'll be our guest and it will be our pleasure to have her.'

Somewhere, I don't know where, I think my father is saying: 'Thank you, Miriam.'

Because that's the way he always wanted it to be in our house and now even though he isn't here to see it that's the way it is.

FRIEDA

What's the Rush?

1974

'Twenty-nine years it's taken him to come and see his grandfather. Now suddenly everything has to be done in a rush and he's the one who's in a hurry.'

This is my mother's opinion of Lenny Lazar who is out here two months and has asked me to marry him. Any other mother would be impressed but mine isn't.

'Don't let all the ritz and the glitz fool you,' she says. 'Whose money do you think is paying for everything? It's not Lenny's.'

What can you do with a mother like this? I'm crazy about Lenny and he's chasing after me and running so hard he's like a man in training for the Olympic Games.

'A man is supposed to chase after a woman,' my mother says. 'If you want my opinion he should even be running a little bit harder. He's a young man. It won't kill him.'

Reuben's pushing. Sadie's pushing. My mother's the only one who doesn't know what the rush is about.

'Give it a little time,' she says. 'You should get to know him better.'

My mother is an open-minded woman but it seems to me she's an open-minded woman who can live without Lenny Lazar.

'A few nice times together, a couple of bunches of flowers and some chocolates and you think you're ready to get married.'

'He wants you to like him,' I say. 'He's trying his best.'

'That's nice and I'm pleased to hear it,' my mother says. 'Now we've seen his best let's see what else he's got to offer.'

My mother may not be impressed but I am. When Lenny goes after a girl he knows how to treat her. What my mother says is right. He's never without a bunch of flowers or a box of chocolates but it's more than that. It's the best seats everywhere. The nicest tables in the fanciest restaurants. Reuben's Caddie backwards and forwards, sometimes with a driver and sometimes without one. He's only been here five minutes and already everybody knows him. It's 'How's it going, Lenny?' or 'What's up, Lenny?' or 'What can we do for you tonight, Mr Lazar?'

The talk around Johannesburg is that the reason Lenny's nearly pushing me through the *shul* door with a bulldozer is not altogether to do with my charms. It may also have something to do with Reuben who we all know is a man who likes to keep a thing in the family especially when the thing we're talking about is such an important thing as a family fortune.

Lenny says it's a lot of rubbish. He wants me and he wants me in a proper way and the sooner we can get it all settled the happier he'll be. He wants to settle down in Johannesburg in Reuben's business which one day he'll take over. He's almost thirty and he wants to have a family and make a life.

This is what I've told my mother which as far as I'm

179

concerned is all there is to tell but still she isn't happy.

'I know what you've told me,' she says.

'So?' I say.

'So?' she says. 'I'm still the mother and you're still the daughter. There are some things I like to work out for myself. Like what kind of a man it is who wants to rush my Frieda off her feet and under the *chuppah* in such a hurry? What's the rush? That's all I'm asking.'

It's not so easy. I know what the rush is. Or at least I think I do.

These days Lenny and I spend a lot of time together in the back seat of Reuben's Caddie and he's getting hotter and I'm no blushing violet. There are some things you tell your mother and some things you don't and I'm getting it from the other side too.

'What's the delay?' Lenny's saying. 'What's the big deal? What are you holding on to it for? It's not as if it's the Crown Jewels.'

No boy has ever talked to me like this before.

'You like me,' he says. 'I know you do. I said I'll marry you and that's what I'm going to do. All I'm asking is a little sample. A little something up front to show how you feel. Is that such a terrible thing? And who's going to know anyway?'

All I know about is looking. Now that I've actually found I don't know what I'm supposed to do.

'You haven't had many boyfriends, have you?' he says. 'That's nothing to be embarrassed about. I'm not really interested in a girl who knows her way around the block.'

'And what's that supposed to mean?'

'You know what it means,' he says. 'You may be holding on to it for dear life and it shows me you're not a fool. In a way I'm quite impressed.'

Lenny has a nice way of looking at a girl. Perhaps he stands in front of his mirror and practises. I don't know if men do but if that's what he does it's certainly paid some dividends.

'You think that's all I'm after?' he says. 'That I can get from any girl. With you it's different. There are girls who are only good for one thing and there are girls you marry.'

What I don't know is that some men are like this too and exactly which kind Lenny is is something I'm going to find out for myself.

FRIEDA

A Girl Who's Nothing
But Trouble

1975

Reuben and Sadie don't think Min being with us is such a hot idea.

'You don't need policemen on your doorstep,' Sadie says.

She'd say more but Reuben shows with his hand that he has something to say too.

'I know how these things work and it won't end here.'

He's never been sure about Min and me being such good friends in the first place and having Min actually living at our house and her not being shy about saying what she thinks drives him crazy. He thinks we should leave political troubles to people other than ourselves to sort out. By which he means *goyim*.

That's his opinion. Not all of us feel the same way but that's nothing new either. When will there ever be two Jews who will be in complete agreement about anything? There are plenty of Jews, people we know who Reuben knows too, who will be more than happy to stand up and be counted right alongside Min and her friends, and they are and they pay for it just the same as anyone else does.

Reuben has no sympathy for them. He thinks maybe they would have learnt a thing or two from Mr Hitler and his friends and not be quite so keen to be seen and heard while they shout their mouths off.

'You think your name isn't already on the files down at John Vorster Square?' Reuben says. 'The minute you let this girl in your door it was on the files and you were in trouble.'

The troublesome girl has her ideas as well. About Reuben and about me.

'Reuben thinks you're wonderful because you never answer back,' Min says. 'You suit him the way you are. Don't you see that? The less you know about what's really going on the happier he is.'

'I know what's going on,' I say. 'I don't need him to tell me. I don't need you to tell me either.'

'You don't know anything,' she says. 'And you don't want to know. All you want to know about is Lenny and your wedding.'

'That's not true,' I say.

'All right then,' says Min. 'If you know so much, do you know Beauty's walking here every day all the way from Alex?'

'It's bus boycott. Everyone knows that.'

We do all know. You can't pick up a newspaper without seeing it all over the front page.

'Never good news,' my mother says. Then she gives a big sigh and puts the paper down again.

Reuben says he doesn't even want to talk about it. He's getting old. His health isn't good and his heart's been playing up lately which he blames on the country.

He says we can forget what the words are the doctors use for it. He could have kept the big fat medical fee in his own pocket and told us for nothing.

What's troubling his heart is watching everything he's worked for over the years going to the dogs. Especially now his grandson's here and willing to lend a hand and maybe some day if he shows he's worth something even to run the businesses.

No wonder men his age and even younger are dropping dead like flies from heart attacks when instead of being able to sit back a little bit and take things easy they're supposed to stand back and see all their hard work flushed down the toilet. All because black people are fed up with living on locations.

They're also fed up with putting bus-fare money in the pockets of people who're already rich and greedy for more. There've been terrible scenes at bus stops. Stones have been thrown and people badly hurt. A bus has been set alight and the police have been called out. Black people are still coming to work but they're walking.

'They'll come to some arrangement,' my mother says. 'They'll see sense. If they think the world's going to stop because a few maids would rather walk than get on a bus they've got a big surprise coming.'

In the meantime winter is on its way and Beauty is still walking. She's stopped saying: 'I'm sorry I'm late, madam.' Every maid in the street has the same story and there's nothing anyone can do about it.

'It won't go on for ever,' my mother says. 'Being stubborn won't get them anywhere. In the end they'll come to their senses and things will be back to normal.'

In the mean time Beauty's ankles are swollen and she's always tired and she tells us bits and pieces if we ask her but you can see she won't tell us what it's really all about.

'Do you know how far it is she walks?' Min says.

Am I walking behind her measuring the miles? The answer is I don't know, not exactly, and Min knows I don't know.

'I said you didn't want to know,' Min says and that's another thing. She likes to have the last word. She can't stand it if she can't make you see she's right.

'You live in Cloud Cuckoo Land. That's fine with me. We're friends and we're not going to have a fight about it. All I'm saying is you can't keep your head in the sand for ever. Something will happen to make you wake up.'

And something does. Beauty has been detained by the police. Her son, Ephraim, comes to tell us. She's been involved in a pass demonstration. On her way walking home from our house to Alex Township there were people burning passbooks on a big bonfire at one of the bus stations.

We don't know what got into her. According to Ephraim she just stopped in her tracks, pulled her passbook out of her bust bodice where she keeps it safe and threw it on the fire with all the others. We think she must have gone a little bit mad.

Ephraim used to come to our house sometimes when he was a little boy. Every now and then Beauty would bring him and his sister, Constance, to show us how they'd grown and my mother and Sadie would say what fine, healthy children they were.

Then they'd play around the kitchen and Beauty would give them tea out of the cleaned-out jars she kept with her things and dry bread with it and at lunchtime they'd share her samp and beans and when she finished work my mother would give her money for their bus fare and they'd go home with her.

But that was a long time ago and when they got bigger and had things to say for themselves they stopped coming so I haven't seen Ephraim for years and he's very different these days. He's grown so much at first I didn't recognize him.

All we saw through the door glass was a tall black man dressed in trousers and a T-shirt and at the front door if you don't mind and not at the back, so my mother said we shouldn't open. 'Just stay quiet so he doesn't know anyone's here and he'll go away,' she says.

That's how things are in Johannesburg these days but even so it doesn't take five minutes for us to find out we know him and open the door and for Min to listen to his story and go off to the police station with him.

'What for?' Lenny wants to know.

He's come to the house to fetch me to go out only I've said I can't go. Not until Min comes back and I know she's safe.

Lenny thinks Min's mad. 'What's it her business?' he says. 'For that matter what's it yours?'

'It's her business because no one will listen to Ephraim. They won't listen to anyone who isn't white. You come from England. You don't know how things work here but that's how it is.'

'As long as you don't get it into your head to join her,' Lenny says, as if he needs to worry about that.

Standing outside a police station getting seen and heard, making a fuss about a maid's release is not the kind of thing I'd ever do. You'd only have to know me for five minutes to know that. No one's ever going to have a sleepless night about me and any kind of political involvement.

Which is not the kind of thing you'll ever be able to say about Min.

FRIEDA

What Lenny Wants

1974

'I had a little talk with Reuben about your friend Min,'
Lenny says. 'He says she's a girl who goes out looking
for trouble.'

'If you wanted to know about Min you certainly
asked the right one,' I say.

Reuben can't find a good word to say about Min and
hardly a day goes by without him letting us know
exactly how he feels. Mostly I let it slide past me but
sometimes I get fed up and let him know it. The way
he pays back is to show as long as I do this he won't
be quite so keen on me as he used to be. Which is not
exactly the situation Lenny wants.

'I'm surprised you haven't worked it out yet,' he
says. 'If you want Reuben off your back just do what
he wants. It's as easy as that.'

'What happens if I don't want to do what he wants?'
I say. 'What happens if I don't feel like sitting around
listening while he runs my friend into the ground?'

The way Reuben goes on you'd think every single

thing that goes wrong is Min's fault. He's not so worried about what goes on in the townships. If black people want to kill each other that's their business. He thinks they get exactly what they deserve. If they wanted things to be different they should be looking to us for an example. He means the Jews. You don't see us worrying about who's in charge and who isn't. In charge isn't your business. Your business is to find a little job somewhere and then to sit down and get on with it and maybe build it into something a little bit better.

When you're busy building up a business you haven't got time to worry about who got here first and whose land it is anyway.

Some of us came to this country not so many generations ago and we didn't just squat around taking hand-outs and waiting for the day of liberation. Unlike some people he could mention we got off our backsides and found some way to make a living and if God saw fit to bless us, we made it good. He means himself.

We pay taxes and although most of our taxes go straight down the drain which we won't even bother to discuss right this minute at least some of them, thank God, are used to pay the police. Sorting out the natives is police business and all he can say is good luck to them. Whatever it takes he hopes they do a proper job so at least we can live out our lives like decent people should.

What's worrying Reuben is that people from overseas are not so keen on throwing their money in our direction any more and the way he carries on you'd think this is Min's personal responsibility. She's doing it all by herself specifically to upset him. He thinks it makes her happy to see him feel things where it hurts most which is in his pocket.

I don't like it when he's like this. It reminds me of Min's mother and the way she is towards Min and I don't like that either. Min acts tough but it's hard on her having these things thrown up in her face just about every time someone who isn't a friend or another student looks at her.

I'd like to tell Mrs Delaney this and I'd like to tell Reuben as well except he's my aunt's husband and about to be my father-in-law so he's my relation twice over and we all know how important family is.

'I've got nothing against Min,' Lenny says. 'But for a quiet life when Reuben's around can't we just keep her name out of the conversation?'

These days all Min's time is taken up at the Baragwanath Hospital in Soweto Township where she's an intern. She's doing shiftwork there or she's studying at home. She doesn't have time to eat. She hardly has time to sleep and the only person she has time to talk to is Davey. It's like living with a ghost in the house.

If Reuben knew how little we see of her maybe he'd get tired of singing the same old song about how dangerous she is and at least give his heart a rest on that score.

Once upon a time the room where Min stays was Sadie's room. We called it Sadie's room. Then when Min moved in we started calling it Min's room and now I can't imagine it being anything else.

Not that she's ever in it. Sometimes, in case she's forgotten I exist, just to remind her I leave something for her to eat.

'Beef on rye and a flask of black tea,' she says when next she sees me. 'I know Frieda passed this way. You don't have to do it, you know. It's bad for me to get used to room service. That's definitely something I'm not going to have where I'm going.'

'And where will that be, I would like to know?'

I would like to know because Min and her future isn't something we talk about all that often and one of these days her intern year will end and she'll have to apply for a hospital post. I've asked her often enough and I think she's always known but she never tells me straight out. At least she never did. Not until this day.

'I'll go back where I come from,' she says. 'My father's clinic's still there. They always need qualified people. Our old house is still there too, you know. I suppose it's so awful no one else wants it.'

Which is exactly what I expected to hear because I know this is what she really wants. When she talks about something that hasn't got anything to do with the townships or politics or putting the world right her old life is all she talks about and it worries me.

No one in their right mind wants to go and live out in the bundu in the black areas and this isn't just Reuben talking, it's me too. Life out there is meant for black people. Maybe once upon a time when Min was growing up and her father was alive it was different but things have changed. Now it's too hard and too dangerous for us.

'Lenny says you can get a good job right here in Johannesburg if you want,' I say.

I've been talking about her behind her back to Lenny. So what? I care about Min and Lenny has some good ideas sometimes and he certainly knows how the world works.

'Is that what he says?' Min says and she seems to think it's very funny.

'I know you don't think very much of him . . .' I say.

'As a matter of fact I don't think of him at all,' she says which is to say the subject of Lenny is closed except I haven't finished yet.

'All the same it won't hurt you to listen to what he has to say. He has some good ideas. You could easily stay.'

'I couldn't easily stay. I don't want to stay. I want to go back where I belong.'

'You don't have to do this. You don't even have to be at a place like Bara. It may come as a big surprise

190

to you but there are other hospitals. You could have asked to go anywhere you wanted.'

'Is that what Lenny says as well?'

'No. It's what I'm saying.'

'If it's you who wants to know then I'll tell you and I want you to listen to me. I know I don't *have* to be there but just the same I did have to because Bara is the place where I can be the most useful just now so I had no choice.'

'You used to say we always had choices.'

'Well, then I was wrong and I'm sorry,' she says. 'When it comes to this I don't have any choice at all. It's no good even talking about it.'

That's all we ever really said and perhaps we should have talked about it more because now Min is in big trouble. We would have heard about it eventually but Beauty is the one to tell us and Beauty heard it from a friend of Ephraim.

'I don't know the exact story,' she says. Her brown paper overall packet is still in her hand and not even opened yet and under her beret her face is wet with sweat from walking to get to us fast.

'It's very bad where we live,' she says. 'The Casspirs come every night. You hear them like elephants. They go past and then they go away and in the morning when we open up our doors people are missing. Our friends, our neighbours, children playing in the street one day and gone the next.'

'What about Miss Min?' I say.

'It's to do with the women waiting for news outside the hospital,' Beauty says. 'That what got Miss Min in trouble.'

Every day there are women outside the hospital looking for missing people and asking anyone who comes past if they have any news. Wives are look-ing for husbands. Mothers are looking for sons and daughters. Old men and grandmothers are looking

191

for missing children and grandchildren. Children leave their houses to buy bread at the local spaza where the neighbour will sell what you need out of the 'shop box' under her kitchen table. They go out looking for half loaf white for supper and are never seen again.

'Yesterday the police came again and asked for passes. Anyone without passes was to be taken away and some people started running straight away before anyone could catch them and ask them to show but some people stayed.'

No one has passes these days. If they do they're too afraid to show them. If you don't burn your pass along with everyone else the way Beauty did, you're in for big trouble with your own people, you get it in the neck for being a sell-out. If you do burn your pass and the police ask for it and you haven't got it, you're in even bigger trouble for breaking the law. For this you get thrown in the back of a police van and taken away for questioning.

Whichever way you look at it, if you're a black person and don't have a pass you count for nothing and your life isn't worth ten cents. You may as well not exist at all.

There's fighting everywhere in the townships and all the injured get taken to Bara. If you want to know about a son or a daughter it's the only place you can go and although Bara's a hospital it's still the same as everywhere else. If you don't have a pass you won't even get past the police cordon and into the door. Not even if you come for treatment.

'How can you worry about a pass when you come for news of a son or a daughter or an old lady neighbour who goes to bed in the night and isn't there in the morning?' Beauty wants to know.

She knocks a finger against her forehead and shakes her head to show *meshugge* and I want to smile because it's just the kind of thing my mother would do and I think Beauty's been working for us for too long. She's beginning to act exactly like us.

My mother and I stand side by side and my mother takes hold of my hand and her hand is cold as ice. For this type of question she doesn't have any answer and nor do I. Nobody does.

We aren't the most Jewish Jews in the world but we have our past just the same as all Jews do and we have reason to thank God that we were spared and are still here to tell our story. We don't talk about it every day but our history has been touched by those black wings that passed over us and in that moment in some way all of our lives were changed for ever.

Sometimes I feel that being a Jew is like having an albatross that hangs around our necks and on days like this, hearing stories like this, I think I hear glass crashing into splinters and see yellow Stars of David floating invisible around us. I think I hear the word 'Juden' being hissed in my ear.

Whether we like it or not we know about such things and we know more than other people do because they have touched us.

'Where's Miss Min?' I say.

She was coming off duty. She could have got a police escort and been taken out of the township through the police cordon to safety but instead she got involved.

The women had had enough. They were shouting at the policemen and the army boys who'd been brought in to keep the peace and instead of getting into the army truck or asking for police protection Min stepped right in the middle of it and said she couldn't care less about passes. She'd give information just whenever she had any to give and she'd give treatment to anyone who needed it. No questions asked.

Someone who saw her passed it on to Beauty because that's the way it works. In the township boys and girls pass you on the street and tell you what you have to know and they hardly stop to do it. It's not the way we do things but when it comes to something like this and a police or army matter it's the only way and you can rely on it.

Min was going around asking for names of those who were missing and might be in the hospital.

'If I know these people I will tell you what has happened to them,' she says.

You can hardly believe that anyone would be mad enough to do something like this with half the defence force looking on but Min was.

'It was definitely her,' Beauty says.

In a black township Min's white coat and her pale hair stand out like a beacon and in Soweto these days a white woman speaking Zulu is not the joke it used to be down in Coronation Avenue. It helps Min with her work but the police and the army boys hate it.

'Give me names,' she says. 'I'll tell you your news good or bad. I'll tell you everything I know but then go home. Go home and stay there. Don't let these men get hold of you.'

'They tried to stop her but she wouldn't listen,' Beauty says. 'They said she was causing more trouble all by herself than all the rest of the women put together.'

So, Min has been taken.

'But why?' my mother wants to know. 'What has she done that's so wrong? Good God! A parent wants to know about a child. A wife is entitled to ask about a husband.'

My mother should know better. These days, if you're black you can't even go to a municipal mortuary to identify your dead and arrange to take them away for burial if you don't have a pass to show but I don't think my poor mother knows about things like this.

I'm planning the no-expense-spared wedding I've dreamt of all my life. I don't want to know any of it

194

myself but Min makes me. This is the price of our friendship. I can ignore the newspapers and turn off the SABC. When other people have something to say I can show with my hands I'm not interested and say perhaps we should talk about something else that's nicer and more pleasant but you can't do that with Min. She won't rest until I've listened to her. So now I know and I can't pretend I don't.

Beauty's crying. Not a lot. Just one tear sliding out from under her new black-framed glasses which Min made her get free of charge from the eye clinic. It's only one tear but from Beauty with all the hardship she's had in her life I think it's all she can spare. If it was from someone else it would be a river.

So now we have to worry about Min.

'We'll talk to Reuben,' my mother says. 'I'm sure it's some kind of mistake. I'm sure it can be sorted out and if there are any strings to be pulled I'm sure he knows where to pull them.'

'Reuben's a sick man,' I say. 'You needn't bother him with this.'

'Who's talking about bothering?' my mother says. 'We'll ask a little favour. That's all. He may have a few words to say but he knows people and he's my sister's husband after all. He'll help us if he can.'

'You needn't bother Reuben because I'm going down to John Vorster Square and I'm going to sort it out myself.'

These mad words are coming out of my mouth. There's no doubt about that but if you asked me why I wouldn't be able to tell you.

'You think this is fun and games?' my mother says. 'Haven't you listened to a single word Reuben or Lenny your own future husband has been saying to you all these months? This isn't our business. We'll do what we can but the further we keep out of it the better.'

I've already fetched my ostrich handbag which Sadie gave me and my shoes to match. My engagement ring is on my finger and a gold chain around my neck which I put under my nice white cashmere jersey because one thing's sure, once you get off the highway and go into downtown Johannesburg you aren't entering paradise.

As far as my engagement ring, my pride and joy, is concerned, it's a different story. I promised Lenny I would never take it off my finger. Never. Whatever I do, wherever I go. Gloves go over it if I should ever have to do washing-up, and a nice gentle soap when I wash my hands. Not only for sentimental reasons but mainly for safety's sake.

It looks very nice sitting on the third finger of my left hand but a promise is a promise and thank God the weather's cold so I can turn the stone back towards the palm where it won't show and pull a leather glove over it.

'You're mad,' my mother says. '*Meshugge*, off your head. Next thing you'll end up sitting right next to Min in a gaol cell.'

If it happens, it happens. What can I say? At least I'll be in good company.

Let me tell you something for nothing. A police station is not a picnic.

You'd be surprised any business gets done there at all. There are people all over the show and uniformed policemen behind desks asking questions and filling in forms and people, all shapes and sizes and colours and kinds, falling in and out of queues. Some wait patiently and look respectable. Others run and shout. Everyone has a story to tell and the policemen behind the desks are taking stories down.

While all this is going on there are other people sitting on benches that run down the sides of the walls and still others sitting on the floor. There are

196

people just wherever you look. I suppose they're waiting to hear what they can find out from the others who are standing in queue and it seems to me no one is finding out anything very much at all.

It smells awful, of people and Jeye's Fluid and floors that need to be properly cleaned and scrubbed and toilets that are too close by and don't work as well as they should and the noise is deafening.

Everyone's talking. Some are shouting and while I'm standing there the door flies open and two men in ordinary clothes come in and they're pushing and kicking a native boy so he lands on the floor on his hands and knees and when he's down they push him and kick him some more although he's already covered in blood. Then they pull him up and push and drag him through a door marked PERSONNEL ONLY and out of sight.

'Excuse me,' I say.

'Join the queue,' a man standing near me says.

'I just want to ask something,' I say. 'Just ask. That's all.'

'Join the queue,' he says.

I may not know very much but if there's one thing I do know about, it's about queues. I don't know what it is. I don't know if it's a Jewish thing. Maybe it is. All I know is that, on my ostrich pumps, I march to the front of the queue. I push a few people to one side to get where I want to be and they can say whatever they like. It makes no difference to me. If you don't ask you don't get and you have to start somewhere and I haven't got all day.

'Excuse me,' I say. 'I'm here to find out about Dr Minnie Campbell. The police took her away last night. From the Baragwanath Hospital. Just as she was coming off duty.'

In my head I can see her name in neat black letters on the label tied on her suitcase by her mother that first time she came to stay with us. I can remember how I envied that label. How I loved the style and the class of it.

'Minnie Campbell,' I say. 'I want to know where she is because I've come to take her out.'

My ostrich handbag between my two gloved hands is on the counter and real ostrich skin may not mean much to some people but it means a lot to me. For those who can see it and know what it stands for it shows I'm a woman to be reckoned with. I don't have a high-class bark like Mrs Delaney or a hands-on-the-hips style of asking other people's business like Mrs Ross in our road does. I have my own way.

'If you'll just hold on,' the policeman says. 'I'll ask.'

He calls to another policeman and they talk for a few minutes and while his back is turned a few remarks are made behind me and I get pushed around a little bit but I stand my ground.

In all my life no one has managed to move me out of the front spot at Silverman's just before early closing on a Friday. Not until I'd got my mother's meat order and checked every single thing for quality and double-checked that the weight and the price agreed with one another. No one moved me then and they can push and shove me from behind just as much as they like, no one is going to move me now.

'What's your interest?' the policeman wants to know.

'I'm her friend,' I say.

He looks at me and his friend he's been talking to steps closer and looks at me too and gives a little nod as if I've just passed some kind of test.

'You can tell her,' he says.

'They've appeared before a magistrate but they aren't formally charged yet,' the first policeman says.

'Which means what?' I say.

'Which means,' the policeman says, 'that while they decide what to do with her your friend can be let out

198

on bail and bail's already been posted so if you've got enough money you can get her out.'

'How much is "enough money"?' I want to know.

The policeman looks at me and can see I'm Jewish which people like him always think means rich. He can see my real ostrich handbag and I think maybe he's not such a fool as I took him for at first because the way I look to him I can see he's willing to do business with me.

'A lot,' he says.

'How much is "a lot"?' I want to know.

'These are very serious charges we're talking about. Incitement to unrest. Resisting arrest. Abusive language towards the police. Standing in the way of an army patrol doing their duty. Do you know how serious this is?'

'How much?' I say.

'Twenty thousand rand,' he says and his rough sandy eyebrows go up a little bit. Serious, I understand. Twenty thousand rand worth of serious. This I understand even better.

'Twenty thousand, you said?' I say. As if to a woman like me throwing around numbers like twenty thousand is actually talking *bubkes* and doesn't worry me at all. 'And where would I pay over this money?'

He points with his pencil to the outside foyer where a woman sits in a glass box.

'Bank-guaranteed cheque or cash only,' he says.

Thank you very much. Having a real ostrich skin handbag is one thing. Having twenty thousand rand to put inside it is another story altogether but if you need it badly enough you can always find money and as it happens I already have an idea in my head and my idea concerns Sonny Emmanuel.

Sonny Emmanuel, 'From Factory to Finger'. That's his motto. He has it printed on a little sign inside his window in Troyeville and there are a lot of women who have stood outside Selikowitz Jewellers on Eloff Street and looked at the rings they show in their window then ended up getting whatever it is they get from Sonny Emmanuel.

Sonny's a man who's seen life. I'm not the first woman to walk through his door needing money in a hurry and no questions asked and Sonny is not a man who asks questions.

'I don't know what trouble you're in and I don't want to know,' he says. 'Let's just call it a favour.'

I wouldn't know a bank-guaranteed cheque if I fell over one in the road. What I need is cash and Sonny Emmanuel is the only person I know who'd be willing to take my engagement ring from me and have this kind of money in his safe and hand it to me over the counter no questions asked.

'If your Uncle Reuben should ask you tell him you were the one who came to me and not the other way around. This ring, which by the way is a real beauty, is safe with me. It's in safe-keeping only. That's the way I look at it. I would like it if this is what you would tell Mr Lazar.'

One day I'll tell about Sonny Emmanuel, word for word what I know from Aunty Fanny, but not today. Today I stand outside the back door of John Vorster Square police station which on a late afternoon in winter is not the warmest place in the world and watch for Min to come out.

Forget about sunny South Africa. In winter the air on the highveld is so cold it hurts when you breathe it in.

It's a very funny thing. The gate these people come through is made of metal but apart from that it's small and quite ordinary. If you didn't know what was behind it you wouldn't even look twice at it. You wouldn't think it would be like this. You'd think a gate that can make a difference in a person's life such as between disappearing into gaol and never being

200

seen again or walking out and being a free person could maybe look a little bit better.

I don't think it makes any difference to them. All they're worried about is getting their money in. Once you've paid your money, you hand your receipt to the sergeant on duty in front of the PERSONNEL ONLY door and he tells you where to go which is round the back.

'You can wait there,' he says. 'If everything's in order they send them out that way.'

I can see in his face that to him I'm no better than the natives waiting for cheap meat outside Silverman's back door on a Saturday morning except I'm not such a fool. I've paid out good money up front and I don't want to let my receipt go.

'You go and fetch my friend first,' I say. 'Bring her right here where I can see her and then you can have it.'

When I say this the lady policeman who's doing the deal looks at me as if I'm mad but why should I care? It's a fair question and twenty thousand rand's a lot of money in anyone's language.

'Just go where we told you and wait,' she says so that's what I do. After all, what option do I have? I'll wait as long as I have to. All I care about is that the gate should open and Min should be there all in one piece because you hear terrible stories and you can never be sure and I don't know who or what to believe any more.

Then the gate opens and out comes Min and I don't think I've ever been happier in my life although at the same time I'm so furious I feel like giving her a piece of my mind right there and then because I should be at home going through my John Orr gift request list not standing here in the freezing cold waiting for some lunatic to be let out of gaol.

All the same when I see her I shout her name out loud and when she hears my voice she turns towards me and I hold out my arms to her and she walks into them and I hold her tight, the way you hold someone you thought you were never going to see in this life again and I burst into tears.

'They wouldn't tell me who paid the bail,' she says. 'I knew it had to be you.'

Of course it had to be me. Who else does she think would be so crazy? A lot of people are going to be so fed up with Min because of what she's done they wouldn't even pay sixpence for her.

Not to mention what some of my own people are going to say about me when they find out what I did to get her out, especially when everyone who knows her would bet their bottom dollar that every word the police say about her is true and gaol is probably the place where she'll be safest. Not just from everyone else but from herself as well.

'Where did you get the money from?' she says. 'You didn't take it from Reuben?'

'I hate it when you do things like this,' I say. 'I wish you'd learn to mind your own business and keep yourself out of trouble.'

Except she isn't going to be put off that easily. 'Where?' she says.

She's creased from head to toe and there's a blood mark and a big gash and a new-looking scab on the side of her leg. Her white doctor shoes are sooty charcoal and her hair badly needs a wash and a brush.

'I hope you weren't so mad as to ask my mother or Gerald Delaney? You didn't go to my grandfather, did you?'

'What is this?' I say. 'You're the one who'd better start practising the smart answers. You're the one who's going to have a whole lot of questions thrown at you, not me.'

'We're not going anywhere till you tell me where you got the money from,' she says.

'All right,' I say. 'I'll tell you. If the alternative is we should stand here until we both die of cold and exposure I'll tell you. I'm tired and I'm hungry and I've had a really terrible day and I want to go home.'

I wriggle my handbag up my right arm and when my hand's free I take it and pull the glove off my left hand and with nothing standing in its way it comes off nice and easy. Then I hold my hand up in front of Min's face and turn my hand around first palm forward and then the other way so she can have a really good look at it.

'My God!' she says. 'You sold your engagement ring.'

The way she goes on usually you'd think there was nothing left that could surprise Min but now I see that there is because I still can.

'Yes,' I say. 'I did.'

I pull my car keys out of my coat pocket and jangle them in front of her which is to say let's get going. I suppose I'm a fool for doing what I did but so is she for doing what she did. I loved that ring but when you get right down to it a ring is only a ring but Min is a person and a person is far more important.

FRIEDA

The Fanciest-Schmantziest Wedding

1976

Min isn't at my wedding. The reason is that as usual she's done exactly what she said she'd do. She's gone to put up her plate in the very same place her father had his and to take up his work at the clinic.

Her grandfather paid back the bail money before the fighting and screaming at our house was even over and I got my ring back. Lenny didn't disappear in the night and we stayed engaged and in the end because of being a student and just about to finish her internship Min got off with a one-time-only warning. As long as she behaves herself. Next time she's for the high jump and there isn't a string to be pulled or any amount of money in the world that will do her any good at all.

Except I don't think this is going to happen. To sit and wait for the day Min changes her ways is just about the same as sitting around waiting for fish to fly which is to say you may have to wait a very long time.

Still it means that on the great day of my wedding although our house is full of women Min is not there.

Everyone else is. Women are putting on my make-up and doing my hair. My wedding things are being laid out and my dress is being taken out of its tissue paper and plastic wrapper. The doorbell isn't quiet for a minute. The phone doesn't stop ringing and one tray full of teacups is hardly taken away before another one takes its place.

When Min phones it's my mother who speaks to her and passes on her message.

'She says in spirit she'll be there,' my mother says.

Spirit is nice and I know it's the best she can do but on this occasion, to be quite honest, flesh and blood would have suited me better.

'Why should it worry you?' Sadie says. 'You know her by now. It comes to a choice between you and the blacks down at the hospital who's she going to choose? You don't need me to tell you.'

Hazel doesn't know why I'm making such a big fuss out of it either. 'This is a Jewish wedding,' she says.

As if that says everything and as if I didn't know. There isn't a Jew in a two-hundred-mile radius of Johannesburg who isn't going to be there and because of Reuben being who he is and well known we even have a few imports. As if there weren't enough already.

'What does she know about Jewish weddings any-way?' Hazel says. 'She just wouldn't fit in.'

'She's only one person,' Sadie says. 'The whole of Johannesburg, all the people who count, will be there. That's the important thing.'

This is quite true. Whichever way you look at it the wedding of Mr Lenny Lazar and Miss Frieda Woolf, lately of Germiston, is as fancy-schmantzy as anyone

205

could possibly wish for and an Occasion no one is going to forget in a hurry.

It's just like Sadie said it would be. Just about the whole world is there and there's an album full of photographs to prove it. No expense has been spared just like Reuben promised but even so it isn't how I imagined it would be.

Who wants to be married in a *shul* full of strangers?

I told Lenny this.

'Ignore them,' he says. 'They're only there to bring presents and because we don't want to offend anyone.'

'Who's going to be offended?' I say. 'How can anyone who's never set eyes on me in their life before be offended because they aren't at my wedding?'

Except it doesn't work like this and I know it. My mother and Sadie and Reuben are all involved and one name on the list leads to another. Sadie's writing out cheques as if they're going out of fashion and Reuben's signing them without even blinking. To make this an Event money's flowing out like water and Lenny knows plenty of people too. He knows who's who. He's had a look at some of the names on the list and he likes them very, very much and when at last even my mother thinks it's getting too much and says so Lenny has his answer ready.

'Don't worry about what your mother says,' he says. 'You better start learning to think the way I think and what I'm telling you is that this isn't money being thrown away.'

What it is in Lenny's opinion is a nice little investment which is going to bring a big fat dividend right into Lenny's and my pocket.

'It's once in a lifetime,' Sadie says. 'For once in a lifetime we make a memorable occasion and it costs what it costs and we don't worry about the money.'

So that's what we do and as it turns out it's far more memorable than anyone ever expected, particularly and especially me.

Lenny's in a tuxedo with satin lapels and underneath a white pleated shirt and at the neck a red bow tie and I'm there too sticking out of a dress that looks like a meringue. It's made from cream silk flown in from Hong Kong and beaded with teardrop pearls and rhinestones.

Out of all this silk which doesn't come any cheaper if you buy in bulk are my bare shoulders and my neck with Lenny's present of a diamond heart pendant around it; and my head with a hired tiara of pearls and diamonds on top of it and a long veil floating down.

Lenny is all teeth and smiling and I'm hanging on to him for dear life. At least that's how it looks in the pictures.

There's a great state of excitement and everyone's looking around to see who exactly is there and who hasn't been invited.

'You won't believe it,' Sadie says. 'Arlene Grossman nearly fell right off her seat when she saw you come into the *shul*. She couldn't believe it was you. She told me out of her own mouth she thought you looked like a queen.'

There are people I've never seen before in my life with parcels in their hands and some of them with a nice fat envelope which slides from hand to hand and it's the envelopes Lenny's most interested in.

'With these we don't take chances,' Lenny says. 'We put them straight into a locked drawer in the hotel manager's office.'

'Let Reuben arrange it,' says Sadie.

'If anyone gives you anything,' Lenny says to me, 'give it straight to me. Don't just put it down somewhere or leave it lying around.'

'What do you think's going to happen if I do?' I say.

'What do you think?' he says. 'You think every *gonif*

207

in town takes the day off just because it happens to be our wedding? What will happen is this.' He puts his fingers to his lips and makes a little blow and a wave goodbye. 'We can kiss goodbye to it, that's what,' he says.

'I thought this was a wedding. I thought these people were our friends.'

'You should grow up,' Lenny says. 'You're a married woman now. You should stop being such a *nudnick* and take a good look at the world around you.'

There are candles and pink and white almonds on every table. There's a board with our name on it in the main marble reception area of the hotel and an ice sculpture of a mermaid at the entrance to the private reception room and pink and white chiffon draped on the table-fronts.

When Lenny and I take to the dance floor the orchestra plays 'Oh, How We Danced on the Night We Were Wed' and everyone claps. Reuben dances past all silver-waved hair and smiles with his beautiful Seidela dressed to kill in his arms and Isaac Silverman gets a push from Ruth and asks my mother to dance.

'Only from your own child can a person *shep* such *naches*,' he says and Ruth Silverman gets up and puts her arms around my mother.

'Lenny's a lovely boy,' she says. 'I just wish Aaron could be with us to see this day.' We know Ruth by now. Her handkerchief is out and her eyes are full of tears.

The ceiling is a mass of pink and white balloons and there are pink and white orchids all over the place. Just wherever you look waiters in black waist-coats are running backwards and forwards with silver trays filled with glasses of champagne, real French for the toasts and local afterwards.

Men with yarmulkas on their heads are clustered around the bar drinking double Chivas Regal on ice and if Rabbi Weisz wants to look he can look and they wouldn't even try to hide the glasses.

'No shame,' my father would have said.

Nothing to be ashamed of these days. Big hands with gold rings are reaching for salmon canapes and caviare blinis and the air is full of talk and the smell of men and food and cigars and Lenny with a key in his hand is running backwards and forwards to the manager's office to put envelopes in the drawer.

'To be on the safe side before something that's ours decides to take a walk by itself and disappear into someone else's pocket.'

This is what Lenny says to Morrie Lubinsky. Morrie is running around with his camera around his neck and one girl has already complained to her mother about him but he seems to understand what Lenny means.

Ruth Silverman's face is pink with Occasion and under the table her satin shoes are off her feet lying next to each other on the floor so her feet in their nylon stockings can have a stretch and at last she can be comfortable.

'It's a wedding to remember and you deserve it, darling,' she says. 'You've waited a long time. You've been a good girl and you've saved yourself.' She has me by the hand and her hair is new-permed and there's a nice lipstick mouth under it and green powder eyeshadow making itself at home in the crease of her eyelid and a little stroke of eyeliner. 'I know that without anyone telling me. I can see it in your face. And a good-looking boy like Lenny, what can I say? All I can say is that there's nothing in the world you should be worried about. You should look forward. This is a day you'll never forget. Something to remember all of your life.'

If everyone says so, it must be so but it still isn't how I imagined it would be.

In the pre-marriage talks Rabbi Weisz says a wife

should be obedient to her husband's wishes. 'I'm not suggesting you shouldn't have ideas of your own,' he says. 'What I'm saying is that what the one wants it should be the other one's pleasure to do.'

It's a very nice idea and it looks very good written down like this. You wouldn't think such a simple thing can be the start of all the trouble but it is.

What Lenny wants is for our wedding envelopes to go safe into the drawer. What I want is to please Lenny. So when Sonny Emmanuel who owes me and my little bit of trouble the favour of bringing him into our family in the first place comes over and wishes me *mazel tov* and hands me a little something the first thing I do is look for Lenny.

When I don't see him I decide to go to the manager's office myself to look for him and all the time I'm thinking what a good wife I'm being and how pleased Lenny will be with me and this is where I make my mistake.

The door to the manager's office is closed and I stand outside in my meringue dress with my hand on the doorknob and that's when I hear it. Hazel's laugh.

Hazel has a funny laugh. It's a sniff and a trill and she thinks she sounds like Elizabeth Taylor. It's a laugh you'd know anywhere and this is what I hear from behind the closed door of the manager's office. This and something else. A scuffling like a burglar and a laugh like someone planning a practical joke out of sight of all the others and for no one else to hear.

Maybe I should walk away. But I don't. Instead I turn the knob and open the door and walk right in and what I see is Hazel standing pushed against the wall and her skirt's right up.

All you see are stockings and white suspenders and there's a man with her standing with his back to me and his hand is up higher than her stocking top right up against her bare leg and I don't need him to turn around so I can see his face.

I know that hand and I know who it belongs to. Which just happens to be Lenny, the man who's my brand-new, fresh-out-the-box, newly married husband, and he hears the door open and doesn't even bother to turn around.

'Excuse us,' he says. 'What we need here is a little privacy.'

His other hand, the one that isn't on Hazel's leg, is up against the wall. He's talking to the space between her neck and the wall and I can't stop staring. All I do is stare. My heart doesn't sink and my world doesn't end. I don't scream or shout or faint. I just stand there in my Hong Kong silk and fake diamond and pearl tiara seeing something I wish I hadn't seen because this is my wedding day and now I have to remember it for the rest of my life.

I think I'm supposed to be hurt or upset or broken-hearted but hearts break for a tragedy not for a joke so I don't even have that.

All I have for a memory is how silly they look. The pink fur sleeve-cuffs of Hazel's bridesmaid's dress are around the back of Lenny's neck.

Her head is against the wall and from the waist up she looks respectable but you can see all of her legs from the white thighs where the stockings end and her suspender belt begins right down to her thin ankles in pink satin shoes and they look ridiculous.

The hand with the big ring Reuben gave Lenny for a wedding present is going about its business and the other hand is spread five-fingered flat against the wall and over his shoulder Hazel's big eyes are looking at me.

'Stop it, Lenny,' she says. 'It's enough.'

She pushes him away and pulls at her skirt and now at last he takes the trouble to turn himself around to see who it is who's standing in the door and getting in the way of him and his good time.

'This has got nothing to do with me,' Hazel says.

'Lenny can't keep himself to himself, that's the trouble,' and Lenny is pulling at his shirt-cuffs and straightening his bow tie.

'I'm sorry you saw that,' he says.

I'm sorry too but I'm not going to say so and I'm not going to say why.

'If you'll excuse me,' Hazel says. 'I'm getting out of here. Just remember what I said. It wasn't my fault.'

After she's gone it's just Lenny and me.

'She's nothing,' Lenny says.

He doesn't even wait until Hazel's out of the door before he says it. He couldn't care less if she hears him. He's smoothing down his hair and checking the buttons on his jacket and in a minute he's himself again, all handsome face and smiles and his hair smoothed back and his tuxedo tailor-made and not put together in some back-street sweatshop.

'I hope you told her that,' I say.

'Told her what?' he says.

'Told her that she's nothing,' I say. 'I'm sure Hazel would like to hear that.'

'Listen, Frieda,' he says. 'Before you say anything else you have to ask yourself a question. What kind of girl is it who comes on to a man the way Hazel does? What Hazel's got she offers on a plate.'

He looks at me and pulls his shoulders straight. 'You know what I mean?' he says.

'No,' I say. 'I don't know what you mean.'

So much for Hazel.

'What about you?' I say. 'I suppose you're so hungry you couldn't wait till it was time for our honeymoon to get started. In the mean time you couldn't say no and it's all my fault.'

You wouldn't think I'd said a single word. Lenny just goes right on talking. Like he's practised his lines and he isn't going to let anyone stop him mid-flow and certainly not me.

'I don't care that she's a friend of yours or what her

212

family are. If you'd like to know what kind of girl Hazel is I can tell you.'

'I know what kind of girl Hazel is,' I say. 'I've known her all my life.'

What I don't say is that now I also know what kind of man Lenny is and he must see this in my face because something about him changes.

'What are you going to do about it?' he says and I know what's worrying him isn't me or how I feel. It's Reuben and what he might say or do if he finds out.

'Nothing,' I say. 'I'm going to do nothing at all.'

It's like standing in another world. There are no orchids or ice mermaids here. There's no chiffon drapery and there are no balloons. There's just Lenny and me standing under a fluorescent light that drains the colour out of everything and makes us look hard and tired and old.

'I'll make it right with you,' he says. 'I just want you to know one thing. Girls like Hazel are nothing. "Disposables", we call them. You use them. Then you get rid of them. Any man will tell you that. They're two-a-penny. A wife's a different thing. You understand that, don't you?'

'Oh, yes,' I say. 'I understand.'

MIN

Going Home

1976

All the way home I remember Justin and the way he
entered the past. I'm driving along and in my head I'm
saying to myself all the things I wanted to say to him
that last time just after he died when I was carrying
the buffalo thorn branch in my hand and believing it
was his soul I held.

'What is it you so badly wanted to say to your
brother?' Marion Davis used to ask me in those days
when she was my doctor in Pietermaritzburg. 'Write it
down. Let me see it. If I know what it is perhaps I can
help.'

I couldn't tell her then. I couldn't tell her now
because it's not the kind of thing everyone understands. I'm not quite sure I really understand it
myself.

All I wanted was to say all of our life together out
loud so my brother could hear it and take it with
him as a gift and a memory into the other world.
That's all. Then I would have taken earth and water

and plastered the buffalo thorn into the side of the big hut in the main kraal and he would be home and safe and part of it for ever.

It's what I'd been taught. It's what I believed then.

Legend says if you don't do this the spirit roams around, endlessly lost, always seeking its place and never finding it. What I have done is the great betrayal because all the responsibility is the soul-bearer's and if he fails as I did all the failure must be his too.

This is what my mother took from Justin and me that night she snapped the thorn twig in two and threw it away into the night and the Great Silence began.

She didn't think it was a very great thing. Just a native legend educated people had no business believing. She thought it was my father's fault for putting our education in the hands of a village schoolmaster like George Morefe.

Who, for heaven's sake, was George Morefe anyway? When you got right down to it he was only a coon after all and not even a very clever one at that. Not in her opinion although there were some people who seemed to think differently.

She thought our attachment to him was unnatural and no one in their right mind could have expected anything but bad to come out of it and in the end that was what happened. We set too much store by him and his half-baked, foot-in-the-bush notions and that was the root of all the trouble.

If she sets her mind to it there are a great many people my mother can blame. She's lucky. I am the betrayer and I have no one to blame but myself. I'm the one who'll go through life and grow older as Justin will not. I'm the one who will have to make peace with it or find some other way that makes it at least bearable.

I'm over the pass and my little car is swaying down the zigzag road. I know the exact place where I'll see the village for the first time and when I get there I pull over and stop the car, pull up the handbrake and switch off the engine.

I open the door and step out and the car door stands open behind me and I look down upon my place and although I thought I'd remembered everything and had vowed never to forget I stand there dazzled and realize I had after all forgotten.

The beauty of it in the late-afternoon light is almost blinding.

I breathe in deep and smell the grass of the flatlands and the heat and the cow dung and all of my childhood, all that has made me, reaches out towards me and enfolds me once again in its embrace.

I see the huts and the scattering of white houses and Father Ignatius's church and the long low Moorish-style building that was once a monastery and is now a hospital and the clinic where I will work and I know this place. Not only with my eyes but with my heart.

When I pull up in front of the clinic Father Ignatius is waiting. I don't know how he does it. He says he can hear a strange car coming from miles away and maybe that's true.

What matters is that he's there and I stand in front of him and my hands are in both his and in his eyes he carries a part of my life no one else knows or wishes to remember and he's the same except older.

'I hear you were in a little trouble in Johannesburg,' he says.

'A little,' I say and he says nothing else and neither do I. Instead he changes the subject and offers to walk around the clinic with me.

'As if you didn't know it,' he says.

But I don't. Not any more. It's small. Smaller than I remember. It seems to have shrunk. The floors are bare concrete and gleam with scrubbing and there are so many people all with needs.

'You know about our lepers, don't you?' Father Ignatius asks. 'Some of the doctors they've been sending from the army base to help out aren't too sure about them. I think the look of them puts people off.'

'It won't put me off,' I say. 'You know me better than that.' And he does.

When our little tour is over Father Ignatius and I stand in the sun together. It's early but the hospital supper bell rings behind us. There will be samp and beans and porridge and bread and a clean bed for the night and tomorrow it will begin all over again.

It's all I want. It's what I've longed for.

'I hope you've done the right thing,' Father Ignatius says. 'We have our troubles here too, you know. Just the same as everywhere else. This isn't a place you can hide away in if that's what you were thinking.'

It's not what I was thinking at all.

BOOK THREE

Strange Songs in a Strange Land

1980–1981

FRIEDA

A Very Sick Boy

1980

Davey's dying. Dr Rosenberg told us but we don't want to believe it.

'He's tired, Miriam,' he says.

Reuben says the best specialists can be called in. If we want we can telephone London or New York. There's nothing money can buy that isn't Davey's for the asking but my mother isn't in the mood for asking anyone for anything. She's content with what Dr Rosenberg's told us.

'I don't understand Miriam,' Sadie says to me. 'You'd think she'd at least ask for a second opinion.'

But what for? My mother is a mother. She doesn't need a second opinion. She doesn't need some stranger to tell her something she already knows. She and Dr Rosenberg have known each other for a long time. He's been Davey's doctor always. Whenever we needed him he came.

In the poor days when there were hardly any cars in Coronation Avenue, on Davey's bad days his green

Hillman Minx stood outside our house and it was like a sign. Everyone knew the doctor was at the Jewish Woman's House and her son was sick again and if there was money to pay Dr Rosenberg that was fine and if there wasn't that was fine too but Sadie forgets.

Dr Rosenberg was the first one who knew there was something really wrong with Davey. He was the one who explained the endocrine problem to my parents. He was with them both at the beginning and he'll be with my mother at the end.

'It's a blessing,' my mother says and Sadie can't believe her ears.

'Your mother's a very strange woman,' she says. 'Davey's dying and she calls it a blessing.'

'It's a blessing because we're with him,' I say. 'He's not alone or among strangers. He's with us where he belongs just like he's always been.'

I don't know if I would have thought to say that a year or so ago but I've come a long way since then and I look at my mother differently these days.

Sometimes before I go into the house I stand in the street for a while and it's the same place but different as if I'm looking down the wrong end of a telescope.

The house is smaller. The street's narrower. There are more cars. All the children are grown-up, the maids are older and they move more slowly as if they're underwater with the weight of an entire ocean on top of them and everything they do is much harder. Beauty's old and her face is furrowed and she walks even slower than the others and mostly she gets left behind.

At the end of the street there's a fence topped with razor wire to keep us safe from the natives or maybe to keep the natives safe from us. These days no one's really quite sure.

My mother should move. Every time Sadie sees her she says how she's got her eye on a nice little flat for her in Yeoville or Orange Grove.

'A maid's room on top,' she says. 'An all-night security guard and a nice garden for you to sit in. Who needs to look at razor wire all day and half-mad natives on the other side of it?'

We don't even bother to tell her to keep her voice down. It's no good trying to keep Sadie quiet and Beauty has heard this story so many times before it isn't worth the effort. There's probably not a single person left in Alex where Beauty lives who doesn't know all about Sadie and Reuben Lazar and exactly how they feel about black people but Sadie can't scare my mother with her stories.

There are other things in life that are far more frightening and until it's all over and the time is right my mother isn't going anywhere.

'Davey likes it here,' she says.

'And one day when he's not here any more?' Sadie says.

'I'll think about that day when it comes,' says my mother.

'You have to face facts,' says Sadie. 'He's a very sick boy.'

'Thank you, Sadie,' my mother says. 'I know that. I don't need you to tell me.'

'You needn't look like that,' Sadie says. 'I'm not saying anything you're not saying yourself. All I'm asking is that you try to be a little bit more practical.'

'All my life I've been in trouble for not being practical enough to suit you. You want I should start now, in my old age?'

'You're the one who mentioned old age,' Sadie says. 'Please God you're spared for many more years but old age will come just like it always does and what are you going to do then?'

'I'm going to get on with my life just the same as I've always done,' my mother says.

*　　　*　　　*

I telephone Min and tell her about Davey and I ask her if she can't make some arrangement so she can come and see him so she can say goodbye.

'I want to be there,' she says. 'I'll do my best. I'll come if I can.'

'If I can' doesn't sound like Min to me. It's not the way she usually is.

'Things are difficult here,' she says. 'You must try and understand.'

'What kind of difficult?' I say. 'How difficult can it be? You get in your motor car, you drive to Durban, you jump on an aeroplane and you come and spend a day or two here with us. They may miss you but believe me the clinic is not going to fall down.'

'It's not so easy,' she says.

It sounds easy to me and then there's what there never used to be between us, which is a long silence, and the long-distance line squeaks and buzzes and crackles and neither of us says anything at all.

'I'll do my best,' she says. 'Just try and understand. I can't talk about it over the telephone.'

'I hope you aren't up to your old tricks again,' I say.

'What tricks?' she says.

'You know what I mean.'

'I'm up to nothing,' she says. 'Except being busy and doing my job. There's too much to tell you. I can't talk over the telephone.'

'What then?' I say. 'Will you let me know by jungle drum?'

'I'll let you know,' she says and then without even saying a proper goodbye she puts the telephone down.

MIN

The Nameless Ones

1980

'You should tell someone,' Father Ignatius says.

It isn't even worth an answer.

Who is there to tell and what is there to say? Things are not good with us. They were once and they aren't any more. Which makes us just about the same as the rest of the country.

'I have you to talk to,' I say.

I tell him almost everything. Even though it's irresponsible, I tell him things it's dangerous for him to know. I don't have this right but I do it anyway.

'You can talk to me any time you like,' he says. 'It's my job to listen but what you need isn't me. For your own safety you need to be sure someone outside knows what's happening here.'

'There's no one,' I say.

What I mean is I don't want to put anyone else in danger. My grandfather is too old. He's earned the right not to be troubled. The Woolfs would worry and wouldn't understand.

Father Ignatius is worried that one day an un-marked truck will come by in the night and when he comes to look for me at the clinic the next morning I'll be gone because that's the way things are these days.

It's happened to other people and it could happen to me. We don't even talk about it any more because there's no point and in any case on this subject we talked ourselves out a long time ago.

I would like to see Davey again. To touch his small hands and talk to him. More than anything I would like to look into his eyes and see again that little bit of goodness and innocence that is his offering to the world.

More than anything, I need that now.

'You should have told your friend the truth when she telephoned,' Father Ignatius says and I can't help smiling. If I'd done that I might just as well have written and signed a full confession.

'I'll write to her,' I say. 'You won't mind posting a letter for me if I ask you, will you?'

I have to ask him this all the time because all my post is opened and read. Sometimes it's resealed and sent on and sometimes it disappears.

This is quite usual. It's not worth the effort of writing any more but sometimes I have to and then I write small things that are not important and hope they'll get through and even sound quite normal to the people outside who know me. Just so they won't worry.

The things that are actually happening here I wouldn't dare write down.

'You'll be watched,' I say. 'But it doesn't matter. If they stop and ask you show them the letter, do it if you have to. Be open about it. Don't put yourself at any risk.'

'I'm not afraid,' he says. 'I'm not answerable to them and nor are you.'

'Thank you,' I say and the letter passes from my hand into his.

'Do you remember when you were a child?' he says. 'You said you'd like to come into church just to have a look but you wanted to be sure to come when God wasn't around to see you?'

I remember. I've forgotten nothing about the funny little girl and her brother who lived here long ago and were happy.

'I told you to make up your own mind about when that time would be,' Father Ignatius says. 'I wonder sometimes if you ever think about that now and if perhaps you're a little bit closer to the answer.'

I know he's trying to be kind but this is something I don't want to talk about and so I change the subject.

'There's nothing in the letter that will offend anyone,' I say. 'I only said how sorry I am not to be there and how much I cared for Davey. That would be all right, don't you think? Even if they opened it. Or do you think I won't even be allowed that?'

The truth is I'm in big trouble and under house arrest. That's what it's called. I'm not allowed to leave the magisterial district where I live and writing letters that have any meaning at all is a thing of the past.

I'm still allowed to do my work but only because doctors are scarce out here and the new young medics drafted to do their national service in the army are reluctant to work with lepers.

So I do it and that's why I'm allowed to keep on doing it. Otherwise all the usual restrictions apply. This is what the officer in charge of the local police post told me.

'You can continue to go to the clinic each day,' he says. 'But you must keep social interaction to a minimum. Only what's necessary to do the job. Do you understand?'

I understand very well. The rules and regulations for the clinic have been explained to us all in careful

227

detail. No patients to be admitted without handing in passbooks first. All gunshot wounds must be reported immediately. Not so much as a tourniquet to stop a person bleeding to death or the tiniest gram of morphine to ease someone out of his agony. Not without a passbook.

There are unannounced police inspections to see the rules are being adhered to. Road barriers have been set up and army trucks roll by one after the other in long convoys and the missing and dead are always with us.

Sometimes it seems to me half the world has taken to walking in search of the other half. The ones who were there one day and then taken away and never seen again.

All deaths to be reported and verified by a government appointee.

I tell the police a hundred times and I tell the army too. We know our own people here. No one is alone or unknown and we can't always wait for a government appointee to get here and when someone dies we have to bury them as quickly as we can because of the heat.

It's not entirely true.

We've become like the rest of the world. We have our own rules which can be changed to suit the occasion. We tell our own lies. We have the nameless ones who are brought in and we treat them the same as everyone else. No passbooks required. No questions asked.

Almost all of them, even when they're dying, won't tell us their names. If they did we could find their families. We tell them this but they don't believe us. They're afraid of the *impimpis*, the informers, who are everywhere, and they trust no one. Around here the price of trust has become exorbitant. One true name can lead to another and in the end an entire cell can be destroyed.

Father Ignatius knows this. The staff of the hospital

228

know it and so do the people who live around here and so do I. Often the nameless ones are brought to us only because they are beyond help and their comrades are desperate and leave it too late and so they die.

We have a special section of ground set aside for them. It was quite small at first but it became very large and was becoming obvious so last spring we planted sunflowers over it and moved on to another place but there are still too many and this spring we will have to do the same.

'You cannot take part in any gathering or public meeting. When not at work you may only have one person other than yourself in your house and that includes servants.'

More than one is considered a public meeting. If the conversation gets heated it can even be called a riotous assembly.

'Are you church-going?' the police post officer wants to know.

'No,' I say.

He seems surprised. He looks up, then he looks down again and makes a small mark on the document lying on the desk in front of him. Whether or not to allow a restricted person to go to church is a big problem. One they haven't managed to resolve yet.

Churches are important now. In some places where the minister is fiery it's difficult to tell the difference between a church service and a public protest.

This idea is Father Ignatius's delight although he says they can ban church services tomorrow for all he cares and it wouldn't worry him at all.

'One person alone with their God and prepared to do His will. That's all it ever takes, Min,' he says. 'That's how little people realize about the power of God.'

I know what he's saying but this is not the way I look at it. I am a scientist and my father's daughter. I'm not a religious person.

'You should think about it,' he says. 'Only think. That's all I ask you.'

I think how long I've known him. All my life if you want to count in days and I look and I listen and think how little it is we know. Not just he and I but how little it is we ever really know about each other.

There's a man. His name is Bill Gordon and he's an army captain but his heart isn't in it.

'When I joined up it wasn't for this kind of thing,' he says and I believe him.

His father, this man he never knew whose residue he is, died in the northern desert and his heart is soft about it. His memories, manufactured by him and nurtured on nothing but a faint nostalgia, have a sepia glow and this is what has betrayed him.

He wanted to be like his father but he's not cut out for soldiering. Not this kind of soldiering. He hates what he does.

'It's the look on their faces,' he says. 'The boot on the door. Shouting out questions, demanding information. Anyone can do that.'

Sometimes he does worse things. I know he does although he won't tell me.

'It's the look on their face I can't bear,' he says.

He keeps on saying it over and over again and his shoulders hunch over and he sits with his hands clasped between his knees and it's all he'll ever say.

What he's seen, what he's done has changed him. It's changed me too. We're all changing. I'm back to the Bible and my days at St Anne's when rejoicing in the truth was all I wanted because it seemed such a good idea to me.

I didn't want to be a liar yet these days I am one. Lies fall from my tongue like honey and I feel no shame at all.

I didn't want to see these nameless dead buried without ceremony, underneath a sunflower field.

When I go past and see those flowers nodding to the sun I avert my eyes. This spring our second field is planted and soon there will be a third and every time I drive past I ask myself how many more there will be before it's all over.

When Bill comes to me it's strange to hear the rumbling of an army vehicle coming down the road my brother and I walked together on our way to school.

It comes defiantly with its headlights blazing when everything else is dark or lit by candles or dying fires or the flickering lemon glow of generator light. It's the wrong time and place. It's the wrong man but all the same my heart quickens.

He comes into my house and we sit together and talk and together we wonder how our world can have gone mad around us and what we can do just to hold ourselves together and keep on doing these things we have to do that neither of us bargained on.

One day, maybe soon, he'll leave. I don't know where life will take him or if he'll live or die or if I will. I can't even begin to imagine how it will be once it's all over and the world is itself again.

Sometimes I think it will never be over but I dare not think that because despair lurks behind that kind of thinking and there's no room for that here. There's still too much to be done and so I have Bill Gordon.

I will not have him always but I have him this moment and he has me and I need him by me now.

FRIEDA

The Things a Mother Knows

1980

It seems wrong that the day that Davey dies is just like any other day.

The cars start up early just like they always do and because it's winter and they've stood out all night you can hear some are not really in the mood for it.

People come out of their front doors bundled in coats and they wipe the condensation off the front windscreens and then they go around to the back and do it all over again.

It's cold and still dark and I'm standing outside in the bow of the stoep. My hands are wrapped around a coffee cup and all of me aches because Davey is dead.

My mother was with him till the end. She wouldn't leave him alone, not even for a minute, and she's still with him, sitting by his bed. Not singing, because the time for songs is past. Not saying anything. Just sitting quietly, holding his hand and waiting for the doctor and the people from the *cherra kadisha* to come and take him away.

The smell of frost is in the air. There's the crack of front gates opening and closing. People who don't have much money are early starters and Coronation Avenue is going to work just like it always does.

My old friend Grief is back and I'm thinking how strange it is that another day is about to begin and the world is waking and Davey isn't in it any more.

Then our gate creaks and Sadie comes and then Rabbi Weisz and Dr Rosenberg and Beauty who puts on the lights and the paraffin heaters and the kettle. Then Sadie goes into Davey's room and comes out and there is only the murmur of men's voices, Rabbi Weisz and Dr Rosenberg talking to my mother, and Sadie makes some phone calls and after a little while the phone starts ringing and it doesn't stop.

MIN

No. 735634 H

1980

They try you with new things. You never know what's coming next and this is the latest. They've brought me all the way from the clinic to the army camp because they need a death certificate signed and when I get there I can't do it.

If there'd been anyone else to do this I'm the last person they would ask but there is no one else. The services of people legally empowered to sign death certificates are too much in demand these days. So they had to come and fetch me.

They come in the night. It's late and bush dark, night dark, and it's the sound of the vehicle coming down our road that wakes me. I know the sound of army transport when I hear it. I'm alert to it, have learnt to listen out for it, become accustomed to it, welcome it even, but not tonight.

It's too late and too dark.

I'm alone except for the guilt and the guilt is always with me. Guilt for the lies I'm telling. My list of deceptions grows daily. From the truly enormous ones to the really very small.

Bill Gordon is married. It doesn't matter but it does. It's a small thing in such an ocean of trouble and we shouldn't even notice it but we do. The day we stop caring about the small things is the day we lose ourselves.

I'm not the only one. There are many of us who sleep lightly and wait for the bang on the door that will be our summons. It will come. It always does. All we have to do is wait until they're ready.

For the ones who come, I think there is some thrill in these late-night, early-hours-of-the-morning visits. They stand there wide awake and immaculate in their uniforms while we're still bleary-eyed and disorientated in our nightclothes, scrabbling around desperately for some suitable lie to tell.

It might make some other person ashamed but it means nothing to them. You can see it in their eyes. All it does is help them feel their own power.

That's the difference between them and us. At least that's what we tell ourselves.

They need have no high expectations of me. I'm not going to astound anyone with my bravery. I've seen enough of bravery to know I'm not brave. If I could I would run away and look for some safe place and that's where I'd stay until it was all over and everything and everyone found themselves again.

I have days when I ask myself what it is that keeps me here and makes me take such terrible risks when I don't have to at all. I have options. I have other places I can go.

The trouble is I know the answer. It's always there right near the front of my mind to remind me of what it might be more prudent to try to forget.

I hate them for what they're doing to this place, to these people, to this country I love. It fills me with white-hot rage and it's rage that keeps me going.

Let them come for me in the night. Let them come for me just whenever they like. Forget about clothes. They can take me stark naked for all I care and do whatever they like to me.

I've done a lot of things I shouldn't have done and I'm not sorry for a single one of them. Given the chance I would do them a hundred times over and then a hundred hundred times over again. As long as I'm allowed the time.

But it's not to be as easy as that. As far as I'm concerned they have something else in mind.

'It's a simple thing.' This is what the officer in command of the main army base tells me.

His name is Evert Brink. It's engraved on a brass plate pinned to his lapel. We're all labelled one way or another these days. On my white surgical coat, thrown on in a hurry over jeans and a sweatshirt, I'm labelled too. They say it makes things easier if we know who we're talking to. I think it's because none of us know who we are any more. We keep having to be reminded.

Brink pushes a document across the desk towards me. A standard printed form with a number in the corner.

'We've had a death in custody,' he says. 'Heart failure. I'm sorry to pull you out of bed for the sake of a signature but that's the way things are these days and there was no one else.'

It's an ordinary-looking form. The kind you see lying around in untidy piles in post offices and government offices. Want to send a money order? Fill in here. Driver's licence lost? Shame. Fill in this form. Sign. Explain. Someone will sort it out for you. That's all.

An everyday kind of form and a man with clean fingernails pushing it towards me. You fill in the details, sign at the bottom. Someone, somewhere, rubber-stamps it and someone else, lying dead somewhere in this building, enters history.

'Am I at least allowed to examine the body?' I say.

The room in which we stand is fully lit, neat and ordered. An ordinary room in which my voice sounds loud.

'Of course,' he says.

Evert Brink.

He stands up behind his desk and I see he's a tall man. Much taller than I am.

'I'll take you. Bring your bag and the form. It won't take long.'

He leans across and picks up the form. He snaps it to a clipboard with a bulldog clip to secure it and hands it over to me so I stand there with my medical bag in one hand and the form clipped to the board in the other.

'Loose bits of paper are always a nuisance,' he says. 'It's easier this way.'

It's three o'clock in the morning. An unforgiving hour. Not yet morning but not fully night. I stand at the edge of darkness and it's not a nice place to be.

The main office is on the upper floor. It has polished wooden floors and good lighting and neat rows of metal filing cabinets.

To get where we have to go we descend cement steps. We go past a guard, awake, alert, with a gun in a leather holster on his belt, but an exchanged look is enough to make a metal door open. No questions asked.

'After you,' he says.

He has to bend down to go through the door. It's an average-size door built to accommodate men of average height and he bends down naturally, gracefully even. Because of his bigness he's accustomed to making these small concessions.

There's a long passage and concrete floors and bare naked light bulbs hanging at intervals from loops of plastic-coated wiring. It's colder than it was upstairs and our footsteps echo.

'It's in here,' he says.

Someone, once a man or woman, now 'it'.

His hand is on the door handle and then he hesitates.

'It's a bit of a waste of time bringing someone in specially for a thing like this,' he says. 'It's routine. That's all. I'm sorry but there you are, but rules are rules.'

'Shall we get on with it then?'

His hand is still on the door and the door stays firmly closed. 'What I'm saying is that we won't be needing an autopsy or anything like that. It won't be necessary.'

'How can we know that?' I say. 'I haven't even seen the body.'

'You know because I'm telling you,' he says.

Slowly, carefully, clearly, so there's no possibility of misunderstanding. His hand is on the door and the concrete chill rising up from the ground is around us.

'Isn't that for me to decide?' I say.

'You don't decide anything,' he says. 'You sign the death certificate. That's all. I want this thing over and done with and I want it over with quickly.'

There's no name written on the death certificate. Only a number. 735634 H. The cause of all the trouble. For him it's over. No haste required in his case. For him there's all eternity.

'Look,' Brink says. 'I don't want to give you a hard time but I don't want you to give me a hard time either.'

I know what he wants. He doesn't have to tell me.

'This isn't Pretoria Central. This is the bloody back of beyond. We haven't got proper facilities here. If we get caught up in red tape the body has to go to the state mortuary. It means detailing a van and a driver. It's a waste of time. The man's dead. It's not going to make any bloody difference to him, is it?'

'Let me see for myself,' I say.

He brings his hand down hard on the door handle and the door swings open but he doesn't move. To get inside the room I have to push past close by him. I can smell him. Man-smell and soap. The top of my head is on a level with his chin.

'Are you up to this?' he says.

'I'm a doctor,' I say. 'Isn't that why I was brought here in the first place?'

I'm ready. My clipboard is in my hand and I look down, detached. Black male. Age: early seventies? Block one and block two of the questionnaire answered. Two simple ticks against the hard wood of the clipboard.

You learn detachment in medical school. It's not part of the regular course. You pick it up along the way. You don't get a course credit for it although it's understood you need it for the job.

You have to work at being detached. That's what the professors tell you. I don't know why they bother. In this country, if we're to survive at all, we learn detachment from the day we're born then we spend the rest of our lives perfecting it.

I know I must try and look at this for what it is. A white woman doctor, alone in a poorly lit room, looking down at the body of a black man, and a white man, truly detached, watching me.

The man has been dead I would think for some four hours or so. An hour for them to make their minds up and three hours there and back to fetch me.

I may just as well be back in Silverman's butcher shop with Frieda Woolf.

Am I up to this? Will I be all right?

The answer is, of course I will, and it's not the medical school at Wits University that taught me this. It's life itself. The life we live nowadays.

No. 735634 H.

There's an ordinary luggage label tied to the

239

metatarsal bone of the largest toe of his left foot. I almost expect to see my mother's handwriting.

'Ladies always travel with properly labelled luggage,' she says. 'You can't trust staff to do a proper job. Not anywhere in the world. Not since the war. You can never be sure when something will go missing and you have to send someone to go and track it down.'

I look again at this once-man laid out neat.

The chill of the room prickles against my bare arms and my white cotton coat which is my only armour is inadequate to keep it out.

I stand level with the dead man's midriff and my eyes scan his body. The feet, the legs, the upper and lower body, the arms and even the neck I can bear to look at but I can't steel myself to look at the face.

I know I will have to but without my willing it my eyes avert themselves and then my mind betrays me also and I think about other things.

Where did they find the table I wonder?

It's a large table, as large as a table has to be to accommodate a big man laid out flat. The wood's good, it's fine wood, beautifully grained and darkened with years of polishing.

I stare at the table because I can't bear to look at the man. I bend down. My hair falls forward and I hold it back with my hand. I look underneath the table. The legs are sturdy and old-fashioned, well-rounded. The kind of legs that delicacy said should be shrouded so the lust of Victorian men shouldn't be too much excited.

'Are you going to take all night?' Evert Brink wants to know. Is his lust excited by what he sees before him?

'I need more light,' I say.

'What for?' he says. 'You can see what you have to see. You can see enough.' At least he's right about that. I can see enough.

'I'm going to need more light,' I say calmly. This is my job. Not his.

'I'll fetch a torch,' he says. 'It's the best I can do. I'll hold it for you and you can do what you have to do.'

I don't need a companion. All I need is a little more light. But I nod my head. 'Go and fetch it then,' I say.

Some people are afraid of the dead. I don't know why. It's the living who frighten me.

There is someone else, I see, who was not afraid. Someone has had the decency to wash this man clean. I can see, without the benefit of a torch, that there must have been blood. There must have been a great deal of blood but it's all washed away now.

Now everything is clean and quiet and we, this once-man and I, are alone and it's only now I lift my eyes to his face and look at him and I see what my heart already knew which is that I know him.

My face freezes and my jaw aches with the effort of keeping it still and the rush of blood up the back of my neck is like a splintering river of ice and there's a terrible rise of bile in my throat.

I'm cold. Cold with a cold I have never felt before. The chill, that small warning chill, that prickled on my skin and through my coat soaks right down deep into my bones and on the way it clenches at my living heart with such violence I think the force of it will wrench it right out of my body.

You can't live without a heart. Yet I'm still here standing in the very same place Evert Brink left me and my shaken heart is still beating inside me sick and slow and my breath is coming in rasps.

I move closer and without my willing it my hand reaches out and lays itself down lightly on the side of this once-loved dead face and I run my fingertips over the features.

Like a blind person in a statue garden I try to remember all it is I know and I think what I feel is some part of me is dying this minute in this terrible place.

I remember my first school and the sun spangling the ground with a pattern of leaves and my knees aching from sitting cross-legged on the ground and the fallen red masasa blossoms all around us like lipstick kisses and our boy-girl voices intoning our children's lessons.

I remember my teacher.

I snatch on to memory as if it is a lifeline. I will myself to remember all I've learnt along the long road that led me to this moment and beg that it will keep me strong.

I take his heavy hand in mine. I run my fingers over its pink palm and look at the tracery of palm lines in which our future is supposed to be secured, safe, as if it was caught in a net, and I wonder if what his future told was true and this, all along, was how it was meant to end?

It's gone the half-hour now. Nearly four o'clock in the morning. I'm weary right down to my bones and I have no answers. Every question breeds another question and none of them is comfortable.

Then Evert Brink is back.

I don't even have to look up. I have been far away in a quiet place, totally deaf to his footsteps, yet I feel him come into the room all the same.

'I've got it,' he says and the torch is in his hands. 'Now, for God's sake, get on with it.'

'What's his name?' I say.

My voice is there and it surprises me. It seems that I, who know all there is to know about silence, can somehow still speak in the face of the unspeakable.

My voice is wiser than I am. It knows it can say anything it likes as long as it never tells what it knows and we, the living, Brink and I, white as snow, stand opposite one another on either side of the table.

He stands with his legs slightly apart, his booted

feet planted firmly on the concrete so the full weight of his body is evenly balanced between them.

'His name?' he says. 'How the bloody hell should I know? Isn't there a number?'

'It says "Name" on the form,' I say.

'Leave it out,' he says. 'The case number will do. These people are such bloody liars they never give you a proper name anyway.'

'As you like,' I say. 'You're the boss.'

Then we begin. 'Start at the top. Shine the torch on his face.'

I bend down to open up my medical bag which is on the floor beside me and Evert Brink doesn't like it. I've bent down and stood up straight and his torch is shining on my face, its light blinding me, but I don't care. I look right into it. If he offers me blindness I will take it. Right this minute blindness would be welcome.

'What are you doing?' he says.

'I'm putting on protective gloves,' I say. 'There are open wounds. It's precautionary.'

'All right,' he says.

The torch is lowered and all that's left is the blind dazzle.

There is no sympathy in this room. If there was it would be for me but I suppose that shouldn't surprise me. Nothing's found in its proper place any more. Why should sympathy be any different?

Evert Brink wouldn't touch a black person living or dead with hands bared or covered. Not unless he really had to. Not when there are so many other ways. The boot. The whip. Electrodes. A sjambok. A rifle-butt.

Bruising. Contusions. A deep indentation at the side of the skull that must have been caused by a terrible blow.

'Why aren't you writing anything down?' he says.

There's not enough paper in the world for me to

write down what I've seen but this isn't what I say. What I say is: 'I need to finish my examination first.'

The light from the torch moves down. It follows my white-gloved hands. I see them moving like ghosts across dark flesh. Flesh with all the lustre of life taken out of it.

'Are you planning to take all bloody night?' Brink wants to know. 'The others don't take this long. They get on with things. They get the job done.'

'I'm not like the others,' I say.

This at least is true. At least, not yet. Please, God. Help me, God. If there is a God. Not yet. Not ever.

'It's all right,' I say. 'I've seen all I have to see. You can switch off the torch now.'

I pull the gloves off and push them into the pocket of my coat. It's not hygienic. Any first-year nursing trainee will tell you that. At our clinic we disinfect and reuse them even though they need to be dumped but here there is nowhere to dump them. They need to be taken away and burnt with the hospital waste.

'You can leave me here alone for a moment, if you don't mind,' I say, which is something he hadn't expected.

'What for?' he says. 'You said you were finished.'

He's mistaken. I said I'd seen all I have to see. Being finished is another matter altogether.

'Just for a moment,' I say. 'You can leave the door open if you like. If you want you can stand outside and watch me.'

I lift my hands and hold them up empty, palms upward, to show I'm not about to do anything untoward. A minute is all I'm asking. How much is a minute in a lifetime?

'OK,' he says.

The gloves are sticking out of the side pocket of my hospital coat and there's a funny smell of death and of violence on them.

I bend down and click my bag closed.

I can't bear to look at the label that sticks out from the large toe of this old man's foot. Even if I could look at it I think my eyes would refuse to see it. There's a limit to what is bearable and what is beyond endurance.

The strange thing is that it's the smallest and least important things that are the most unbearable of all.

He leaves the door open and stands in the doorway. The pallid light from the passage outside filters in and gives the room an eerie illumination. It glows with the dull gleam of phosphorus but I'm not afraid of the eeriness because I've seen a terrible darkness and I fear that more.

I go up to the table and lay my ungloved hand lightly on this man's forehead. On his hair which is thick with grey. He's an old man, just as they said, but he didn't die of heart failure. I lay my hand against his cheek. Africans do not leave the dead alone. It is a great disrespect. I wish someone in this place knew this and knew this man as I do.

No one should be made to wait this last wait alone. There should be someone to mourn. To say the last farewell is the greatest privilege and I have to think that this at least is one good thing to have come out of this terrible time. This privilege has been given to me. It is like a benediction.

'*Hambani Kahle*,' I say.

Goodbye, kind master, old friend, giver of the gift of learning. Go well on your great journey.

FRIEDA

Facing the Facts About Lenny

1980

I have to face facts about Lenny. My husband is a womanizer. He likes women and they like him.

I got over the business with Hazel and after we'd made it up she tried to tell me.

'Lenny Lazar is like a dog peeing against every pole he passes,' she says. 'Excuse my language but that's the way it is.' She says it's nothing getting the business from Lenny because there've been so many women before and so many will come after. 'Believe me, Frieda,' Hazel says. 'If every woman Lenny went with went through the gate at the Rand Easter Show they'd say they had a bumper year.'

The latest is Lorraine Katzeff.

The story about her is how she dances naked for my husband with nothing on her body but a pair of red high-heeled slippers with ostrich-feather fronding on the front.

Perhaps he likes this. I wouldn't know. You have to draw the line somewhere but she's lasted a little bit longer than any of the others. So maybe she's got what it takes. How should I know? All I know is I wouldn't dance for Lenny Lazar clothed in feathers and jewels on the centre stage of His Majesty's Theatre never mind stark naked in some tired hotel room on the wrong side of Benoni.

I'm not the first woman with a husband who doesn't know how to keep his flies zipped up. I don't know what these other women do but I suppose we all do the same. What choices do we have?

You know about it and for as long as it suits you turn a blind eye. Then one day something happens and you're not in the mood to be so blind any more. You take a look at your life and you face facts. You know it's not what it should be and you decide that maybe the time has come for you to do something about it.

For me this is the day. Mrs Lorraine Katzeff, the dancer, decides she can spare five minutes away from my husband. It's the day when I get out of my car at Thrupp's and there she is in big hair and a navy-blue suit making it clear that it's me she's waiting for.

'I think you know about me,' she says. 'I'm sorry to do it this way but I didn't think I should come to the house. I wasn't sure you'd see me but I think it's time we had a little talk.'

One thing you can say about Lorraine. For someone who's only the girlfriend she's got a lot of chutzpah. Or maybe times have changed. I thought when a girlfriend sees a wife coming she's supposed to vanish like mist before the sun but not Lorraine.

Lorraine is standing at the end of a row of cars right close to Thrupp's entrance and she's got something on her mind that she wants to get off it and you couldn't move her not even with a bulldozer but it doesn't matter.

I know what she's here for. She's come all the way from the other side of town to ask me if I feel like giving her my husband although if you listen to her you'd think it was going to be something quite the opposite.

'This is nothing to do with Lenny,' is the first thing she says. 'He doesn't know I'm here. I didn't tell him. He'd kill me if he knew.'

I have nothing against Thrupp's parking lot. As parking lots go it's very clean and tidy and nice and it works very well but I don't think it's the place where I want to hear what it is Lorraine Katzeff has come to say to me.

'Can we at least sit down?' I say. 'There's a nice little tea room inside. I don't think what we have to say to each other we should say out here in the road.'

I don't know what she expects. Maybe she thinks there's going to be a scene. Maybe hysterics. When a girlfriend only knows a wife from what the husband tells her there's one thing you can be sure of: she doesn't know the wife at all.

In a situation like this how is a wife supposed to act?

Not even the wife knows this. Not even me although I suppose while you're still above ground with the wedding ring on your finger it's still all right to be Mrs Lazar and known by your name to the nice young waitress that shows us to a table?

Is it bad taste to think that whatever you're about to hear you aren't so sick to the stomach that you couldn't still think about a nice piece of Thrupp's cake to help the bad news go down? Would a nice slice of chocolate cake be the wrong thing? What about tarts? Tarts in all their flavours are very good at Thrupp's but I suppose on a day like today asking for tart is what Min would say is not really an 'appropriate' kind of thing to do. As far as tarts go I happen to know there's a glut on the market but I only found that out after I married Lenny Lazar.

'Won't you sit down?' I say.

248

She sits down and I sit opposite her and there's a neat square of white tablecloth between us and I look at her and wonder what it is she sees when she looks at me. I can just imagine. Poor plain Frieda Lazar, an ordinary kind of woman in good jewellery and an imported coat.

I order lemon tea. She orders coffee. No cake. No tart. I sit back and I look some more. It costs nothing to look and there's plenty of time for it. She fusses about settling and her perfume slicks out to meet me.

She's not as young as she'd like people to think. Her hands are hands with hard beauty-parlour nails. Her hair's thick and puffed out thicker. There's lots of it and it's flecked with gold. She has Cleopatra eyes and there are brass buttons on her jacket.

'Please listen to what I have to say,' she says.

Do I have an option? Am I going anywhere? What should I do but listen? Do I look to her like a woman who's got something so important to do I will suddenly get up and leave and in any case where can I go with Lorraine between me and the door?

'I'm sorry about the way things haven't worked out between you and Lenny,' she says. 'Truly I am. But you and I are both grown-up women. I think we'd agree that when something's over maybe the time has come to stop hanging on to it. Maybe the time has come to call it a day.'

Hanging on to Lenny? Is that what I'm doing?

'You've probably heard I'm divorced now?' she says.

I heard. The whole of Johannesburg heard. This is what happens when your husband is a man people know who is named co-respondent in a not very nice divorce case and there's still a newspaper published every day.

'I heard,' I say.

What I heard is that the minute Boykie Katzeff found out about his wife and Lenny he made it his business to see she was out on the street with her luggage out next to her. What she came in with, she went out with. Nothing more and nothing less.

The tea's in front of us, set out in small silver pots, and there's a flurry of black dress and white apron that's the waitress and there's a single yellow rosebud in a cut-glass vase.

'It's over,' she says and she makes a small swiping movement with her hand. It's her divorce she's talking about. 'What's past is past. Who needs to dwell on it? What I need now is to get on with my life.'

Am I stopping her? Am I the one standing in her way?

She feels sorry for me. I can see that. She makes sure I see it. The way she does it is not the kind of way you can easily ignore. She has big eyes and she opens them bigger for my benefit. She wants me to know she's not a woman without feelings and what she feels for me is pity.

'Lenny won't speak to you himself,' she says. 'You know how he is.'

I don't know what it is she thinks she's telling me. I know how he is and she'd get a very big surprise if she knew exactly how much 'how he is' it is that I know.

'I know this isn't easy for you,' she says. 'I know you love him. I can understand it. But I think we both know you're not the kind of woman a man like Lenny needs.'

There at least we're in agreement.

'What exactly is it you're asking?' I say.

'That you should let him go,' she says.

Is he shackled I wonder? Is there a leash? Is the leash only long enough to get him as far as a woman like Lorraine Katzeff and no further?

'You want Lenny to have a divorce?' I say. 'That's what you want? That's what you came here to ask me?'

There are tears in her eyes and she's all doe-eyes

and anxiety because the way she sees it her whole future is in the balance and before I can stop myself I think how funny it is. When I think exactly what it is she's doing for me some terrible weight rises up off my shoulders and although she doesn't know it I think I will be in debt to her for the rest of my life.

'If a divorce is what he wants,' I say. 'Why shouldn't he have it?' I snap my handbag closed and I get up.

'Just like that?' she says.

'Just like that,' I say. 'You can have him and *mazel tov*. I hope you have each other for a very long time. Enjoy him with my compliments and in good health.'

She sits at the table and her mouth falls open and just for a change her nervous hands are still.

'You mean it? You're serious?'

'I've never been more serious about anything in my life,' I say.

I do mean it. I walk out of Thrupp's tea room feeling like a queen and I don't even turn back. I don't have to. I'll remember the look on Lorraine Katzeff's face for the rest of my life, till the day I die, and I haven't finished yet. I've only just begun.

MIN

A Little Piece of Paper

1980

'This is the biggest lot of rubbish I ever heard in my life,' Brink says.

He's not alone now. There are two others in the room and they're not tired like we are. They're fresh from a good night's sleep.

We're sitting in the same office with the clean polished floors and metal filing cabinets, some with keys dangling out of their locks and some not. We've been brought a big pot of fresh coffee and thick white cups to drink it out of. It comes on a tray. Everything is scrupulously clean and there's plenty of milk and sugar.

The man who brings it is a 'trustee'. A thin black reed of a man with a skeletal face and sunken eyes who walks carefully. He's wearing a white tunic, clean and crisp and freshly ironed straight from the prison laundry with no hint of the day in it yet. There are shorts to go with it. His feet are bare and his head is shorn.

252

'Leave it,' Brink says and the tray is put down.

Then Brink turns to me. He's tired. I can see he is. But so am I.

'What do you mean you bloody well won't sign?' he says.

The coffee's hot and good and heavy with milk.

'I mean what I say,' I say. 'Without a proper autopsy it's hard to say exactly what this man died of but it wasn't heart failure.'

'Tell me,' one of the others says. 'When you were down below a little while ago doing what you're supposed to do, what did you find?'

He's the joker in the pack. You can see it on the faces of the others. They're holding coffee saucers in their hands, cups raised to their lips, waiting for the punchline so they can laugh before they drink.

'Did you find a man with a heart beating away like a piston?' the joker says.

'No,' I say. 'I didn't. I found a man who'd been beaten and kicked and very probably manacled. There were cuts and contusions on his wrists that certainly gave that impression.'

'Contusions?'

'Markings. Bruises,' I say. 'They're called contusions.'

I'm tired. I lap up these people's coffee as if I were a grateful dog. What I would much rather do is throw it steaming into this man's face.

I can't trust myself. I put the cup down neatly, as though getting it into the round in the centre of the saucer where it belongs is the most important thing in the world.

'There were other things too. Congruent with electric shock being administered by some or other instrument.'

'Is that so?' the joker says. 'Perhaps a light switch shorted or he had a little dance with the electric fence. It happens sometimes.'

'I wouldn't know. Perhaps an autopsy could establish that.'

Apparently my jokes aren't as funny as his because no one laughs.

'You listen to me,' he says. 'You think it's a picnic keeping these people in check? You think it's a bloody picnic? You've got to watch them. They're the biggest bunch of liars the world has ever seen and they take any chance they can.'

I don't think it's a picnic.

'We use a *beesprodder* sometimes. You know a *beesprodder*?'

I know a *beesprodder*. A *beesprodder* gives a small electric shock to a cow reluctant to go into a cattle dip or be loaded on to a truck destined for the abattoir.

'We're not running a convent here,' the joker says. 'The people who get sent here aren't angels. Most of them are hardened criminals.'

That's what they always say.

'What did he do?' I ask just by the way.

'Who?'

'The one downstairs. The one with the number.'

'None of your bloody business,' the joker says.

'Nothing you'd like to hear about or need to know,' Brink says. 'He was an activist. A cell leader.'

'You don't even know his name. How can you know he did these things?'

'What the hell difference does it make? No, we don't know his name. They don't give us their bloody names. Sometimes they'll give us practically everything else they have to give but not their names.'

Names get put on record. Names lead to other names. Names given or ungiven open up a trail that leads to places like this and the unmourned dead lying in the phosphorous glow alone while we, who have power in life and it seems in death, decide what ought to be done with them.

'Look,' Brink says. 'It's been a long night. Just sign.

We needn't make a big thing out of it. We're tired. Just sign and get it over with. Then we'll take you back and we can all just forget about it. It's over and it never happened.'

'I can't sign,' I say. I can't. I know how it works but I can't sign.

'What the hell's "can't sign" supposed to mean?' the joker says.

It isn't me he's talking to but it's me who answers.

'It means this man was tortured and beaten. There are probably internal injuries. There's certainly been a very hard blow to his head which probably caused cerebral haematoma. Any one of these things could have been the cause of death.'

'Wait a minute . . .' someone says.

I can't wait. The things I have to say have all got to be said and there's no time to wait while I say them.

'You need a proper post-mortem to establish cause of death. You'll need to go to Stanger for that. Or maybe there's somewhere closer. I don't know.'

I don't know because the police and the army have many kinds of facilities civilians don't know about and are not meant to know about.

'You haven't been listening to a thing I told you,' Brink says and he sounds regretful.

'I know what you told me,' I say. 'What I'm telling you is you need a proper post-mortem. Then you'll have to find the person culpable and he will have to take responsibility for what he's done and he will have to be punished.'

What I want to say is: 'Find this bloody murderer and see he gets what's coming to him.' But I can't do that.

There's always a strange smell in a room full of white men. I've noticed it before. It's a smell of salt and man and you never find it quite so concentrated as you do among men like this. It's a peculiar smell. Perhaps it's the smell of power and more prevalent now than it used to be. I suppose like everything else it comes and it goes.

I reach down for my medical bag. I've said what I have to say and am no help at all here now. My plastic gloves are still in my pocket. They smell of death but no one in that room except me seems offended by it.

'I'd like to go now if I may,' I say.

They look at each other and then they look at me and the soft light of morning is coming in at the window. It's gentle but getting stronger. It's going to be another hot day.

'You better take this back,' I say.

I put the clipboard and the form clipped to it down on the desk. In a world of paper such things are important but nobody looks at it. It's the object of least interest in the room. What interests them is me.

FRIEDA

Mr Right is Dead

1980

'I've had a hard day and I'm not in the mood for complaints so don't start now. Whatever you've got to say save it for later.'

That's what Lenny says. He's saying it from the minute he comes through the front door.

'You pick your time, don't you?' he says. 'You wait till I've had a day like I had today, then suddenly you want to talk. Well, whatever it is you have to say, it can wait.'

'Suit yourself,' I say.

His car keys are slammed down on the hall table. He's shouting into the yard to Evalina to ask where the evening newspaper is and he's got the look of a man in a hurry.

'You know why I don't want to talk right now?' he says. 'Because from you it's always complaints.'

'I said it was fine. If you haven't got time to listen I'm not complaining. It's all the same to me.'

'When I get home I want peace and quiet and a

257

little respect. I think you owe me that much.'

This is not a new song.

'And by the way I'm eating out tonight,' he says. 'I don't know what time I'll be home.'

This is not a new song either. I can mouth the words without having to hear them out loud. He's on his way out to see a business associate. There's a deal that's being finalized. There's some new business that might be coming his way.

'You think all business is conducted nine to five inside an office?'

He always asks me this.

'No,' I say. 'I don't.'

That's what I always say but I may just as well keep quiet. He never listens to a word.

'That's where you're making a big mistake,' he says. 'But what's the good of talking to you? You live here like a queen. You never worry about where the money comes from and what would you know anyway?'

'Not very much,' I say.

Everyone's gain is someone else's loss. That's true about Lenny the same as it is about anyone else and I'm not talking about Lorraine and I'm not even thinking about me. What I'm thinking is that the stage lost something really wonderful when Lenny decided to become a businessman because you can always rely on him for a good performance. No one in this life is as hard done by as Lenny is when he puts his mind to it.

'I haven't got time for nonsense,' he says.

'You haven't got time, you haven't got time,' I say. 'It's fine with me.'

He goes upstairs to change his clothes and I sit at my accounts desk in the corner of the kitchen and wait for him to come back.

The shopping list for the next month is made up. All the accounts are paid up to date. The fridge, the store cupboard and the liquor cabinet are stocked and

I haven't wasted my afternoon. The dry cleaning's back from the laundry. The wages for the maid and the gardener are drawn and ready to be paid.

It's getting dark outside and Evalina is going around the house drawing the curtains and putting the lights on just like she does every day at this time. I sign the last cheque and look at the grocery list one last time and then I put the cap back on my pen and the pen back in its place and I wait.

When Lenny comes downstairs he's still in the same clothes and he's changed his mind. He's seen the suitcases on the upstairs landing and the empty cupboards in the bedroom.

Now, all of a sudden, I'm not hysterical any more and he's ready to talk and if his associate has to wait five minutes or so it's not the end of the world.

'So?' he says. 'I'm listening. What's this all about anyway? If you've got something to say, why don't you say it?'

So I do. I tell him everything there is to tell and he listens and doesn't even try to chip in. He looks away. He brushes non-existent dust off his coat-sleeve. He pushes at his hair. He looks at his fingernails as if he's never seen them before and I look at him and never take my eyes off him. Not once.

'What can I say?' he says. 'If you believe her, you must be off your head.'

'I don't think so.'

'You don't think so?' he says. 'I'm telling you it's so. You're absolutely, totally *meshugge*. Some mad bitch fills your head with a lot of crap and now you want to walk out on me. Is this what I'm hearing?'

'I don't think she's a mad bitch,' I say. 'I think she's perfectly fine in the head and she loves you, Lenny. *Mazel tov*. You should be a happy man.'

'What a load of shit,' he says.

'To you, maybe. Not to her.'

He's walking up and down. All I see are smart

Italian shoes on smart Italian floor tiles and I think about what my mother said: 'You dress up a broom and it also looks good.'

His hand with the big ring on the finger is in a fist and he's slamming the fist into the open palm of his other hand. I've seen this before too. It's supposed to show he means business. I'm supposed to take notice of it and be careful what I say. Perhaps once I would have, but not any more.

'Between us, Lenny,' I say, 'knowing what I know, I think you could do worse than Lorraine.'

'What shit is this?' he says.

'No shit,' I say. 'I hear she's a great dancer.'

I suppose I shouldn't mention it but this is a once-in-a-lifetime opportunity. It may not come my way again.

Evalina is coming downstairs carrying my suitcase and Lenny's stamping up and down and I'm half looking at him and half sorting through house keys and separating them out and hanging them up labelled on the hooks behind the kitchen door.

'I know what women are like,' Lenny says. 'You want me to take notice of you? I'll take notice of you.'

'The only thing I want you to take notice of is the list I've left for Evalina and Jackson.'

Everything's set out on the desk. Keys and shopping reminders, staff instructions and even a list of emergency telephone numbers. I can see on his face if Lenny didn't think I meant business before, he does now.

'Joke's over, Frieda,' he says and he's right.

The joke is over although not in the way he means and he looks at me and I look him right in the eye and I keep on looking and he looks away first.

'Where the hell do you think you're going anyway?' he says. 'Where am I supposed to find you?'

'Will you be wanting to find me?' I say. I don't think so.

'I know what this is about,' he says. 'Where am I supposed to send the flowers and the letters begging you to come home? Where am I supposed to send all that shit?'

'I don't think you'll be able to send it anywhere,' I say. 'And frankly if I was you I wouldn't waste my time or my money.'

'What's that supposed to mean?'

'It may take a few months but it means I'll be tying things up. My lawyer will be talking to your lawyer. In the mean time I'll be looking for a place of my own.'

We stand there my husband and me in the show kitchen he renovated for my wedding present and I look at him and what I see is a total stranger.

MIN

The Right Way

1980

'Come here,' Brink says. 'There's something I want to show you.'

We're still there, all four of us together. I want to leave. I've asked to go but they won't let me.

Brink puts his arm heavy around my shoulders and draws me close to him in a casual, confidential way as if we're comrades and somehow bound together.

'Look here,' he says.

There's only one window in the room but it's large and if you look beyond the yard and the encompassing fence it has a pleasant panoramic view. We stand together in front of it. Outside the sky is tinted with the beautiful hues of a mid-summer morning. It's almost Christmas, a day very close to my brother's birthday.

'Do you see those men?' he says.

Beyond the compound itself, beyond the steel fence with the spiked wire rolled out on top of it, is a field and there are men at work in it. I see them stooping and bending, dark figures against the early light. Stooping and bending and shovelling and throwing the fresh-dug earth over their shoulders behind them into a pile that's already quite high.

It shows how early they must have started their digging. They must have begun almost before the sun was up.

'Do you see what I see?' Brink says.

His voice is soft and easy. His arm, still around me, is not confining me in any way and I should move away but I can't. It's strange. We are four but there might only be the two of us alone in the room.

'Those men are digging a grave for the man downstairs and whether you do as we ask you or whether you don't, in about half an hour's time that man is going to be in that grave and that's going to be the end of the story.'

'That's your affair,' I say. 'Not mine.'

'Whoever he is, he's dead,' Brink says. 'He's not coming back. Put your signature to the form and that's the end of it. It's not much to ask, is it?'

'It's very much indeed to ask,' I say and it is. 'Why did you ask me? Why do you want it anyway? He's dead. He's not coming back. You said so yourself. You could just have buried him and been done with it.'

It's happened before. It happens all the time, all over the country. We all know it.

'Because some fool in Pretoria wanted it,' the joker says. 'Bloody fools. Don't know what's going on half the time and then they wake up and want everything on paper and stamped and nice and legal and above board.'

'I see,' I say.

I do see. What it means is this is an important man and people are asking about him. Where is he? Why has he disappeared? What happened to him? Is he alive or is he dead?

You never know where the questions will come

from. Sometimes they come from Amnesty International or the International Red Cross. Sometimes there's a strong enough local lobby, one that doesn't know when it should leave something alone and refuses to be silenced.

'Change your mind,' Brink says. 'We aren't going to change ours.'

'No,' I say. 'No, thank you.'

'It isn't as if you're so lily-white yourself,' he says.

'I don't know what you mean.'

'I think you do,' he says. 'Sign that piece of paper. Walk out of here. Forget you were ever here in the first place and I can turn a blind eye to what we both know goes on in your village.'

'I'm sorry,' I say. 'I can't do it.'

'I'm sorry too,' he says and by the way he says it I know that in a funny way he means it and I know something else too. From now on things will go badly for us.

I will have to write to the Medical Council. I know that. I also know I can write as much as I like to whoever I like. No letter from me will ever reach them.

All the same they've allowed me to leave. I can hardly believe it but they've let me go. They're sending me home with a driver to take me.

The roads are bad. The tyres can find no proper purchase. We're going faster than is safe and the vehicle sways giddily from side to side. The driver is young. A national serviceman drafted into duty. I think he's some small-town boy who would rather be anywhere in the world than here but thankful all the same for an easy assignment.

I'm in the back. I can see his eyes in the rear-view mirror. He isn't looking at me. He's keeping his eyes on the road just as he's been taught, probably by some small-town, small-time father when he was teaching him how to drive and not so very long ago either.

He has no idea what he's taking me away from or the kind of thing I can expect now. It's not his job to know. Evert Brink and men like him are his masters. All this boy does is what he's told.

'They could at least have given us a vehicle with an air conditioner. Don't you think so?' he says.

'You're in the army now,' I say.

'The big brass all have air conditioners,' he says.

It's not an accusation, just a fact. He glances at me in the mirror and smiles. Normal. I have to make certain everything is as normal as possible.

I must write to the Medical Council. I have to do it. It's not a question of choice. It's my responsibility. But the Medical Council don't know about us out here. We're too far away. We can stretch out our hand as far as we like but it's still too far for them to grasp it and offer us help.

I could telephone but by the time I get back there will be some inexplicable repair that needs doing on our line and men in overalls will be there doing it. Or they will already have been and gone. Always obliging. Always with an explanation, plausible and incomprehensible all at the same time. Always apologetic.

Sorry, folks, life in the bush is like this. We're not talking Jo'burg here, you know. This is the back end of beyond. The arse end of the country. That's what they sometimes call it.

Sometimes we're without telephones for days at a time. We complain at the army post and at the police station and the answer is always the same.

'Damn nuisance,' they say. 'Never mind. Perhaps they'll get it sorted out eventually and just for a change they'll get it right.'

They're always very nice about it. Regretful, sympathetic, obliging. We don't know how much they know or how much of what we try to do is still safe. They know we don't know and it increases their power over us.

Bill Gordon is gone. He's been transferred. He doesn't know where to. They don't tell them, not even the officers know, and he doesn't want to go.

'Destination unknown,' he says.

'You'll know when you get there,' I say.

It could be life itself we're talking about. These days it's true of all of us.

'I hope it isn't the townships.'

They all dread this. It isn't easy to stand on top of an armoured vehicle and shoot down children with nothing more deadly than stones in their hands but we don't talk about it because he can't look me in the face and tell me that if this happens, when the order comes, he won't do as he's told.

He doesn't want to say it and I don't want to hear it and it leaves each of us alone in our private anguish, unable to comfort each other, unable to offer any help.

I suppose he's like me. People like us make deals with ourselves all the time. What will we do in a certain kind of situation? At what point will we draw back? How far can we be stretched before we break? These are the things we keep on asking ourselves.

We do it because all we have is ourselves. We have no one else to turn to and there is no one else who has any answer to give us anyway.

However it turns out he won't be the same when this is over and nor will I but all the same I don't like to say goodbye to him because farewells make what we were so commonplace.

I dash tears from my eyes. I don't want to. They're there uninvited and there's so much else that's so much more important that I should be crying about.

He's a man to whom words don't come easily so he

hides in banalities and doesn't say anything at all but it makes no difference. I know what he feels.

I will miss the smoothness of his body in the night. It's like my home. It's the lie of the land I know and I trust it. These days we may love as we wish and our desire may be urgent but the knowledge that we will not be allowed to keep what we have is always with us.

It isn't something written down somewhere. It's just the way it is.

'Do you know this road?' I ask the driver. 'There used to be a motor rally over it, something like the Roof of Africa, but then they stopped it.'

'I'm not surprised,' he says.

'It's called God Helps Me Pass. Did you know that?'

'I come from Port Elizabeth area,' he says. 'I don't know this part of the world at all.'

The road sign, shots pot-holed into it, fell down. Eventually it was dragged away bit by bit. I don't know what happened to it exactly but nothing here is ever wasted. Part of it will be someone's roof. Some other part may serve for a corner post of a kraal. I don't know. All I know is I shall never see it again.

'Just around the corner, there's a slight shelf on the side of the road. Do you think we could stop there for a minute? It's the best place.'

'I don't think so,' he says.

He looks at me in the rear-view mirror. His eyes are the expectant eyes of a child. They still have a kind of innocence in them. All these boys are like that and this is what hurts me. I wonder where they find them and what will be left by the time they're finished with them.

'They said to take you straight back,' he says. 'No stops anywhere. Those are my orders.'

'I'm afraid your orders aren't going to be very much

267

use to you,' I say. 'I'm sorry but you're going to have to stop. I need to pee.'

He's very young. His face reddens slightly as if I've spoken a profanity but at least he slows down and stops at the place I told him, the highest place from which you can see the full lie of the land. All of the flatlands painted on the horizon with a delicate brush and the place where the river runs, where there are palms dense to the water's edge and papyrus.

It's beautiful here. The wind sings in the grass and the rocks are dusted in a golden glory of sun and the only movement is a monitor lizard sliding rock to rock out of indolence into further indolence.

Sometimes there are peach moths and I've seen the Masked Weaver here and the Red Bishop and heard his *chizz-chizz* call but not today. Today all I see is the flatland rolling away from me towards the hills. This is and always will be the most beautiful place in the world to me and I drink it all in because I don't think I shall be here again soon.

I will not write to the Medical Council. For the one thing I have to tell them there are too many other things I would need to conceal. Evert Brink knows this.

Before they come for me I will pass on what I know in the usual way. Mouth to ear. Whispering from person to person, house to house, to each one who needs to know and each one who knows will be made more unsafe because of knowing.

Even so I will tell them that my old teacher George Morefe is dead. I have seen it with my own eyes. I have seen him lying dead on a fine old table in one of the terrible cellar rooms under the main building at the army base camp.

I can tell that I've gone to where they are and seen what they do and I've come back and even as I say it I will also have to tell that when the time comes, I'm going to pay for what I know and what happened this last night. We all are.

268

FRIEDA

Getting Unmarried:
The Beginner's Guide

1981

The story in our family is that I have gone off my head.

Reuben is backwards and forwards talking to Lenny and pleading with me. In between he's asking God what it is that he's done to deserve this? Why on the one hand give so generously and then decide to take almost all of it back? Reuben is taking it personally. It's something he simply doesn't understand.

He's raising his voice to Lenny and Sadie is telling him please darling to remember his heart is not what it should be and it isn't helping anyone that he should get so excited.

He's asking Lenny if he thinks this is the right way for a man to carry on in this life. Then he's telling both of us that our good name is already in the mud because of Lenny's goings-on and the Katzeffs' break-up and a divorce is the last thing we need in our family.

'If you build up something and put it together for your family to enjoy, inside the family is where it belongs and that's where it should stay.'

We don't need a *nafke* like Lorraine Katzeff trying to work her way into something that looks to her like a very nice arrangement.

'Do you think it's your brains or your looks she's after?' Reuben says. 'This is not what she cares about. It's your chequebook she sees.'

He says Lenny should already have given Lorraine her walking ticket and been on his knees to me trying to talk some sense into my head. A marriage is not a thing you throw out of the window just because something with a 38C brassière at one end and a nice little *tochis* to go with it feels like giving away a few free samples in your direction.

When my turn comes he talks quietly and nicely. He even pleads a little bit.

'You're a girl with brains,' he says. 'You know what side your bread's buttered on. Lenny's got his little faults. Who hasn't? What I'm saying is turn a blind eye and we can all be happy. Is that such a big thing to ask? Will it kill you to do this?'

The words are coming very smooth out of Reuben's mouth and I'm listening to every one of them and everything's just as fine as it could be except for one thing. I'm not buying.

Lately I've had a few thoughts of my own about the Lazar family, Reuben included, and never mind the presumption, I'm thinking that maybe on this matter God and I are of the same opinion. Reuben's not so well these days but apart from that He's given Reuben plenty in his life. He doesn't deserve to have me with my eyes turned blind and my mouth shut thrown in extra like a little cash discount.

Sadie's crying. She's been crying since the minute

she heard I'd had enough of Lenny and as far as I was concerned Lorraine had danced her last dance.

She's been crying in my mother's house and at the mansion in Houghton which was the wedding-present house she chose herself where once upon a time I lived with Lenny in the days when I still thought he was a prince.

Right this minute she and my mother and I are together and she's crying in the front room of the cottage I found for myself to live in by myself in Sandton. All you can see is what you always see when Sadie cries, which is her lace hankie flying around in the diamond light from her fingers, and all you smell is the Ashes of Violets she scents it with.

My mother's not crying. What my mother is is a completely different story. She doesn't say, 'I told you so.' She did tell me so and I wouldn't hold it against her if she reminded me she did. She doesn't say I've made my bed and now I must lie on it. I think she knows without my having to tell her that my particular bed is getting a bit crowded and I draw the line when it comes to Lorraine Katzeff.

'You're a grown-up woman,' she says. 'You'll make up your own mind.'

Husbands come and husbands go. Death, divorce, what difference does it make? One way is only another way on a road that's going in the same direction. For a woman like me it means only one thing. I'm going to be a woman alone again right back where I used to be. Which when you come to think is not the end of the world. There are worse things that can happen.

We're sitting there the three of us and my mother hasn't said very much. Then suddenly her whole attitude changes. She sits straight up and you can see she's been thinking about a few things and decided the time has come for her to get them off her chest and say what she thinks out loud.

'You'll be better off without him,' she says. Those are her words. From her mouth to my ears and in front of Sadie who's stepgrandson Lenny is. My mother, for once in her life without any arguments or any free advice, is saying she thinks I've done the right thing. Which, to me, is like a gift.

MIN

The Day of the Locusts

1981

They make us wait but they come as we know they must.

You think when the time comes you'll be ready. You do all you can to make things safe but they choose the time and you're never ready and you can never be safe.

They come at harvest time in the late afternoon just when people are packing up for the day and coming in from the fields. In helicopters and it's the sound you hear first.

It's the sound that makes people stop what they're doing and draws them out because it sounds like locusts. Like many thousands of locusts come to lay waste to the land. The sound alone is enough to make you afraid.

People run out of their homes. Mothers scoop up the smallest of their children. They clutch the larger ones by the hand or whatever they can get hold of and pull them not into the houses but away from them.

Inside the houses is the first place they come to look for you.

They pull them out towards the small newly harvested fields as if they'll be safe among the corn stubble and the cabbages. Chickens cluck everywhere, high-stepping on anxious claws, and dogs lope away, tail between the legs, the way dogs do. Animals already penned up chafe up against each other. Head to head, one head pushing the other up, their eyes rolling in terror.

I didn't know they had so many helicopters or that they'd commit them all to one 'clean-up operation'. Usually they use them sparingly. If they asked me I could have told them we aren't worth so many but as I'm the cause of all the trouble I'm the last person they would ask.

Dust rises up. Animals push and the wire around wood-poled kraals strains and goes taut. In some places it buckles but it doesn't yield.

'Keep the patients in their beds and tell everyone to be as calm as they can,' I tell the sister on duty. 'They're doing this to frighten us. Don't be afraid.'

This is a warning to us all but it's me they've come for.

There's a terrible sound now. The helicopters are looking for flat ground to land. Their rotor blades are spinning like creatures possessed and beneath the underbellies in which the men are carried dust is boiling up enveloping everything.

There are people running everywhere. Grown-ups pulling at children and helping old people along. People screaming at one another or at nothing at all and I'm walking among them telling them not to be afraid and when I look again Father Ignatius is walking next to me.

'Jesus, Mary and Joseph,' he says.

His cassock is dust-stained almost to the waist. He's moving fast and the heavy black cloth is getting in the way. Under his cassock his feet in old leather sandals are bare. I never noticed this but I notice it now.

'God help us,' he says.

I doubt whether this is His intention. I don't think He's going to help us not even now when we need all the help we can get but I don't say so. I just keep on walking.

Once there was peace here, now the air vibrates with panic and fear is all around me.

When the women here are afraid they make a strange involuntary sound. It's something like an ululation but far shriller. White people don't like it because it goes to the spine and lingers there and refuses to go away.

'Don't be afraid,' I call out as I go. 'They're doing this to frighten you. Don't be afraid.'

'Dear Christ,' says Father Ignatius.

The underbellies are opening and men in combat uniforms are coming and their boots hit the ground with a thud and they come falling out holding rifles to their chests and running.

'You have nothing to do with this,' I say to Father Ignatius. 'They're only doing this to teach us a lesson and show they mean business. I think they'll make their show but then they'll go away and leave you alone. Keep these people as calm as you can. Explain what you can to them. It's me they want.'

It's Evert Brink. It's between him and me. It's me he's come for. If it hadn't been this day it would have been some other. This is his job and he will see it's done. I know that and I've always known it. All this time I've been waiting for him. Waiting far more ardently than I ever did for Bill Gordon.

I don't think I'm a woman very good at love yet given the chance I think I might have been good enough at loving Bill but Bill is gone and in his place is Evert Brink.

He steps out of the helicopter dust cloud clean. He

bends down the way people do to avoid the down-draught of the helicopter's rotor blades and when he's clear he stands up broad-shouldered to his full height and he's clean.

In this matter it is me and it is him. One pole and the other. That is all there is.

'Dr Campbell,' he says. 'I hope we haven't alarmed you. I thought it was time I gave some of my boys a little exercise. We like to keep them on their toes.'

He has the calm measured voice of an educated person. His tone is unruffled and I sense in it an undertone which might be real regret and the hot unnatural stirring of the air whips at my hair and lashes it across my face.

The sky is a strange colour. Still light but getting darker. Purple tinged with yellow. Crocodile time. The time before it's quite dark when the yellow's still in the sun. Before it deepens into purple and night begins to fall. This is the moment the crocodile likes to strike.

It's what my father used to say to us. 'You better get home before crocodile time, especially if you come by the river path.'

There are still crocodiles in these parts although you hardly ever hear of them these days. They're strange creatures. Hoarders. They wait their time and strike when it suits them. Then they carry their prey still living down to the dark places of the river that only they know and that's where they keep them, living, dying, dead, to snack on at their leisure.

I don't look at Brink. I look at the others and my eyes fill with tears because these are not men. They're still boys.

'If you don't mind,' he says. 'We'll set up some lights and get ourselves organized. We have some digging to do.'

He knows. He knows what we've been doing and we

know he knows. Father Ignatius touches the crucifix at his waist.

'They're not keen on night exercises,' Brink says. 'But they have to learn the same as we all do. You can't always have things just the way you want them.'

They will go straight to the sunflower patches but it's only the dead they will find. The wounded have been moved to other, safer places and the living are long gone. It's the dead under their canopy of sunflowers he's come for. They have their own story to tell and their story even mute is enough to get me into very deep trouble.

It will be enough for him. It will enable him to secure me and this is how it will go.

The rotting dead, hastily wrapped in plastic and buried, will be dug up. The young boys who do it won't like it. Some of them will be sickened. Some will vomit. With others it won't be so obvious but something inside them will break and never be mended again.

He'll tell them later they're not supposed to like it. They're soldiers. They have lessons still to learn. This is only one of them and not a very big one at that. It's all part of being a soldier. That's what he'll say.

When my turn comes he'll ask me, very politely, if he can look at the hospital records. He'll sit in my small office and go through them with great thoroughness and his hands and his fingernails will be clean. Then he'll ask me if signing death certificates and doing things through proper channels is something I generally have trouble with.

Every act against the state has a number. I don't know how many I have transgressed.

Treating people without demanding they show their passbooks.

Not reporting gunshot wounds or other suspicious injuries.

Assisting and playing a part in the activities of banned organizations.

Giving sustenance to terrorists.

He will have a copy of my student file. People go missing but such things don't get lost. He'll have a copy and keep it in one of those metal cabinets that line the walls of his office. Small stuff if you look back from where I am now but even so it will count against me.

We both know this needn't have happened. I'm not that important. Not really. Just as long as he knew, he could have left me for a little while longer. It might even have been useful to him.

No one's safe. People talk. People always do. We all have it in us to be an impimpi. Brink is a clever man and sometimes the clever way is not to stop something but to let it continue. This is not what this is about.

I think there's been some trouble about George Morefe's death and its ripple has reached out and touched him. If it was his choice I think he would have left me alone. I don't know why I think this but I do.

'You should have signed. It would have been the easiest way,' he says.

He says it even now and he stands in front of me and I hear the sound of spade on earth but his body shields me from what is happening behind and he has light clear eyes and he holds my face in them.

I couldn't have signed. He knows I couldn't and he knows why. He understands everything. He knows it absolutely. This is his tragedy and it draws us together because despite my revulsion at all the things he is in some strange way I am drawn to him and as for him, if he knew how to protect me I think he would but he only knows one way.

FRIEDA

The Journey

1981

I'm a fool. On all the long road to Min I'm thinking what a fool I am.

'You don't go anywhere without an invitation.' That's my mother's golden rule but if I wait for an invitation to visit Min I'll wait for ever.

There's a joke they tell in Johannesburg about a Jewish girl who got carried away by King Kong. I heard it at the hairdresser. King Kong carries her off and terrible things happen between them. You can imagine. You don't need me to paint you a picture but eventually she's rescued.

She comes back to her nice house in Houghton. Everyone hears the terrible stories about what's happened to her because this girl is quite happy to tell these stories herself. She'll tell people who never even asked to hear them. That's the kind of girl she is. Her shrink tells her to talk it out. So that's what she does but she doesn't tell everything. The most important thing she leaves out.

She takes Valium. She has plenty of girlfriends who can't get enough of her story. She tells it twenty-five different versions and they're always willing to listen but nothing seems to help. She's losing weight. She can't sleep. People are getting worried about her. The word is going around and we all know she had a bad time with this gorilla but enough is enough already.

'A person puts the past behind them and gets on with their life.'

This is what my mother says to me. I suppose the gorilla-girl's mother says the same kind of thing to her. Anyway. One day when her best friend takes her to Balducci's, over *caffe latte* and a nice slice of Black Forest cake to share which the gorilla-girl isn't even touching she tells her friend what the trouble is. The real trouble.

'You want to know the real trouble?' she says. 'The real trouble is that three weeks we were together he and I. We went through things. You know what I mean?'

Her friend knows. By this time the whole world knows.

'The trouble is that after all that what do I get? I'll tell you what I get and the answer is nothing. He doesn't phone. He doesn't write.'

This is a man joke. About men and how awful they are. The kind of joke women tell one another over coffee in Sandton. It's a stupid joke but on all the long road to Min's clinic I'm thinking about it although not in connection with King Kong. Min is a real-life person and she doesn't phone and she doesn't write either. Some people would say I could count the letter she sent me when Davey died. But how can I? It didn't sound like Min at all.

'She's busy,' my mother says. 'What did you expect? She can't drop everything she's doing just like that just so she can be here for a funeral.'

280

This is exactly what I expected. You don't drop everything just for nothing but for a death you do. Death is just about the most important thing there is. Min, crying her eyes out with her face to the wall, knows this.

I, on the closed toilet seat with my father's shaving mirror in my hand and the handkerchief Sadie put over it lying on the floor, know this too but when Davey dies what do I get? I get this stupid letter and then nothing at all.

I saved the elephant bangle. Davey loved it and her brother loved it and I thought maybe she'd like to have it back for a keepsake. I wrote to her and asked her. I asked her when she was coming to Jo'burg for a visit. I said she's so scarce these days, if she does decide to come I'd be willing to roll out the red carpet. I said I'd like to see her. That I was having a few troubles. But not too much about that.

She's never around at the hospital either. Out, busy, away. I know because I tried to telephone even though it's terrible trying to get through. The wires buzz. The sound comes and goes and when eventually you get a human voice it doesn't even speak English and click-clack is no use to me. My maid Evalina is still with me and I put her on the phone.

'Just tell them I want to speak to Miss Min,' I say. 'Say it's urgent.'

'Yes, madam,' says Evalina and she clicks and clacks away and no matter how many times I try the story is always the same. Out, busy, away.

'Say she must phone back straight away. It's very, very urgent. I'm talking life and death here. Tell her that. She's a doctor, she'll understand.'

So? This is at least my twentieth try. If she doesn't think it's all that urgent she can sue me.

'I told them, madam,' Evalina says. 'They say they'll do it.'

Thank you. Pesach and Rosh Hashanah are also

coming and I'm getting old while I wait for Min to call back and she never does.

My mother doesn't think this whole idea is what she would exactly call the best thing in the world and we all know what Reuben says about me making up my mind and wanting to get in my car and go off and see Min.

Reuben may not be such a well man these days, but he still has his ideas and with the little bit of breath squeezing in and out of his body he doesn't mind letting us know what they are.

'Now I know she's gone right off her head,' he says. 'What does she think she's going to do on a kaffir location in the middle of bloody nowhere?'

'I'll make a deal with you,' I tell my mother. 'This is what I'll do. I'll go and I'll say hello and how are you. She'll offer me a cup of tea and I'll take a Thrupp's hamper so we should at least have something to eat. She'll say she's glad I came. I'll say I am too and that will be that. Then I'll come back.'

'I have a bad feeling about this,' my mother says.

This is what Jewish mothers have. When nothing else works, this is what they say and it's a daughter's duty to listen and I do and I'm sorry she feels this way but I can't help it. Good feeling, bad feeling, I've made up my mind. I'm going anyway. There's something Min's not telling me. I know this because I know her and she's not like this and how big can the story be that you don't even share it with your supposed-to-be best friend?

That's what I'm going to find out.

'Sit down,' my mother says.

'Not now,' I say. 'If I'm going I need to get started.'

'Sit,' says my mother and I sit. 'If I can't change your mind the least you can do is sit with me for a few minutes. For good luck and a good journey. You'll do it to please me.'

I sit in one chair and she sits opposite me and I

make a joke and point to my watch like I'm in a hurry but we haven't done this for a very long time and it reminds me of being a child again and because five minutes here or there isn't really going to make such a big difference I stay where I am until when she's ready my mother stands up.

'Now you can go,' she says and she may not be happy but at least she's satisfied. Then she does something else she hasn't done in a long time. 'Come here, darling,' she says. She takes my hand and pulls me close and kisses me on the cheek. 'You look after yourself,' she says. 'It's enough one of you is out looking for trouble. Trouble doesn't need company. You listen to what your mother tells you.'

It isn't like her and I should have known then. Your mother is your mother and always will be. There's nothing that can ever change that. When she has a feeling that's not such a good kind of feeling and tells you about it and it's not a thing she does every day, you should maybe take a bit more notice of it.

But who ever does? No one. So, I get into my car. My AA map is on the seat next to me and in my head are all the stories Min ever wrote or told me about the clinic in the back of beyond. Which according to Min is a place that's like heaven on earth.

I should have listened to my mother.

You can change your mind even at the last minute but not me because I always know better. I set out to do what I want which is to see my friend, Min, and all of my life changes and I love my mother but if I had my life over again and had a second chance I'd do exactly what I did all over again too. I wouldn't change one bit of it and there would still be no regrets on my side. No regrets at all.

When you start to run out of what any normal person would call a proper road you have to ask yourself something. Is there some kind of St Anne's rule I don't

283

know about living in Parktown or Sandton? Couldn't Min be a doctor just as well at the Park Lane Clinic?

God forbid I should hold departed Lenny up as an example of common sense but this is what he suggested in the first place. I thought it was a good idea then and the more I see of the bundu, the better idea I think it is.

A woman has to work. I understand this. Doing some good among the blacks I understand too. I've got nothing against people helping each other. It's a nice thing to do. What I can't understand is why, if you have to do it, it has to be done in the back of beyond.

Johannesburg is jumping with black people. They need doctors just the same as anyone else does. Would setting up a nice practice somewhere closer to town have killed Min?

Every now and again I stop at a roadside shop to buy a cold drink and check I'm going in the right direction. Twice I got stopped at an army post and they asked me all my business and I told them and they looked at me and shook their heads as if I was crazy. Then they said I could go on my way.

Everyone you ask gives you the same answer. 'Just follow the road.'

Which is easy to say but we're not exactly talking Jan Smuts Highway. Here the road is grey dust. It seems to go on for ever and it's so narrow you couldn't turn around and go back even if you wanted to but that's all right because I've made up my mind now. What I'll do when I get there, please God in one piece, is just what I told my mother I'd do.

I'll say hello and how are you. I'll give the Thrupp's hamper and have a cup of tea and Min will say she's glad I came and I'll say I am too and that will be enough. Then I'm going back. My mind is made up about that even though it gets a bit better the closer you come.

There are more houses. The fields have things

growing in them. Chickens keep the goats company and cows sway along with herd boys next to them to make sure they keep themselves to themselves. The road isn't so dusty and there's a shop and a school and although it looks a little bit the worse for wear there's even a postbox. People have shoes on their feet and there's even a sign that shows where the clinic is.

There's a hedge of red honeysuckle and a dog who looks at home and well-fed and an open piece of ground where cars are supposed to park and I park my car and lock it by remote just in case anyone gets any ideas.

There are people outside sitting on the lawn. They have bits of food out and chickens cluck past them as they eat. I hold on to my bag. My sunglasses are on top of my head. My blouse is sticking to my back and the two-tone brogues that looked so good in the Bally shop in Sandton seem surprised to find themselves first of all on a rutted path and then on a strip of threadbare grass and now on a concrete floor without even a piece of mat to make it look a bit better.

What can I say about this hospital of Min's that she's so wild about except that it is not the kind of place Dr Kildare is going to apply to for a job but if it suits Min I'm happy for her.

You can see they don't get many strangers here. People stop what they're doing to have a look and it's not a quick look either but I can live with this. I've got this far and it's going to take more than a few looks and some children clustering around to put me off.

I get hold of a young nurse-looking girl dressed in white and tell her to find Dr Campbell and tell her her friend from Johannesburg's come to see her. Which isn't such a big thing.

Maybe you're supposed to pay them to do something like this. I don't know. In town they wouldn't move two inches without at least twenty cents in their hand but here maybe it's different because when I look up the girl has gone off to look for someone and she seems to know where she's going.

I go right inside the foyer and sit down and I take my sunglasses off and put them away and when my eyes have adjusted to the light I take a good look around and we're not talking the entrance foyer of the Park Lane Clinic here.

There are natives sitting around on wooden benches. There's a nurse with a clipboard in her hand and all the time in the world moving around and taking down particulars. There's no coffee bar or cold-drink vending machine. There are no magazines lying around, not even very old ones, and everyone who goes by has a look at me.

Through the door I can see women sitting on the ground with babies on their backs passing bits of fruit to each other and chickens strolling past pecking at the grass as they go and a vegetable seller sitting on the ground and not much to sell and no one buying.

But I'm here now and what can I do?

I settle myself. I pull my handbag tight next to me and wind my hand around its straps and I wait and I wonder what the *shul* women at Waverley would say if they could see me now.

I sit there and think about Min and the trouble I've taken to come all this way to see her and what I'm going to say to her when I eventually do and I'll wait. I'll wait for ever if I have to but as it turns out I don't have to wait very long at all.

'Are you the lady who's looking for Dr Campbell?' a voice says.

A man's voice. A nice voice. In English, thank God, and the man is standing in front of me and he's a priest, dressed in black priest's clothes and the whole thing and a cross with a dying Jew on it tied around his waist.

'Yes,' I say. 'I am.'

Out of respect I stand up and a little bit out of

286

thankfulness too. It's fine to say you'll wait for ever and nothing will budge you but for ever is a very long time to wait.

'You expected to find her here?' he says.

If I didn't expect to find her here what would I be doing here myself? I don't say it but he can see it on my face.

'You better come with me,' he says. 'You've come a long way and I think we should talk.'

Priests drink. I don't hold it against them and I'm not going to make a big thing out of it but they do and I'm not surprised.

In all the holy pictures they have to look at every day, everyone looks so sad. I suppose in the end it just gets too much for a person. They tell you themselves that Jesus Christ, who is in one way of looking at it their boss, carries all the worries of the world on his shoulders. I suppose if I was in that kind of business I'd drink too.

'No, thank you,' I say when he pours one whisky and offers to pour another one. 'But I wouldn't mind a cup of tea.' At four o'clock in the afternoon tea would be better for him as well but it's not my job to tell him this.

'I'll arrange it,' he says and he goes off to the back of the house.

What can it be about a cup of tea that's such a big 'arrange'? You tell the maid and in the time it takes for the kettle to boil you get a cup of tea. I don't know.

I suppose I could sit down but I think you have to be careful. The plain chairs don't look safe and in a house like this you don't know what you could come across behind the armchair cushions which is what I'm thinking about when he comes back with a cup and saucer in his hand.

'Why don't you sit down?' he says.

He shows a big leather chair with no cushions.

'That's the most comfortable. Why don't you sit

there and drink your tea and I'll tell you about Min. How long since you were in touch with each other, by the way?'

'About eighteen months,' I say. 'I've written and I've telephoned. I wouldn't even like to tell you how many messages I've left but I never get any answer.'

He nods his head and gives me the tea and sits down in the chair opposite me and picks up the whisky glass from the side table and he doesn't even have to turn his head to do it. His hand shoots out like a homing pigeon and by the way I wonder if the reason he drinks whisky at this time of day is because the tea is truly terrible.

'She wrote me a letter when my brother died.'

'I know,' he says. 'I posted it for her.' He takes a little sip and then he takes another and then while it's still half full he puts the glass down.

'She felt very badly about your brother. She wanted you to know that. She was very anxious you should.'

If she felt so badly and wanted me to know it she could have got in her car and driven to Durban Airport. From there Johannesburg is only an hour away. She could have got on a plane and come to say goodbye to Davey. Face to face. While he was still with us. I gave her plenty of time to do it.

Never even mind about Davey, she could have come to see me.

'I can see there's a lot you don't know,' Mr Ignatius says.

If there wasn't a lot I didn't know would I be sitting on the edge of a chair in a priest's house drinking tea, which in all honesty in my own house I wouldn't expect my maid, Evalina, to drink? Would I be as quiet as I'm being while I wait for him to open up his mouth and speak? Would I be so patient?

I hate not knowing things. When I was a child I always needed to know everything. Not knowing something or being left out used to make me half crazy.

'Let me tell you something,' my father used to say. 'You want to know everything there is to know and that's the way it should be but if that's the way it is there's one thing you have to accept. There are going to be times you're going to find out things you'll wish you didn't know and what are you going to do then?'

I don't know. That's the only answer I could give him then and after I finish listening to what the priest has to tell me it's the only answer I can give now.

'She should have told me,' I say.

'What do you think you would have been able to do about it?' Mr Ignatius says.

It might just as well have been my late father's voice coming out of the old priest's mouth because the answer is, I don't know.

'I could have arranged a lawyer,' I say.

He shakes his head. 'She didn't want one.'

'Excuse me?' I say.

I know I can't be hearing right but he says it again and it really is too much for me. In a case like this any sane person would take the best lawyer they could lay their hands on and money could buy. Here I'm not talking some tuppenny-ha'penny divorce lawyer. I'm talking the really big guns that a person needs in a case of this kind. I'm talking Sidney Kentridge QC and George Bizos.

I'm not a poor woman. Not lately, and since Lenny I'm really very comfortable thank you very much and Min isn't poor either. She doesn't like people to know but I know. She was an only grandchild and her grandfather left her very nicely looked after, may his soul rest in peace.

So, don't talk to me about not wanting a lawyer when you're in the mess Min is in unless in the same breath you mention that what she needs even more than a lawyer are the services of a good psychiatrist. Because she must have gone mad.

I may be very stupid but I don't understand it and

poor Mr Ignatius explains and then he explains again but the more he explains the less I understand.

'Don't you see?' he says. 'She did all those things they said she did. There was no point her saying she hadn't done them because she had.'

'She let them lock her up?' I say.

'She went before a magistrate,' he said. 'The charges were read out in an open court and she pleaded guilty. If that's what you mean.'

Guilty-schmilty. It's not what I mean. I mean what I said. Min let them lock her up. Some country magistrate's idea of guilty and Sidney Kentridge's idea of guilty and George Bizos' idea of guilty can mean very different things.

'What I can't understand,' I say, 'is why Min just gave up. It isn't like her.'

'She didn't "just give up",' Mr Ignatius says. 'In fact she didn't give up at all. Quite the contrary.' He stops in his tracks and looks at me as if I've just newly arrived from Mars. 'It's a very important issue,' he says. 'You have to understand that.'

'She's in prison, isn't she?' I say. 'For an "indeterminate time", "at the State President's pleasure". Isn't that what you told me?'

'Yes,' he says. 'It is. I told you that and it's true but that's not giving up. It's nothing like giving up at all.'

I may seem very stupid to him but this is not how I see it. Where I come from people talk things out. They give their side of the story. They don't plead guilty and put out their hands for the prison key so they can lock themselves in without troubling anyone else to do it. It doesn't make sense.

'Being in prison for what you believe in, when you believe in it as passionately as Min does, is a form of protest,' he says. 'It's a privilege really. Or, at least, that's one way of looking at it.'

That may be so but it's not my way of looking at it. I look at what's happened to her and listen to Mr

Ignatius going on and on and I put my teacup down and think that all this time she's been away from us Min has been mixing with some very funny people.

'I'd like to see Min,' I say.

'It might not be so easy,' he says.

He says it all quiet and nice. It isn't so much what he says but how he's saying it which is the point at which we're parting company.

'She's not allowed visitors,' he says. 'Well, she is and she isn't. She's allowed one visitor a month and even for that there has to be special permission.'

So? We ask for special permission. How big a thing can it be?

'I'll telephone,' he says but he doesn't look very happy about it. 'I'll talk to a few people. I'll do what I can.'

'Thank you,' I say.

'In the meantime you'll need somewhere to stay. You can stay at Min's house. I'm sure she wouldn't mind. I'll send a girl over to take care of you. The girls here are country girls but willing. I'll send one of my own girls. A Christian girl with good English. You'll be all right with her. I'll send some food too. Nothing fancy. Just a few basic things.'

'No, thank you,' I say.

I've had his tea and I'm grateful for it but that's quite enough for me. The Thrupp's hamper, my present for Min, is, thank God, in my car.

'I'll do my best,' he says. 'But I want you to understand how difficult all this is. You do see that, don't you?'

In fact I don't. Not really. All I see is that I allowed the wool to be pulled over my eyes for far too long. I should have got here sooner. A lot sooner. Maybe then I could have done some good.

MIN

No Gifts Allowed

1981

Frieda's coming to see me.

He takes a special interest in all things concerning me, so he came to tell me himself. Evert Brink.

'She's very insistent about seeing you,' he says.

I can imagine it. I can just imagine it and imagining it makes me smile and it comes to me that I haven't smiled for a long time. I can just hear her. I can see her face in front of me.

'She tells me I should make an exception in her case and what are rules for anyway except to be bent in exceptional cases. It surprises me that a friend of yours could talk like that. She's not like you.'

What he's saying is that no matter what tack he takes I won't yield. Frieda is more sensible than I am and I want more than anything to see her.

'She's here now,' he says. 'Upstairs. The priest's with her. He keeps telling her she's wasting her time. He says you refuse to see anyone. She says you hasn't got any time to waste and as it happens she isn't just anyone, so you'll see her.'

I want to.

'She sent you this. She asked me to give it to you.'

He has a small plate in his hand with a white napkin over it.

'Here it is,' he says. 'I promised I'd see you got it and you know I'm a man who keeps my promises.'

He pulls the napkin aside and underneath it is a Thrupp's apple cake. With poppyseed. I don't believe it.

'She says it's your favourite. I would never have known that. It's strange to think how long we've known each other and how much you know about me and how little I know about you.'

This is the way it is between us. He's the one who made it this way. It's he who said I'm allowed one visitor a month. It's me who told him I don't want anyone at all.

They don't know me here.

I'm quite happy with myself, without anyone else at all. The Great Silence and I are friends of long standing. It's almost a relief to go back to it but Evert Brink won't allow it. He comes to see me almost every day and what he wants is for us to talk.

'You can call me by my name,' he says. 'You know what it is.' Of course I won't do it.

He comes whenever he chooses. So I never know when to expect him. At first I thought he did it to make me uncomfortable. I don't think so any more. There are worse things he could do if he wanted to. I know this but I also know that because I'm white and known and there are people who would miss me he would have to think twice. Imprisonment is good enough for me. It's all I'm worth. Solitary confinement even better.

I tell them nothing. Only because I have nothing to tell that is of any importance to them. Nothing they

293

haven't already heard from other people. Nothing they don't know. They know this but they send me back into solitary anyway.

Some people can't stand it but I don't mind. I'm used to it. My mother sent me here long before they even knew I existed. By the time they arrived and decided solitary was to be my fate they were offering nothing I hadn't savoured before and found to my liking.

All they got were my mother's leavings. 'Serve them right.' That's what she'd say.

I hear these days my mother goes around telling people as far as she's concerned I'm dead and she has no daughter. She won't say my name. It's forbidden in her house. Since this 'disgrace'. This latest 'fiasco'.

'What are these black things?' he says.

'Poppyseed,' I say.

I speak to him for a reason. To have him think he's the one who's driven me into the Great Silence is too great a gift to give him. I can't allow him to be important enough for that. None of this is.

'I'll tell you what I told your friend,' he says. 'I told her technically you're not allowed casual visitors but because of the circumstances I'd be prepared to make an exception.'

'What circumstances?'

'Because you're leaving soon,' he says. 'Soon you and I will be parted.'

He asks if I will miss him and of course I won't answer but he doesn't need me to.

'I'll miss you,' he says. 'I've got used to having you close to me.'

I know he has because so have I.

I know things about him now. I know he was brought up on a farm in the Transvaal and how much he loves the land. I know his mother was a music teacher; that he was one of three brothers and could run faster than either of the others. He is a natural athlete. He has silver cups to prove it. His mother keeps them in a mahogany display cabinet in the front parlour of their house.

'Did you think I was so very different from you?' he says. 'We all begin somewhere. We all have a past.'

It is the ordinariness of his past that unnerves me. I think he knows this. I don't want to know about the farmhouse and the coolness of the big front parlour and the silver cups polished each week and put back behind the glass of the mahogany cabinet.

What I am prepared for are monsters. Nothing has prepared me for this unnerving assault of ordinariness.

On the days he doesn't come, when he's sent away and can't give me any advance warning, he comes back apologetic and tells me how much he's missed me. He always does that.

Sometimes he comes in the night. There's the sound of a single pair of boots and the click of the door opening and then the click of it closing and there he is, standing in front of me, looking at me, and after a while I look back and we can be like this for a long time, wondering at each other in silence.

I'm not afraid of him. What I'm afraid of is that there is something in me that wants to reach out to him.

He has a nice voice, nice and slow and even, and sometimes when he talks he tells me things. Terrible things. The kind of things only a man like him would know. Things he's seen. Things he's done himself and things he plans to do.

'Just so you know it all,' he says. 'I want you to know everything.'

At first I thought having to listen to what he said was part of my punishment. I thought he made me listen to sicken and to hurt me. Now I know more of him I think differently. I think he's reminding himself that he does know right from wrong and it's himself he's punishing.

'If we were outside,' he says. 'If this is ever over. Knowing what you know. Knowing what I've told you. If you could, would you betray me?'

I don't know. Once I could have answered but the more I know of him the less certain I am. What I want to ask him is if this is what he'd like me to do.

He lives alone and is very neat. He doesn't smoke or drink although sometimes he takes women. He told me this and I think they go to him willingly but he doesn't tell them anything about himself.

'I'm in a special section of the defence force,' he says. That's all they need to know. He's tall and strong and there to keep them safe. That's all he offers them and it's more than enough. The rest he saves for me.

He is a long-distance runner. He will run uncountable miles, pushing his body as hard as he can long beyond the point where it calls out to him to stop. He will ask nothing of anyone else's body he does not ask of his own and he can do this because he has learnt the power to endure. We both have.

He's always alone. Yet he has given himself to me.

He has been a student of philosophy and when his work is done he likes to sit in his flat in the dark and listen to Bach.

When he was a boy he played the violin and he still has the instrument but he doesn't play it any more.

In bits and pieces he gives all of himself to me and then from time to time he stops mid-sentence and asks if I will one day remember any of it or if he is wasting his time. Will I remember him? he asks although he needs no answer.

He knows I will never forget. Not him crouched down on his haunches, or me as I am now, or the strange half-light, twilight which is prison light or his pleasant voice and the gentle even flow of his words.

He has gone one way and I the other. I am entrusted

to him by the state and he by his own choice is entrusting himself to me. He is putting all of his life into my hands and giving me all he has to give. It is meant to be the other way around.

On one hand there is the ordinariness of it and then a thousand and one tales of horror told with the special tenderness reserved for the beloved.

'When we get right down to it, we're not that different,' he says. 'We both believe. We're on different sides. That's all.'

This is what he says. My greatest fear is that there might be some truth in it and, worse than this, that there is something of him in all of us.

'I think you should see your friend,' he says. 'When you get to Pretoria Central it might not be so easy.'

'I would like to see her,' I say.

It is a hard, hard thing to say but I want it very much. I want it more than water on a hot day.

'Then ask me,' he says. 'Say, "I'd like to see my friend, Evert." It's as easy as that and then it's done. You can say "please" if you like. I don't mind if you don't. It doesn't matter to me.'

'I should like to see my friend,' I say.

'Not good enough,' he says.

'Please,' I say. 'I should like to see her.'

The door is open and he stands aside so there is room to pass and he shows with his hand that if I want to I can step out. It's the same as it always is. He only ever gives enough room so I will have to pass close to him and smell him and feel the warmth of his body and this time when I do he takes hold of my wrist and jerks me even closer.

'Say my name,' he says. 'Before I go I want to hear you say it.'

I know he does and he knows I won't. I never will. Not for any prize he chose to offer me. No matter how badly I wanted it.

*   *   *

I don't come up blinking like a rat out of a sewer. It's not like that.

I have a washbasin and a mirror. I have a brush and comb and plenty of soap. I have a blue prison dress and underneath it blue prison underwear which is clean every day.

I don't know what Frieda expects but I know there's nothing very alarming about the way I look.

'My God, Min,' she says. 'What have you done to your hair?'

We meet in an upstairs room set apart but in sight of the glass-partitioned offices where people go about their duties. I'm there before she is.

There's a grille but it's electronically controlled. It slides open at the push of a button. There's a table, clean and dusted, and a straight-backed chair on either side of it. I sit down and settle myself in a chair and I wait. High up is a pair of windows, closed against the cold of the afternoon but the clear, bright light of the winter day falls through them and to me it's like a gift from another world.

There's a policewoman in the room with us. She's wearing a khaki uniform, neat and becoming to her. It suits her fawn-coloured hair. She sits in a chair in the corner.

'The Commander says you're allowed fifteen minutes,' she says. 'You know the rules.'

I know the rules. General conversation only. No tricks. No messages hidden between the lines. I know the rules but Frieda doesn't and they don't know Frieda.

'What happened to your hair?' she says. As if it's the most important thing in the world.

'I cut it off,' I say. 'It just came to me one day that I didn't really have any use for it any more. So I cut it off.'

Every word of it is true but there's something else

298

too which I don't tell Frieda and will never tell anyone. He liked my hair. He told me so.

'You have beautiful hair,' he said.

It's the only personal thing he ever said to me. So I asked for a pair of scissors and he brought them to me and while he stood and watched I cut my hair off. Because he admired it. For no other reason.

'I'll have to get used to it,' Frieda says. 'I'm not going to say it suits you but I think it does. I'll get used to it first. Then I'll tell you.'

She looks good. She looks lovely. She has on gold earrings and a necklace and the famous engagement ring and a cashmere coat with a fox collar. She's beautifully made-up. Her fingernails are painted and she's wearing a great many gold bangles. They go so high above her wrist they disappear into the sleeve of her coat, so I suppose that must be the fashion now.

She's wearing perfume with a rather sharp undertone. The kind you have sprayed on you by shop girls and don't really want. She's moving forward with her arms outstretched. She wants to embrace me.

The policewoman stands up and shows 'no' with her hand.

'Not allowed,' she says.

'What does she mean, "not allowed"?' Frieda says.

'She means this isn't a contact visit,' I say. 'You're not allowed to touch me. No one is.'

'Why?'

'I don't know why,' I say. 'But those are the rules.'

'Excuse me for the rules,' Frieda says.

'You can sit down on that chair and let me look at you and tell me how you are,' I say. 'That's allowed.'

'Thank you very much,' Frieda says. 'I'm happy to hear it.'

She's the same. The straps of her handbag are hooked over her shoulder. The bag nestles under her arm like a sleeping chicken. I think for a moment she's going to take out a handkerchief and dust off the chair before she sits down but she doesn't.

'Listen, Min,' she says. 'This whole thing. It's not a joke.'

'No,' I say. 'It isn't.'

'You've got no idea how these people carry on. I brought you something. A little something from Thrupp's. All I wanted to do was give it to you. You'd never believe how they carried on.'

I would believe it.

'God forbid I should say it but I actually wished Lenny was here. He's not good for much but he knows how to deal with this kind of thing.'

She makes a charade with her eyes and her hands like an envelope changing hands and a wink and a little smile.

'I know you don't like that kind of thing,' she says. 'I don't like it either but believe me, whether we like it or not with a certain type of person it takes you where you want to go.'

That is something I would like to have seen. I would like to have seen Evert Brink's face if Frieda offered to bribe him but she doesn't know about Evert Brink and the family pew in the big white small-town church and the wrath of God on Sundays and the everyday evening prayers with three boys on their knees before their father.

Our destiny is in God's hands. He will direct us. He will deliver us from evil.

'If I knew what was going on here, which I would have known if you only would have told me, I would have brought a lot more things with me,' Frieda says.

'I got the apple cake.'

'Forget the apple cake,' she says. 'I was never so wild about it in the first place. You were the one who liked it which is the only reason I brought it.'

'Thank you, Frieda,' I say. 'You and no one else but

300

you would ever remember a thing like Thrupp's apple cake.'

'The cake's nothing,' she says. 'What I mean is that if I'd known what was going on here I would have brought a decent Jo'burg lawyer with me and you would have been out of here by now.'

'Not allowed,' the policewoman says.

This is so unexpected Frieda turns right around in her chair.

'Excuse me,' she says. 'But what exactly is this "not allowed" business? I'm here having a conversation with a woman who happens to be my best friend and all I'm hearing every five minutes is this is "not allowed" and that is "not allowed".'

'Frieda . . .' I say.

'No, Min,' she says. 'I have to say what I have to say. I'm a grown-up woman. I make up my own mind what I want to say and what I don't want to say. I don't need someone chipping in all the time to help me.'

She's really affronted and although it's all so terrible just for a moment it's also very funny and there's no one in this world who could make it so except Frieda.

'So, excuse me,' she says. 'But while you're at it perhaps you should tell me what it is I'm actually allowed to say and what it is I'm not allowed to say. I'd like to hear it.'

'General topics, personal news, health issues, nothing pertaining to the case or the sentence,' the policewoman says.

'Thank you,' says Frieda. 'If this is what I've come all this way to hear I might just as well have stayed at home.'

'It's quite true,' I say. 'You shouldn't have come.'

'What I should have done is come much sooner,' she says. 'You should have sent for me.'

She reaches across and takes one of my hands in both of hers and I expect a bark because this isn't allowed but it doesn't come. So we sit there holding

301

hands, looking at each other. Smiling. Glad of the touch of each other. Glad of each other's presence.

'If you'd sent for me I would have come,' she says. 'You know that.'

I do know and I know it wouldn't have helped but I don't know how I can explain this to Frieda.

'In any case,' she says. 'Now that I do know, I'm not going to leave it at this.'

'Please, Frieda . . .' I say.

'Oh, don't worry,' she says. 'I'm not going to say anything "pertaining to the case or the sentence". All I'm saying is that it's in my hands now and the minute I leave here I'm going to jump on the telephone and phone a few people and sort something out.'

'You can't,' I say.

'You don't know me,' she says. 'At least you do know me but you don't know me lately. I'm not the woman I used to be. These days there's nothing I can't do.'

I'm glad she thinks so but I could tell her if she'd listen that there are some things that are too big even for Frieda Lazar on the warpath to take on. Not even with her mother and Sadie and the entire congregation of the Waverley *shul* behind her.

'Anyway,' she says. 'This is not your problem. It's my problem now and I'll sort it out and in the mean time to show there's no hard feelings between us because you couldn't be at Davey's funeral, which I now understand, I've brought you a little something.'

Her handbag is on the table and she's opening it up.

'No gifts allowed,' the policewoman says.

'Excuse me,' Frieda says, 'but this isn't a "gift". Not in the way you people understand "gift". This is something that belonged to a dead boy and was very precious to him.'

The policewoman is on her feet now and so is Frieda.

'Here,' Frieda says. 'Look at it. Take a good look.'

In a see-through plastic packet is the elephant-hair bangle and Frieda holds it up and goes right up to the policewoman so she can take a really good look at it.

'This lady was my late brother's best friend,' she says. 'He wanted her to have this to remember him by and I said I'd make sure she got it and not you or anyone else is going to stop me.'

'Don't, Frieda . . .' I say.

'Don't you start,' she says. 'It's for you from Davey and you're having it. I'm giving it to you and you're taking it and that's the end of the story.'

I have to get up now and because I'm so big these days it's not easy. When I put my hand on the table to help myself and push myself free of the chair and stand up in her presence for the first time Frieda understands everything.

Her eyes are enormous and the elephant-hair bangle keeps waving up and down in her hand as if it was battery-operated and running amok with no one to remember that somewhere there was a switch that could switch it off.

'My God, Min,' Frieda says. 'My God!'

'You don't have to make such a big thing out of it,' I say.

'My God,' she says. 'You're going to have a baby.'

My stomach is enormous. Under the blue prison dress and with Frieda staring at it it feels as if it's getting bigger by the minute.

'Women have babies every day,' I say.

This is not an easy thing and I don't want Frieda to get over-excited and make it even harder than it already is because I know what she's going to say. She's going to say that a gaol is not a place for a baby to be born. I know it isn't. I don't need her to tell me.

She's going to say over her dead body will such a thing be allowed to happen. I hope it doesn't come to that because even that won't stop it happening the way it's going to happen. There's nothing very much

303

anyone can do to change things and dead bodies don't count for very much around here.

She's going to ask me what I think is going to happen to my baby after he comes into this world. I can't keep him with me. It isn't allowed. Who will take him? Where will he go?

I'm asked this every day and the answer I give is that I have no proper answer. I can't think about it because thinking about it hurts too much and I simply don't know and the squabble over the elephant-hair bangle has been forgotten in all the other excitement.

'You never said,' Frieda says.

'No,' I say. 'I didn't.'

'It doesn't matter,' she says. 'Don't worry about it. We'll sort it out.'

As if it was as easy as that.

Then I feel something. Something quick and smooth. With sleight of hand that surprises me and takes me off-guard the elephant-hair bangle slips from Frieda's hand into the pocket of my dress.

'For luck,' she says quick and fast so no one can hear except her and me. 'Do you remember how Aunty Fanny loved to play cards?'

Of course I do. Why poor old Fanny? Why now?

'She knew how to cheat, you know,' Frieda says. 'I'm not actually saying she did it herself. All I'm saying is she knew how to do it. She showed me and I never told anyone. "One day it'll come in useful." That's what she always said.'

'You never told me,' I say.

'You never asked,' she says. 'Which is a big problem with you in some very major areas. Which is why there are some things about me you don't know.'

We may not continue to touch each other but we may speak and I look at her and what I see is Funny Frieda, my friend who brings the light in with her and it touches me in a way touching hands could never do.

304

'I love you, Frieda,' I say.

I don't know why I say it except it's what I feel and it needs to be said and it just comes out.

'Thank you,' she says. 'Excuse me for not knowing this before. But what am I supposed to be? A mind reader?'

She turns to look at me and there are tears in her eyes and in mine and the bracelet is safe in my pocket.

'You never asked,' I say. 'If you asked I would have told you.'

Then our time is up.

FRIEDA

The Most Natural Thing
in the World

1981

Now I know about the baby I have to stay for a while. At least until it gets here and it's time for us to go because this is what we'll have to do. This is not the place for me and it's not the place for Min's baby either.

Min and I have talked about it.

'What about the father?' I say.

She hasn't said anything and I can see she's not going to but someone has to. You don't need a medical degree to work out that somewhere along the way a man has something to do with this.

'Does he know about this?' I say.

'No,' she says. 'He doesn't know. He's not going to know and he can't help me if that's what you're going to ask next.'

Why should I even bother with questions when she already has all the answers?

Am I asking for names? Am I asking for details? Does she think I've got nothing more on my mind than having a nice heart-to-heart chat about the ins and outs of how she got in this condition in the first place?

'Min,' I say, 'all I'm saying is you need help and maybe this man, whoever he is, can help you.'

'He can't,' she says. 'I don't want him to.'

Unknown, uncaring, married, vanished, uninterested, disappeared, dead. I can see she isn't going to tell me. I may just as well do a lucky dip and take my pick.

'It's not important,' she says. 'He was good and he cared and it mattered but he's gone and I won't see him again. It's the baby that's important now.'

When the time comes for her baby to be taken away from her I'll take her or him back to Johannesburg. Home with me. There would be no point our staying. I've telephoned until the wires between here and Johannesburg are hot. I will keep on trying. People, very important, very expensive people, tell me there is little that can be done to change Min's fate.

She will have to serve her sentence.

'I accept it,' she says. 'Why can't you do the same?'

I can't because I'm me and the way I am. I'm not like her and she's not like me. That's the answer and we both have to learn to live with it.

She will go to Pretoria Central and the same rules will apply as apply here. No one will be allowed to see her except with special permission and special permission will not be given very easily. Until then Min has her six weeks with her child after it's born. That is allowed and then the baby comes to me.

I think it's the cruellest thing I ever heard and if it were up to me and I could make that six weeks last for ever so Min could keep her baby I would.

Except it isn't up to me.

No amount of money or influence is going to change

this and I have to do exactly what Min said in the first place. I have to accept it.

'You need to be there when the baby's born though,' she says. 'It's important. He has to bond with you just as much as he does with me. After all, you're the one who'll have him.'

I can't look at her.

'I'll ask them,' she says.

She never asks. She hates asking but because it's for the baby she'll ask.

'I would like my friend Frieda with me if that's possible.'

She has to say why and she says it's because when the time comes for her child to be taken from her I'm the one who'll be taking him. They know this. Yet we have to keep telling them.

'You don't have to do this,' Min says. 'It's a very big thing to ask. You can change your mind if you want to and I would understand. It wouldn't make any difference between you and me.'

'You didn't ask,' I say. 'I offered and of course I have to do it. Besides which, I want to.'

Who else should do it if not me? I don't say it but what does Min think will become of her baby if he doesn't come to us, to a place already being prepared for him where he will be so much loved and wanted? There will be no last-minute change of heart here.

She's been told how it will be. She has the baby for six weeks and then some plan must be made for him. If she can't make her own arrangements and there's no family to take him a social worker will do what has to be done and her child will go into foster care.

They won't change their minds. I've only been here a few days and I know this and even if she can't face up to it she knows it too. I know these people are supposed to be human beings just the same as we are but all the same they're very strange.

I think it's the baby. I think it's a problem to them.

Until it's actually born it's beyond the rules and there's nothing they can do about it. I think they find the idea of it peculiar and difficult to understand. I think it's because until the moment of its birth it's free. It's only after it's arrived that the rules of the South African Correctional Authorities apply to it. Until then it's beyond them and they're not used to that.

Min thinks about her child all the time. It's her reason for living. She told me so. She couldn't care about anything else. She couldn't even care about playing her part in changing the world. Not the way she used to.

There are plenty of other people who can pick up where she left off and go on with that job but there is only one person who can bring this child into the world and that's Min herself and suddenly her world which was once such a big place has become a very small place indeed. It centres on one thing.

She still wants the world changed. She wants it more than ever. Only now she knows exactly why she does. This small kicking person who shares her solitary life keeps on reminding her. It will never let her forget.

She doesn't tell me this. It isn't the kind of thing we're allowed to speak about but it doesn't matter. She doesn't have to tell me. I know Min. I know how she feels about things. I can see it in her eyes.

Her time is very close and because of this and the arrangement we have about the baby I'm allowed to see her. Compassionate reasons. Fifteen minutes only. Three times a week. It says so on the form I have to sign.

I'm signing anything these days and in between I'm on the telephone to my mother who thinks what's going on is the most terrible thing in the world.

'For God's sake,' she says. 'To separate a mother

from her child. What kind of monsters are these that you're sitting with there?'

I wish they were monsters. Monsters are things we all understand. What I'm sitting with here are people who look just the same as any kind of ordinary person does. They look neat and tidy. There's a little bit of jewellery here and there. There are flowers on some of the desks and funny pictures pulled out of magazines stuck on the walls.

At teatime they drink tea. Sometimes someone brings in something nice to eat and they all share it. They make jokes. They talk about each other behind their backs. They're polite and they smile and they do their job.

These people may be monsters but the worst part is you can't tell by looking. Which makes them, I suppose, monsters in their hearts and that's the worst kind.

I don't know. In a way my mother's right and in a way she's wrong. In a way they're ordinary people and in another way they are monsters, the very same monsters who are going to take my friend's baby away from her and give him to me.

When I talked to my mother about it there was no doubt in her mind what the right thing was to do.

'This poor child will come to us,' she said. 'Where else should it go? That's the one thing she'll never have to worry about. I'll have everything ready. Dear God, that such a thing should happen.'

Min tries to make me feel better. She tells me that the women who come to her clinic are having babies every day of the week and it's no big thing. In fact it's the easiest and most natural thing in the world. When the time comes these women come walking up the road. They arrive at the hospital and say they're ready. Then they do what they're told. They put their legs in the air and the baby jumps out.

This is the story according to Min and if you believe what Min tells you you'll believe anything.

'It's the easiest thing in the world,' she says.

She sits opposite me on the hard-backed prison chair. Her stomach is enormous. The baby is swimming around inside her impatient to come out. Which if it knew what I knew it might not be quite so keen to do. Our watchdog is sitting on a chair in the corner. Her eyes are down but she's tuned in to every word we're saying and you'd think Min who is a doctor herself and a doctor's daughter would have more sense.

I've heard this story of hers before and I know what's coming next. The next thing I'll hear is how women have babies out in fields. They squat down for five minutes. The baby comes out. Then they get up, tie the baby on their backs and go right on working. *Mazel tov* and I'm happy for these wonderful women. Min should be so lucky when the time comes. Every woman should.

This is a story that sounds very unusual and nice when you tell it at a coffee morning in Parktown. When a mother can hardly stand on her two feet any more without falling over backwards and a baby's kicking as though he means business it doesn't sound quite so wonderful.

'It's a natural thing,' Min says.

She keeps on saying it and every time she says it I believe it less and less because I haven't just taken her word for it. What I've done is ask about it and the kind of thing I'm hearing doesn't make me feel any better.

'I'm not happy with just a nursing sister,' I say. 'I think a proper doctor should be there.'

They think I'm mad. Around here babies arrive every day and they need doctors for other, more important things. A nursing sister with a diploma in midwifery is good enough to deliver a baby and you can forget about any fancy equipment.

I'm happy about the baby. I really am. All I want is that it should come out alive and kicking and in one piece and that everything should be well with Min. That's all I'm really asking.

I don't think I have to be there but she wants me.

'Don't say no,' she says. 'It wasn't easy to get permission. You know what they're like here but you're going to be a big someone in this child's life and I'm asking you because I want you with me. It means a lot to me.'

I enjoy being a 'someone' in someone's life just as much as the next person does and it's nice to help a friend out but is it such a crime if you'd rather be a someone at a hospital where doctors have beepers and there's a paediatric consultant just around the corner?

'You'll be there when the time comes,' Min says. 'I'm not even going to ask you again. I know you will.'

She's right. I'm there and I'm cross with her for landing us somewhere neither of us should be at all and I'm cross with me for allowing it to happen just like I always do and it's a Sunday and it's freezing cold.

I'm standing in a makeshift little delivery room and my cashmere coat is on my back and there are two pairs of pantyhose under my slacks. There should have been a doctor here. I should have spoken to my mother and to Sadie. Between them they know the whole world. They could have found someone who would have been willing to be at this confinement.

Min wouldn't hear of it.

'How come you always know better than anyone else?' I say. 'Why do I listen to you?'

'Because I make sense,' she says. 'That's why.'

I hate this. Min's sucking in air and sweating and grunting and no one tells you this is what babies are really about and I have other problems too. I don't think a decent baby should be born in a place like

312

this. It isn't right. It isn't the kind of thing you would ever like to mention in later life even if it's not your fault.

Who but a madwoman would end up in a place like this with only a nurse to help her and no one for miles around unless you count the army and the police and about half a million natives who right this moment can all probably live quite happily without another white person in the world?

'Breathe,' I say.

'Why do you keep saying "Breathe"?' Min says.

Her face is wet with sweat. Her tufts of blond hair that are all she's got left are going brown with wetness. Her face is bright red with heat and effort and the way she's been pushing.

'I don't know what else to say,' I say. 'If you told me in the first place what you wanted me to say I'd be saying it.'

'Don't say anything,' she says. 'I'm the doctor. I know what to do.'

'That's fine,' I say and it's a big lie. At least as far as I'm concerned.

She may think it's fine but from where I am it doesn't look so marvellous. She may be the doctor but it's hard to run the show when you're flat on your back with your legs in the air and a baby half-way out.

'Don't worry,' Min says. 'Regina's done this more times than anyone can count.'

I'm happy to hear it. I've got nothing against Regina, the nurse, whoever she may be. For myself I like a doctor with a nice surgery with comfortable chairs to sit on and all his certificates framed and hung up on the wall.

'We're nearly ready,' Regina says. 'It won't be long now.'

She shows three fingers to Min. Then she bends her head down between Min's legs.

'Push some more,' I say.

313

Poor Min's red in the face and pushing as hard as she can.

'Come over here and have a look,' Regina says.

She stands back so I can get a better view and I don't think it will be polite to say, 'No, thank you,' so I look and what I see is the crown of the baby's head sticking out.

'It's almost here,' Regina says and everything seems to be going faster.

Min's breathing and yelling. Regina's giving instructions. Min's pushing and crying and nothing's going to stop it and there's no room for me now and I stand back and look and the baby comes out squealing and crying and before I know it I'm crying too. I'm pushing tears out of my eyes with my hand and my hand keeps knocking against an earring and half my mascara floats away.

So what? We're not on the stage at His Majesty's Theatre. This is real life.

'It's a boy,' Regina says. 'A lovely little boy.'

She has him by the ankles in the old-fashioned way and he's crying for which you can't blame him and I'm crying and Min's laughing and crying all at the same time and holding out her arms for her baby to come into them.

'Come and have a look here,' she says. 'Come and see how nice he is.'

I don't know about babies. You have to think twice before you look. You never know what you're going to see. Not every baby who arrives in this world looks like Paul Newman.

'Look at his hands,' Min says. She takes hold of one and spreads it out. 'Aren't they just perfect?'

I don't know about perfect but I look at Min's baby lying in his bit of white sheet in the crook of her arm and he's not so bad. His face is a bit crumpled and right this minute it's a sad old person's face but it'll straighten out the way babies' faces always do.

314

What I think is he may be small but he's smart just the same. You have to be smart to wish yourself into this world and then all by yourself find your way here.

Min looks pleased with him and I think I could like the look of him and he lies there and I don't know him very well yet but if you asked me I'd say he even looked a bit pleased with himself.

'What do you think?' Min says.

'What should I think?' I say.

She holds the baby out so we can both see him and together we look into his crumpled face.

What should I think about this small new life who's going to be taken away from his mother so soon? Maybe I think life is unfair and that this is an adult matter and it isn't right that a child should have to find this out so young.

What I think is I wish he knew how much I wished it could be some other way because this is not the best way. It's just the way things have to be.

I wish he knew how welcome he's going to be in our house. His place is already prepared for him. For as long as he needs us he will have in my mother the very best *bubbe* this world has to offer.

How do I know this? I know because of the good mother she's been, and wife and daughter and sister. All her life she's been in training for being a first-class, top-of-the-range *bubbe* and now she will have her chance. He will have at least two good Jewish *tantes*, me and my aunt Sadie, and in addition there will be the whole of the Waverley *shul* who will for sure by now know all his business because Johannesburg is not such a big place as it sometimes seems to be.

When the time comes all these women will want to come and have a look at him for themselves and not one of them will walk through the door without bringing with them a little something meant just for him. So in that way at least he will be lucky.

If I could tell him what was in my heart and he could understand I would tell him that even so, I know it isn't the best way for a baby to start out in the world. A mother is a mother. Ask me. I know. If your mother is taken away from you there isn't a present in the world that can make up for it.

'I was thinking of calling him David,' Min says. 'I wasn't sure though. I didn't know what he'd come out like.'

Between us lies the baby wrapped in his sheet. He looks small and cross and probably has his own ideas but even so it's up to us to decide.

'David's good, isn't it?' Min says. 'What do you think?'

What I think is that for someone so small and a newcomer and not even a Jew David's not such a bad name and Min's baby, now that I take a proper look at him, is not such a bad kid. I think Davey would be happy and he would be proud and this is what I tell Min.

316

FRIEDA

A Strange Song in a
Strange Land

1981

I have to say how it was the day I took David from
Min.

Six weeks is not a very long time in the history of
the world. It's not a very long time in the history
of one person's life either.

'We hope for the best,' my mother says. 'Perhaps
there will be a miracle and it won't have to be this
way.'

She's tried everything. She's spoken to everyone she
knows. She's gone to people she doesn't know from
Adam, sometimes with a telephone call beforehand,
sometimes with a letter of introduction in her hand.
Sometimes she's gone to total strangers without any
introduction at all.

I look at my mother with new eyes these days.
To think I've known her all my life and had to wait
till I was a grown-up woman to find out that all this

317

time my little mother had a will like iron.

'Don't give up hope,' she says. 'You should never give up hope. I'll keep on trying and you keep on hoping for the best.'

There's a Yiddish proverb that says not to hope is to insult the future. I mean the future no disrespect but I know something my mother doesn't know. I've seen for myself the way things work here.

So, I hope and I speak to my mother by kind courtesy of the General Post Office when the telephones feel in the mood to work in the way a decent telephone should. I see Min on the allowed days and I see David and am allowed to touch him. The social worker says I can but only because he's coming to live with me and we need to get to know each other.

I count the days and wait for the moment when Min and I will see each other for the last time. I wait for it although I wish it will never come. Just thinking about it makes my heart ache.

Sadie is sending the Caddie.

'For goodness' sake, Frieda,' my mother says. 'What were you expecting? You thought your aunt and I were going to let you get in your car and drive back alone with a baby lying on the back seat?'

I hadn't thought about it at all.

'She'll send the Caddie,' my mother says. 'And a few things for the little one just to get him started and one or two things for Minnie.'

I know my mother and I know my aunt Sadie even better. Half the baby department from The Belfast will have been bought out and be in the car. The other half will be all packed out in the room at my house that's already been set aside for David.

'Minnie isn't allowed to have things, Mama,' I say.

'You'll see she gets them,' my mother says. 'I'm sending jerseys. Decent stuff. And some socks and a good-quality dressing gown with plenty of padding on it.'

'Please, Mama,' I say. 'You don't understand.'

'I don't understand?'

I stand in the living room of Min's small house with the phone in my hand and my mother's voice crackling over the line and I see her face in front of me.

People talk about those TV telephones that will be all the fashion one of these days. The ones that will make it possible for us to see the person we're talking to. As far as my mother and I are concerned this won't be necessary.

'Don't tell me what I understand and what I don't understand,' my mother says. 'Maybe you think Pretoria Central Prison is the Holiday Inn Hotel. What I'm telling you is it isn't.'

I know this. I never thought it was.

'You'll find a way,' my mother says. 'As far as the little one is concerned Joshua will be driving up and I'm sending Wanda Schumacher's girl's sister with him. Her name's Elizabeth.'

'Please, Mama,' I say. 'It's not necessary.'

'It's necessary,' my mother says. 'She's a trained nanny. Well, they call themselves trained but you never know. Anyway, I've seen her references and interviewed her myself and I'm satisfied.'

'Excuse me asking,' I say. 'But will that be all or are you sending the rest of Johannesburg as well?'

'No,' says my mother. 'All I'm sending besides these two is old William to drive your motor car back. He's not young but he's dependable and I've told him he can take his time.'

Thank you for telling me.

'You and Elizabeth and the baby will be taking the aeroplane from Durban. Joshua will take you straight to the airport.'

'Thank you,' I say.

'Don't thank me,' my mother says. 'I'm your mother. What do you think I'm here for?'

Only my mother can say this in the way she does.

319

So you should know where you stand without taking any pleasure in it.

'You just do what you have to do and tell Minnie to be a good girl and be brave.'

'Mama,' I say. 'Minnie is thirty years old. She's a grown-up woman. You're talking about her as if she was still a child.'

'Listen to me, Frieda,' my mother says. 'I don't care if she's a hundred and thirty years old. From where I'm standing she isn't looking all that grown-up and neither are you.'

I think I sometimes forget it myself. I know I don't always remember to tell her but my mother will never change and I'm glad she won't because I will always love her and I love her just the way she is.

It's arranged. Min's leaving early afternoon on Friday and she'll give David to me before she goes. He will have his new Belfast baby clothes to leave prison in and the carry-cot my mother sent. Everyone around here's talking about the car and the three servants in their uniforms and about all the boxes of baby things. All neatly packed with the baby's name on them.

MR DAVID CAMPBELL. In my mother's handwriting. I didn't think she'd even heard me when I said it. I never thought she'd remember it. Not after all these years. 'Classy people have classy luggage.' That's what I thought. I was fourteen years old and trying to sort out the way the world worked and where I fitted into it. I thought classy people had luggage with name labels on it. I thought it showed they had style but that was a very long time ago.

I thought Julia Delaney had class and style but I was wrong. She didn't have either. When class and style were handed out it was her daughter who got it all. It isn't a thing you buy into or marry. Either you have it or you don't. Or, with some people, it's just there because it's bred in the bone and Min has it and it's something no one will ever be able to take away from her no matter how hard they try.

'I wish you'd stop crying,' Min says.

I can't help it.

'It'll only be for as long as it takes and then it will be over.'

I know, but that's true of life as well. Except I don't think this is the time to mention it.

It's all arranged. We'll do the handover at the prison hospital. Min is allowed no contact with me but she can hold her baby one last time before he's handed over into my care. There will be a social worker with us the entire time.

'It's all right,' Min says. 'It's not the end of the world. If I can bear it so can you.'

Then I'm to go away with David and Min will go by special van to Pretoria.

'My mother sent you some things,' I say.

'I know,' she says. 'They told me. Please say thank you but I'm not allowed to take them.'

'I told her.'

'When you see her please tell her I'm fine. I have everything I need. I'll be perfectly all right. Really, I will.'

'Listen, Min,' I say. 'I'll be in contact with Pretoria just the minute I get back. I'll find out what's allowed and what isn't. I'll come whenever they let me. I'll never just let you go.'

'I know,' she says. 'I know that.'

We look at each other. I cry. I can't help it. I'm worse than Ruth Silverman ever was. It's because things are different now. David has changed everything.

'Listen,' Min says. 'Please listen to me. What I have to say is very important.'

'I'm listening,' I say.

'No,' she says. 'You're not. How can you listen

properly when you're crying and making such a noise I can hardly hear myself?'

Who needs jokes at a time like this? Certainly not me.

'I don't want you to bring David to see me in Pretoria.'

'If they let me I will. Of course, I will,' I say.

'No,' she says. 'Please listen to me. I don't want it to be like that. I don't want him to know me like that.'

'You don't have to decide now,' I say. 'You can change your mind.'

'I have decided,' she says. 'I'm not going to change my mind. You come. Come just whenever you can, whenever they let you. You come and tell me all about him. It's enough. Don't bring him with you.'

Min. She can look at you and into you or right through you if she wants to. She's always been able to do that.

'Will you promise me?' she says.

Then she does a funny thing. A small thing. She turns over her hand, palm up on the table. The movement is so small our minder isn't even disturbed by it. She doesn't look up at all. Across her wrist, so slight that if you don't know it's there you wouldn't even see it, is a very fine white scar thin as a thread of cotton.

I have one too.

'I promise you,' I say. 'I give you my word.'

'Thank you,' she says. 'I know I can trust you.'

It's Friday night. Min's gone and David's with me. He and Wanda Schumacher's Elizabeth and I are together in Min's house.

The two drivers have found some people who'll take them in and in the morning we leave.

Fridays come and Fridays go but I will never have another one quite like this. I know that.

Every *shul* in Johannesburg and all over the world for all I know could be packed to the gills with devout

Jews and no one would even notice I wasn't there. No rabbi is going to stand up and say the service can't take place because Frieda Woolf, once Frieda Lazar, is not there.

No one except my mother and Sadie is going to ask what I may be doing when everyone else is singing Friday-night songs and sitting down to their chicken soup and they can ask if they like because I may be out in the bush in the back of beyond but on Friday I make *shabbas*.

I've always done it. I always will. From the very first Friday since I've been here this is what I've done and it's my pleasure to do it. For *shabbas* I will even take on the mambas in the garden and go out myself to look for vegetables and a nice salad because on Friday wherever I happen to be I serve only the best so it's no good asking the girl Mr Ignatius sent to help me and go out and choose food instead of doing it myself because what I call 'only the best' only I would know.

They know me by now down at the native shop. I'm the white woman from Johannesburg with my basket over my arm and my big handbag lying in the bottom of it. I know what I want. I don't take the first thing I see and I take my time.

There are a lot of life's lessons I still have to learn but how to shop is not one of them. People here stand back while I go about my business. They smile behind their hands and they watch me and they can watch as much as they like.

Friday is my day and when it comes to choosing food for the people who'll be at my table the shoppers can smile at me as much as they like. I'll pick and I'll choose until I get exactly what I want and if it takes all day that's all right too.

I shop until I'm satisfied and when I'm done I go back to Min's house with my basket and my handbag and David is asleep and the native girls are passing the time of day with each other and there's only room for two of us and I chase Elizabeth out of our way and back to the baby.

Then I put on an apron and I begin.

Adelaide sets out all the things I ask for and my shop purchases and my basket of garden salad stands on Min's scarred old table. The back door is open to let in the light and the air. The knives and the mixing bowls and the chopping boards are ready.

I'm happy when I cook. It doesn't matter where in the world I am or what a strange and sad thing it is that has happened to me right this very day, I can still rejoice for who I am and for what God sees fit to pass in my direction. Good and bad both.

Out of the pots come the smells and the memories of my childhood and all of my life. Today, on this day on which I've said goodbye to my friend, I'm ready.

I have a few herbs and some carrots and potatoes and the pots steam on the stove and there are two small breads baking in the oven and even if I can't eat them I can bake them anyway and out in the yard Adelaide is singing and washing the dishes in a big plastic bucket.

There's a dish of water and I wash a few pieces of fruit and I polish them. I see Aunty Fanny in front of me saying what a work of art my fruit always is and I lay the table and set out candles and glasses and put bush jasmine and lilac in a glass jar and I change my dress and make up my face and brush my hair and the sun goes down fast like it does in the bush especially in winter and before you know it the stars are in the sky like jewels in a velvet box.

'Come, my friend, to meet the bride,
Let us welcome the sabbath day.'

I light two candles and hold my fingers flat against my eyes and it doesn't matter that I'm alone and among strangers because I'm never alone and I know now that this is what *shabbas* is all about.

David's little fists clench open and closed above the rim of his blanket and he lies in his carry-cot warm and safe. He's not a Jewish boy and never will be but it doesn't matter. He's under my protection now and I stand at the head of my table with a Gucci scarf over my head and my head is bowed. I stretch my arms out as far as they'll go and I draw the sabbath to me with half-cupped hands, once, twice, and once again.

I say the blessing and in front of me is a small glass specially prepared and out of the very bottom of the Thrupp's basket is a special bottle of *kosher* wine I brought for just in case my stay was a little longer than I intended and because there is no man I say the *broche* for this myself.

It is my own voice sounding very small in all of this great wilderness but this is not the voice I hear.

I am a child again. It is my father's voice I hear and I feel his hands on my head.

'God make thee like Sarah and Rebecca. God make thee like Rachel and Leah.'

I hold my hands to my eyes and I wait.

I'm here in this strange place far from where I belong but they are here too. I know they are. I can feel them. They look down in their flight and they see me just like they always do wherever I happen to be. *Bubbe* Rochel and my father, Davey and Aunty Fanny.

They don't stay very long. They never do. Just long enough to remind me and then in a whisper of wings they're gone and I am who I am and I am blessed and I am the one who kindles the sabbath lights.

BOOK FOUR

The Small Door in
the Wall

1986–1987

FRIEDA

Life as an Unmarried Woman

1986

Life as an unmarried woman is not so bad. I have my small house in Sandton that suits me with a nice little garden for David to play in and there's a park just down the road where we like to go with a small pond in it with ducks who like to be fed. There are swings in one section and other children to play with and lots of opportunity to be the king of the castle.

At home there's Elizabeth to take care of David and Evalina is still with me and old William comes in twice a week to do odd jobs and look after the garden and at the same time he's teaching David about plants and also a few words of Zulu.

This is as a surprise for Min, for when she comes back to us, and he learns fast. Everything he does he does fast. He's that kind of child.

This may not be everyone's kind of life but I've seen other kinds and it suits me.

Sadie doesn't agree. She's without her Reuben these days and a widow but Reuben went just the way he

329

would have liked and we were ready so it wasn't so bad.

One evening he was lying in his bed listening to the six o'clock news and the weather report. Listening with his head back and his eyes closed just like he always did, waiting to hear the worst and just how fast the country was going to the dogs. But just for a change it was all good news and we don't know how much of it he heard and we can't say if that was the thing that killed him but by the time the three pips came for the weather report he was gone.

Gone, God rest his soul, but not forgotten because Sadie is still speaking for him just like she always did.

'I don't understand this new life of yours,' Sadie says. 'I don't think I ever will and I know Reuben wouldn't either so maybe when you've got the time perhaps you'd like to tell me exactly what it is that's so wonderful about living the way you do.'

I don't know. Perhaps some day I will and it will be the story of David and me that I tell and it won't be a very long story.

David goes to Sandton Primary. Sometimes I walk him to school and sometimes Elizabeth does. When it's raining we go by car and the car days are the days I like best. Not because I mind the walk. It's a nice suburban walk under trees and past gardens and David knows every dog by name. People greet us and sometimes when I walk back there's a little shop I stop at to buy a newspaper and whatever fresh vegetables are looking good that day. Even so, I like the car days best.

I like the sound of the wipers going and the rain pouring down. I like the way the mothers' cars stand bumper to bumper outside the school and children in all shapes and sizes wearing mackintoshes, wellington boots and rainhats jump out. I love the colours. All the colours in a paintbox on small heads and bodies and feet.

I like the way there's no apology for holding up all the traffic so the children can get safely into school. Having David as my guest has taught me something about myself I never knew. I like children. I like the way children light up the day.

David is a runner. He never walks if he can run. It's the way he is and I think he will be like this all his life and he likes the rain nearly as much as I do although for different reasons. What I like is the way he runs through the puddles. What he likes is that suddenly there are puddles, specially put down for him to run through.

For him it's like a miracle and for me too.

Best of all, I like the way he stops at the school gate and turns around and waves his hand to show me goodbye before he goes inside. It's our signal. He knows I won't go till I've seen it. He knows he's safe with me.

'If you played your cards right and listened to some of the things your Uncle Reuben told you you could have been a comfortable woman today,' Sadie says.

What she's really talking about is Lorraine Katzeff, now Lazar.

If you come to Johannesburg and you've only got time to see one thing, the thing you have to see is the house out on Parktown Ridge that Lenny built for the new Mrs Lazar. Sadie can't get over it.

'It's a palace,' she says. 'I don't even know why we're wasting our time calling it a house. It's a palace and it could have been yours. Lorraine Katzeff shouldn't be sitting up there with her *tochis* in the butter acting the Queen of the May. It should be you.'

Some things never change and nor do some people and Sadie is one of them. She's not a young woman any more but she never gives up hope.

'You could still find someone,' she says.

'Please, Seidela,' says my mother. 'We don't need to go through all this again. Frieda's happy as she is.'

'I'm talking a nice widower,' Sadie says. 'Or maybe someone who wants to settle down a little bit later in his life.'

'Thank you, Aunt Sadie,' I say. 'I'm happy just the way I am.'

I may not be the Queen of the May up on Parktown Ridge but since David has come into my life God has seen fit to heap blessings on my head.

It's no secret about his mother or where she is or why she's there. We talk about it and he knows. He's always known.

There are people who say she should stay shut up and perhaps with a bit of luck in the end they'll forget where they put the key and she'll stay where she is and everyone will forget about her.

There are other people who say she's a very brave woman and some day people will say she's a hero.

Right now it doesn't seem very important who's wrong and who's right. Time will decide and I think I know what the decision will be but in the meantime David is the important one. Min and I are in agreement about that.

I go and see her when I'm allowed to and this is how it works.

You get a telephone call and are given a day and a time and when the summons comes you grab it with both hands. Anything you'd planned is put off or changed or adjusted. When the telephone call comes you take whatever time you're offered because such opportunities don't come twice in a row. If you miss one it can take a long time before it comes round again.

It drives Sadie mad. 'What I'd like to know is who these people think they are and why they think they can treat us this way,' she says.

My mother shakes her head to show I should leave

it alone. We've explained a hundred times to Sadie and a hundred times she hasn't listened to a word we said. These people don't need to think about who they are. They know who they are. At the moment they're lords of the universe but times change. We all know that.

Sadie sits at her Patience board and snaps the cards down.

'Of course,' she says, 'she was a girl who always wanted to do things her own way. I don't have to tell you how many times Reuben tried to warn her. He should have saved his breath. He spoke nicely but she just wouldn't listen. That was her trouble. She wouldn't listen and look where it got her.'

She snaps the cards over and my mother looks at me and we smile at each other. We know Sadie and if Reuben was a wise man who could say and do no wrong in life, in death he has become a sage. If we'd all only listened to what he told us the country wouldn't be in the mess it's in today, we'd all sleep safe in our beds at night and our money would still be worth something. God forbid she should need to remind us of how Reuben warned us all about this but she does it every day.

When I go on these visits to Min, David knows where I'm going. I always take something of his with me. Crayon pictures of our house. Not very flattering drawings of me and his *bubbe*, Miriam and Sadie and William and Elizabeth and his friends and his dog and the cat next door that keeps coming in through the fence.

He and William choose the best leaves and flowers for Min and press and dry them so I can hold them up to show her and that way she can see the seasons outside are changing and work out for herself how time is going past.

I take packets full of photographs. Always more pictures than there is time to show them.

This is how it works at Pretoria Central.

You're searched on your way in and again on your way out. I don't know why. You have to leave your coat and handbag behind anyway. They give you a slip for it. The bits and pieces you've come to show on your visit they check through before you show them. If they're approved then this is allowed.

Visitors wait on long benches. There are two policemen to keep an eye on them and usually they stand between them and the door to the visiting room. It always smells of Jeye's Fluid. Too much Jeye's Fluid. I'll never in my life smell Jeye's Fluid again without thinking of this place. I suppose they've got some contact and get it wholesale.

Your name is on a list and you go in when you're called. As you go through the door you get a tick against your name. The person you've come to see is always there ahead of you, ready and waiting, and there's always someone whose visit has just ended going out as you go in and they always look dazed.

Fifteen minutes is a very short time.

There's a glass panel. Someone, another waiting visitor, told me it's bullet-proof. I don't know why.

I sit on one side and Min sits on the other and we speak to each other on a telephone. We aren't allowed to touch. The things I have to show her I hold up pressed against the glass and I give a running commentary.

'This is David with William. In our garden,' I say. I slap the picture up against the glass. 'You remember old William? I keep expecting someone to come and tell me he's no longer with us but every week he turns up.'

Up goes another picture. *Slap.* Like Sadie's Patience cards. You can tell your life in cards as well. At least you're supposed to be able to.

'That's a frog in David's hand,' I say. 'Between them he and William rescued it from the pool filter.'

Min nods her head. *Slap* goes the next picture against the glass and out comes the next story.

We have a watchdog. Never the same one twice. I suppose their job is to listen for state secrets and by comparison what we have to say is such a disappointment and so ordinary no one would want to have to listen to it more than once.

We know the rules. We don't say anything pertaining to the case or the sentence. We give no secret verbal messages to each other. We say nothing the whole world isn't welcome to hear.

The pressed flowers, the gifts of leaves, the crayon pictures that are a child's account of his life with people who love him but are not his own go *slap, slap* against the glass but that's not all there is to it. With our eyes and silently from her heart to mine and mine to hers we say all that has to be said and know all that needs to be known.

'It's time,' the policewoman says. 'You can say your goodbyes now.'

Min puts her hand palm-up against the glass and I do the same. Sometimes I put a kiss on my two fingers and press them against the glass and she does the same.

'Thank you, Frieda,' she says.

It's I who should thank her because she's the one who has given me a life but I wouldn't even know where to begin so I push my bits and pieces back into the paper packet they came in and I say nothing and hope she understands.

FRIEDA

Circumstances and Conditions

1987

I don't know what I expected. Special delivery to the door? Bells, banjos? I don't know what. An announcement in the newspaper? A ball of fire in the sky? Any of those things? All of them?

What I didn't expect was the quietness of it. The quietness and the courtesy.

The invitation into the prison superintendent's office. A carpet under my feet. The offer of a chair. An apology for taking up my time. I didn't expect that.

He's a small man and round. Pleasant-faced and polite. Not what I expected. Min warned me. She told me they never are.

He begins by telling me that as I know cases like Min's are reviewed from time to time. I didn't know and I tell him I didn't.

'Oh,' he says. He sounds surprised.

Do I look to him like a woman who knows this kind of thing without being told? When it comes to knowing I'm the same as anyone else. I know what

336

people tell me and what he tells me is that Min's case has been reconsidered and under certain circumstances and conditions she may be released.

I can't believe it. Just like that. Why? I don't understand but I'm not asking any questions.

She must stay in the magisterial district of Johannesburg. She must report to a police station once a week. She may not be a member of any political organization or party. She may not attend public meetings of any kind. She may not make public statements or allow any public statements to be made in her name.

He keeps looking at me to make sure I understand and I don't understand at all but I keep nodding my head yes to show that actually I do.

She's restricted to the place where she chooses to reside. Such residence will require advance approval by certain people and he himself will nominate these people.

I can't believe what I'm hearing.

'Does she know this?'

'Yes,' he says. 'She knows.'

'When I see her,' I say, 'can we talk about it?'

'Yes,' he says. 'You can. It's permitted.'

Min will hate me and I'll never tell her but I'm so grateful to this funny little man in his off-the-peg suit and bright polyester tie that I could kneel down on the floor in front of him and kiss his really terrible grey shoes.

'Dr Campbell is a very fortunate woman,' he says. 'I hope she realizes that.'

I suppose that's one way of looking at it but you'd have to be the same kind of person he is to understand why.

There's a file on his desk and he lifts it up to show me. So much of it. Pages and pages. So many folders. All kept in a brown cardboard box file tied with pink tape that's so old it's beginning to fade. All of her life I suppose they think it is but what would they know?

I think of my father. In this strange, awful place I feel him close to me. 'A life is only a life after all' is what he would say. It may be all mapped out for us but it isn't given to us to see it all. It isn't right. Day by day is how we have to live.

I don't care about the file. All I care about is Min and how we're all going to go mad with making arrangements and how soon I can take her home and how at long last I will come away from this place with good news and what pleasure it will give me when I get home and tell David.

MIN

The Voice of the Beloved

1987

He came last night.

It's been a long time but I knew it was him.

It wasn't the sound of his boots on the concrete. He has risen up in the ranks. He doesn't wear boots now. Now he looks just the same as everyone else but all the same I knew it was him. I knew it was him long before the key turned in the lock and the light went on.

'It's been a long time,' he says.

He's wearing ordinary clothes. A navy-blue blazer. A light blue shirt. Fawn-coloured twill trousers. Brogues highly polished. Everything pristine.

'I missed you,' he says. 'I never missed any of the others but I missed you.'

He can stand still in one place for a very long time. We both know that but that isn't what matters now. It isn't what the visit's about.

He can give freedom if he wants to. He can just as easily take it away again. The lack of uniform, the change to blazer and flannels makes no difference to that.

They do this sometimes. Say that you can go and then change their minds. But I don't think he's come for that.

'Did you think I would forget you?' he says.

He bends down on his haunches with his knees slightly apart and his hands clasped loosely between them.

'I'd never forget you. That's why I came. Just to see you.'

It's been a long time but he still has that slow quiet way of speaking.

'So much has happened,' he says.

'I know,' I say. 'We hear things even in here. You'd be surprised how much we hear.'

'Not the things I can tell you.'

I don't want to hear them.

'You don't mind, do you?' he says.

Once the lights are put out for the night we are supposed to stay in darkness. Prison dark is very dark and it can go on for a very long time. Sometimes, when you can't sleep, it feels as if it will be for ever before you see light again.

He can change all that.

While he is with me the single pale light in my cell is on. It shines cold on both of us.

Hunched down he is level with me. I look at him and am not afraid. He knows this. What I feel for him is something else. Something deeper and far more disturbing than fear. And then he begins to talk.

'I've been promoted,' he says. I didn't know.

He has been given a medal. It was pinned on his uniform by the State President and his father and mother were there to see it. There was a photograph and they have it, framed. It hangs above the cabinet with the silver cups in it.

His mother cried. She cries a lot these days. Not in

340

front of his father. She would not shame him in such a way but one of her sons, Evert's youngest brother, a national serviceman meant for theological school, is dead in the war on the border.

These are bad times. They touch us all and our lives are changed for ever.

Slowly and evenly and terribly just like he always does he talks to me and when he speaks even when he tells the very worst it is the voice of the beloved I hear. He stays until he's said what he has to say and when he's said it and knows I have heard it all and can never forget, he stands up.

'You're going at the end of the week,' he says.

'They didn't say exactly when.'

'On Friday.'

I didn't know.

'Tell me,' he says. 'Once you leave. You'll never come to me. I know that. But one day when you're free again will you remember everything I've told you? Will you tell it?'

I don't know.

'I didn't think so,' he says.

I will never forget him. Never.

'I will always be close to you,' he says. 'Always. Closer to you than anyone else. You won't always know it but I'll be there. One way or the other I'll be there. So, I don't think there's any need to say goodbye, do you? What we'll do is part company just for the moment.'

He's so very tall. His hair is flat, cut close to his head. His eyes are light and clear. I know the smell of him and the feel of his hand, heavy-boned around my wrist, from a long time ago.

It's the only time he ever actually touched me and it was like fire on my skin stamping me branding me drawing me even closer to him.

'I'm sorry it has to be like this,' he says. 'It's a strange thing really. I can set you free but I can never

341

let you go. If I could, I would, but I feel as if you're part of me now. I hope you understand that.'

He comes towards me then and takes my face in his hands. The palms meet at the base of my chin one on either side of my face. There we stand. A lover's cup. A lover's touch; gentle and tender.

'Remember me,' he says.

He needn't say it. I'll never forget him, never. No matter what he thinks, when he's close by I'll know and I'll never tell anyone. Not any of it. Not ever.

FRIEDA

The Small Door in the Wall

1987

We've been through the arrangements a hundred times. Everything's been checked and double-checked and is ready. David's been blowing balloons until his cheeks nearly burst. He's been practising his Zulu greeting on poor William who must have heard it at least a hundred times by now and he's had a flower-pick and every decent flower that was once in the garden has been cut and put in the house.

'You'll have to explain to him that this is not the easiest thing in the world for her,' my mother says.

'It'll be all right,' I say.

'It's been such a long time,' my mother says.

David's lifetime. It is a long time but it doesn't seem long to him. He's an open child and loving. He likes excitement. That's what his mother coming back means to him.

Nine months Min waited for David. Six years, nearly seven, he has waited for her.

'It should be here,' my mother says. 'Let it be here.

343

I'll do a nice table. We'll have a few flowers and some tea.'

'I don't think so,' I say.

'I'm not talking a party,' my mother says. 'All I'm saying is it will be just ourselves.'

'We've talked about this,' I say. 'And this is the way I want to do it.'

'This is David's home,' my mother says. 'A child's place is in a decent home, not standing outside a prison gate.'

I won't budge. Min has waited for too long. She's missed too much. All she ever said is that if she can bear it so can I and I have borne it as long as I can. I kept my word. I said I would never bring her son to see her in prison. On the other hand I never said anything about not taking him with me to greet her when she steps out into freedom because I think there are some things that are important in life. Things you want to remember always. Like the time you see someone properly for the first time.

My time is up. I have had David long enough, held him long enough, loved him long enough. Now it's her turn and I want it to be right for her. I want it to be just right.

Poor David. He's dressed and dressed again. He's not a baby and he's not a proper boy yet and I'm never quite sure what I should do with him when it comes to clothes. He's always got a lot of complaints. Everything I like is either sissy or baby or worth nothing more than a face-pull.

'You choose then,' I say.

I'm in a hurry. I don't have to be. Our instructions are clear and simple. We should be waiting at the side door and at a certain time the door will open and Min will walk out. I believe it and yet I can't believe it. I think it's because I'm too scared to.

I look at my watch at least every five minutes and I know we have plenty of time but even so I'm in a

344

hurry and David chooses blue shorts and a green T-shirt with enormous frogs on it.

Of all things he chooses native sandals. Tyre tackies we used to call them long ago but how can he know this? All the kids have them now. You buy them on any street market and they're all the fashion.

'It beats me,' my mother says. 'I never know how they're supposed to stay on a person's feet.'

I don't know either. I suppose it depends on the person.

'Please, David,' I say. 'For this big occasion you should look like a decent person. You'd be doing me a favour if you would. You'd be doing us all a favour. Do me a favour right now and change your mind.'

'This is what I want,' he says.

One thing you can say about David. He's a boy who knows his own mind. Over his head I look at my mother and she lifts up her shoulders and I sigh but I give in.

'If that's what you want then that's what you better wear,' I say.

After all, on such a big day, what do clothes matter?

I've been allowed to take clothes to the prison for Min.

Her coming-out clothes she calls them. As though she's a débutante.

I have all her clothes. I packed them and I kept them for her. I kept them for this very day and when I asked what she'd like me to bring her she said: 'Any old thing will do.'

Min's funny clothes. Jeans and shirts and shorts and jerseys that not even a self-respecting char would be seen dead in. I've had Elizabeth wash them and hang them out in the sun to dry and then iron them and air them properly.

'Do you think I care what I look like?' she says.

I suppose she's right.

'You'll come straight back here,' my mother says.

'Straight back,' I say. 'As arranged.'

I pull a brush through David's hair. It's blond like Min's but thick and no matter how short it is it always fights back.

'I'm not talking about a party,' my mother says for about the twentieth time. 'We'll keep it nice and quiet.'

'Come along, David,' I say.

'She'll take it day by day,' my mother says. 'This isn't a thing you get over in five minutes.'

No. It isn't. This isn't a thing you get over in a lifetime.

'Will we have long to wait?' David wants to know.

'Not long,' I say.

He's at the time of his life where patience is not his greatest virtue.

'It's a funny place, isn't it?'

'Yes,' I say. 'It's a very funny place.'

All you can see is a high wall and an enormous gate that slides back when a car draws up to it. You think you'd see a guard but you don't. All the guards are inside. On this side you get in on electronic pass only and a computer inside decides whether you're *kosher* or whether you're not but that doesn't matter to us. All we're interested in is the small door at the side.

'Is that where she'll come from?' David says.

'Yes,' I say. 'That's where she'll come from. You just keep your eyes open and give a shout when you see her.'

I don't know what will happen after that.

She has a house of her own. That is allowed and my mother and Sadie and I found something we thought would be right. We thought it was a place she could be happy in. She didn't seem to care.

'Anything's fine with me,' she says. 'Anything at all.'

David may live there with her. That is allowed but

346

she is not allowed to practise as a doctor. She knows this and she knows the other restrictions that will be placed on her. They may not exactly be everyone's idea of freedom but she's accepted them. Or, she says she has. All we can do is hope.

'Will it be long?' David says.

'Not very long,' I say.

For a child time has a different meaning. When you are six years old going on seven 'not very long' can be a very long time but eventually the door does open and Min steps out. Just like that. By herself. In brown jeans and a white shirt and sandals on her feet and the rest of her things in a canvas bag which she carries in her hand.

'Is that her?' David says.

'That's her,' I say.

I raise my hand. First only as high as my shoulder but then higher, high above my head and I wave.

There's a perimeter between the door and the place we're allowed to wait. A kind of no man's land made of tarmac. Wide enough for large police and army vehicles to go by except there's no traffic now. The road is absolutely empty.

'You go along, David,' I say. 'Go and say hello to your mother.'

He's a nice boy, David, and friendly. He's not a skirt-clinger or the kind of child who shies away from people he doesn't know well. He'll go off at a walk but I know him. Even when he's not as excited as he is now he's not a very good walker. He likes to run.

'Do you think she'll know it's me?' he says.

'I don't see any other little boys around,' I say. 'I think she'll know it's you.'

He has Min's eyes. Clear eyes, like glass. Eyes that see everything and miss nothing. Eyes that see more than they should.

'Hurry up,' I say. 'Don't keep her waiting. She's waited so long already.'

He's off and running. He's flying towards his mother on his funny shoes and Min is watching him and waiting. She's standing quite still and giving him all the time he needs, all the time in the world, all the time it takes him at his own pace in his own way to reach her.

THE END

DANCE WITH A POOR MAN'S DAUGHTER
Pamela Jooste

'IMMENSELY MOVING AND READABLE'
Isobel Shepherd Smith, *The Times*

*'My name is Lily Daniels and I live in the Valley, in an old
house at the top of a hill with a loquat tree in the garden. We
are all women in our house. My grandmother, my Aunt Stella
with her hopalong leg, and me. The men in our family are
not worth much. They are the cross we have to bear. Some of
us, like my mother, don't live here any more. People say she
went on the Kimberley train to try for white and I mustn't
blame her because she could get away with it even if we
didn't believe she would.'*

Through the sharp yet loving eyes of eleven-year-old Lily we
see the whole exotic, vivid, vigorous culture of the Cape
Coloured community at the time when apartheid threatened
its destruction. As Lily's beautiful but angry mother returns
to Cape Town, determined to fight for justice for her family,
so the story of Lily's past – and future – erupts. *Dance With
a Poor Man's Daughter* is a powerful and moving tribute to a
richly individual people.

'HIGHLY READABLE, SENSITIVE AND INTENSELY
MOVING . . . A FINE ACHIEVEMENT'
Mail and Guardian, South Africa

'TOUGH, SMART AND VULNERABLE . . . EMBLEMATIC
OF AN ENTIRE PEOPLE'
Independent

'I COULD HARDLY PUT THIS BOOK DOWN'
Cape Times

WINNER OF THE COMMONWEALTH BEST FIRST BOOK
AWARD FOR THE AFRICAN REGION

WINNER OF THE SANLAM LITERARY AWARD

WINNER OF THE BOOK DATA'S SOUTH AFRICAN
BOOKSELLERS' CHOICE AWARD

0 552 99757 9

BLACK SWAN

HUMAN CROQUET
Kate Atkinson

'VIVID AND INTRIGUING . . . FIZZLES AND CRACKLES
ALONG . . . A COMPELLING STORY WITH EXCURSIONS
INTO FANTASY, EXPERIMENT AND OUTRAGEOUS
GRAND GUIGNOL . . . A *TOUR DE FORCE*'
Penelope Lively, *Independent*

Once it had been the great forest of Lythe – a vast and
impenetrable thicket of green with a mystery in the very
heart of the trees. And here, in the beginning, lived the
Fairfaxes, grandly, at Fairfax Manor, visited once by the
great Gloriana herself.

But over the centuries the forest had been destroyed,
replaced by Streets of Trees. The Fairfaxes had dwindled
too; now they lived in 'Arden' at the end of Hawthorne
Close and were hardly a family at all.

There was Vinny (the Aunt from Hell) – with her cats and
her crab-apple face. And Gordon, who had forgotten them
for seven years and, when he remembered, came back with
fat Debbie, who shared her one brain cell with a poodle.
And then there were Charles and Isobel, the children.
Charles, the acne-scarred Lost Boy, passed his life awaiting
visits from aliens and the return of his mother. But it is
Isobel to whom the story belongs – Isobel, born on the
Streets of Trees, who drops into pockets of time and out
again. Isobel is sixteen and she too is waiting for the return
of her mother – the thin, dangerous Eliza with her scent of
nicotine, Arpège and sex, whose disappearance is part of the
mystery that still remains at the heart of the forest.

'READS LIKE A DARKER SHENA MACKAY OR A
FUNNIER, MORE LITERARY BARBARA VINE. VIVID,
RICHLY IMAGINATIVE, HILARIOUS AND FRIGHTENING
BY TURNS'
Cressida Connolly, *Observer*

0 552 99619 X

BLACK SWAN

SISTER OF MY HEART
Chitra Banerjee Divakaruni

'CHITRA BANERJEE DIVAKARUNI IS A TRUE STORYTELLER.
LIKE DICKENS, SHE HAS CONSTRUCTED LAYER UPON
LAYER OF TRAGEDY, SECRETS AND BETRAYALS, OF
THWARTED LOVE . . . [A] GLORIOUS, COLOURFUL
TRAGEDY'
Daily Telegraph

Born in the big old Calcutta house on the same tragic night that
both their fathers were mysteriously lost, Sudha and Anju are
cousins. Closer even than sisters, they share clothes, worries,
dreams in the matriarchal Chatterjee household. But when
Sudha discovers a terrible secret about the past, their mutual
loyalty is sorely tested.

A family crisis forces their mothers to start the serious business
of arranging the girls' marriages, and the pair is torn apart.
Sudha moves to her new family's home in rural Bengal, while
Anju joins her immigrant husband in California. Although they
have both been trained to be perfect wives, nothing has
prepared them for the pain, as well as the joy, that each will
have to face in her new life.

Steeped in the mysticism of ancient tales, this jewel-like novel
shines its light on the bonds of family, on love and loss, against
the realities of traditional marriage in modern times.

'DIVAKARUNI STRIKES A DELICATE BALANCE BETWEEN
REALISM AND FANTASY . . . A TOUCHING CELEBRATION
OF ENDURING LOVE'
Sunday Times

'A PLEASURE TO READ . . . A NOVEL FRAGRANT IN
RHYTHM AND LANGUAGE'
San Francisco Chronicle

'DIVAKARUNI'S BOOKS POSSESS A POWER THAT IS BOTH
TRANSPORTING AND HEALING . . . SERIOUS AND
ENTRANCING'
Booklist

'MAGICALLY AFFECTING . . . HER INTRICATE TAPESTRY OF
OLD AND NEW WORLDS SHINES WITH A RARE
LUMINOSITY'
San Diego Union Tribune

0 552 99767 6

BLACK SWAN

A SELECTED LIST OF FINE WRITING
AVAILABLE FROM BLACK SWAN

99313	1	OF LOVE AND SHADOWS	*Isabel Allende*	£6.99
99820	6	FLANDERS	*Patricia Anthony*	£6.99
99619	X	HUMAN CROQUET	*Kate Atkinson*	£6.99
99687	4	THE PURVEYOR OF ENCHANTMENT	*Marika Cobbold*	£6.99
99767	6	SISTER OF MY HEART	*Chitra Banerjee Divakaruni*	£6.99
99587	8	LIKE WATER FOR CHOCOLATE	*Laura Esquivel*	£6.99
99755	2	WINGS OF THE MORNING	*Elizabeth Falconer*	£6.99
99770	6	TELLING LIDDY	*Anne Fine*	£6.99
99795	1	LIAR BIRDS	*Lucy Fitzgerald*	£5.99
99721	8	BEFORE WOMEN HAD WINGS	*Connie May Fowler*	£6.99
99656	4	THE TEN O'CLOCK HORSES	*Laurie Graham*	£5.99
99774	9	THE CUCKOO'S PARTING CRY	*Anthea Halliwell*	£5.99
99801	X	THE SHORT HISTORY OF A PRINCE	*Jane Hamilton*	£6.99
99757	9	DANCE WITH A POOR MAN'S DAUGHTER	*Pamela Jooste*	£6.99
99736	6	KISS AND KIN	*Angela Lambert*	£6.99
99771	4	MALLINGFORD	*Alison Love*	£6.99
99712	9	ANGEL BIRD	*Sanjida O'Connell*	£6.99
99814	1	AN INNOCENT DIVERSION	*Kathleen Rowntree*	£6.99
99777	3	THE SPARROW	*Mary Doria Russell*	£6.99
99781	1	WRITING ON THE WATER	*Jane Slavin*	£6.99
99788	9	OTHER PEOPLE'S CHILDREN	*Joanna Trollope*	£6.99
99780	3	KNOWLEDGE OF ANGELS	*Jill Paton Walsh*	£6.99
99673	4	DINA'S BOOK	*Herbjørg Wassmo*	£6.99
99723	4	PART OF THE FURNITURE	*Mary Wesley*	£6.99
99761	7	THE GATECRASHER	*Madeleine Wickham*	£6.99
99591	6	A MISLAID MAGIC	*Joyce Windsor*	£6.99